FRENCH KISSES

David R. Poe

FRENCH KISSES

David R. Poe

SERVING HOUSE BOOKS

French Kisses

ISBN: 978-0-9913281-7-8

Cover design: Alexander Poe

Photos: Stevens-Poe, except fountain by Jean-Marie Hullot, Eiffel Tower by Cherry X, "Kisses" by Valerie Crochemore, "Bisous" by Swen Diguet

Serving House Books logo by Barry Lereng Wilmont

Published by Serving House Books
Copenhagen, Denmark and Florham Park, NJ
www.servinghousebooks.com

Member of The Independent Book Publishers Association

First Serving House Books Edition 2014

For Candy

And for Bob Tischenkel,
since our writing days at Syracuse
my wonderful friend with the keen eye
and endless enthusiasm

My deepest gratitude to
Tom Kennedy and Walter Cummins
for providing my orphans with a loving home
at Serving House Books

Acknowledgments

"Frederico's Wife" appeared in *Prairie Schooner*; "Playing Above the Rim" in *Cimarron Review*; "Wilson's Last Gardener" in *StoryQuarterly*; "An Easy Day at Easy Red" in *The Literary Review*; "Feast" (French version) in *Cahiers de Nuit* (France); "My Red Desdemona" in *The Girl with Red Hair*; "How It Works" in *Winter Tales: Men Write About Aging.*

"French kisses in the darkening doorways."
—DIRE STRAITS

"It is not what France gave you but what it did not take away from you that was important."
—GERTRUDE STEIN

Contents

FREDERICO'S WIFE

The very first time Avril and I had coffee we were sitting in the shade of a red awning in the Latin Quarter. This lost tourist came squinting along and stopped to ask us directions. He was an American like myself. I told him in French, "I'm sorry, I don't speak English."

Avril however leaped from her seat at this chance to offer directions. Her eyes beamed as if to light the way, her hands turned corners in the air. She looked beautiful, giving directions. Having set the lost person aright, Avril demanded to know what I was anyway—a joker? a misanthrope? Jesus no, I said. I just don't like giving directions. Her eyes bore down on me, seeking some truer truth. Maybe I'd fail in the theatrics, I said. Maybe I'd get some poor soul more lost than he already is. The fact is, I couldn't direct a moth lost in the dark to the nearest light bulb. So then and there we agreed, whenever a lost person approached she'd give directions. And in the many months that followed I never once had to.

Until I met Frederico.

That was some two years after the cafe with the red awning. By that time Avril and I were engaged. It was her first marriage, my second. I'd just dropped her off at Charles de Gaulle. She was flying to Dublin for ten days to see her mum, a strong-minded woman who thirty-two years earlier overrode the protests of her husband and gave their daughter a French name. We hadn't set the date, but Avril was thinking fall, maybe sooner.

I parked the car on the quay, just down river from the Eiffel Tower, where I paid a man with a houseboat three-hundred francs a month for the space at the end of his gangplank. At my front door I realized I'd forgotten to buy bottled water and turned around to head for the grocer's.

It was a March evening and getting dusky. A man was standing at the corner of my street, rue des Cygnes, and Avenue du President Kennedy. A stocky dark-haired man, perhaps mid-fortyish, he studied a piece of paper in his hand, glancing up and turning his head one way, then the other. He looked befuddled. A brown suitcase heeled at his feet. I assumed he wanted Hotel Guimard, just around the block. He was eyeing me now, raising his hand and about to speak, and I was set to declare, "One street over!"—for even I could manage that—when he stumbled over his own suitcase, knocking it flat, and caught me by the arm to recover his balance.

He apologized profusely and, without actually touching me, waved his hands all about me, as though he were fanning away smoke. He had a thick accent I took to be southern, maybe out of the Pyrenees, maybe even Spain. He railed about what a day it'd been—late train, busted suitcase (I looked, sure enough it had been secured with clothesline), and now he couldn't find rue des Cygnes though he knew it was around here somewhere.

"This is the rue des Cygnes," I said, pointing at the sidewalk.

"This?" He calmed down and pointed at the same spot on the sidewalk. He had big black sad eyes I thought for a moment were filling with tears. Then his round face broke out smiling.

"Wouldn't you know, right under my feet!" He laughed loudly as he picked up his suitcase. "I must report that," he added, pointing up at the corner of a building. There was a blank where there should've been a street sign. He thanked me and walked away.

I couldn't imagine why he thought to take it upon himself to report a missing street sign. And I still couldn't place his accent. Placing accents had become something of a hobby with Avril and me. We were both translators at a news bureau. Sometimes, on a sunny afternoon, we'd go sit in one of those glitzy cafes that has an inexplicable global attraction, maybe along the Champs Elysees or

Boulevard Montparnasse, just so we could hear the many different languages and accents fluttering about. Then, like lepidopterists in a field of butterflies, we'd try to see how many we could identify. Of course, we didn't always know when we were right or wrong.

On the way home with my bottled water, I turned the corner to see the same man in front of my apartment building, again befuddled. When almost to the door, I heard him curse a set of keys—in Portuguese!

"You need some help?" I asked him in Portuguese.

"Ah, the directions man—you know Portuguese, eh?"

"Some."

"You'll excuse my cursing then."

He took a breath, then patted his pants—right and left, front and back; his coat—right side, left side, inside breast, right and left, outside breast— "It's no goddam use." And his eyes watered.

He took the coat off, an old green tweed, and shook it. We both heard the rattle of keys. From his pants he withdrew a pocketknife and opened it. By this time I realized he smelled badly, like a bowl of old onion soup.

"I knew I left the office with them," he said.

"You mean Madame Heursault's office?" She was the building manager.

"Sure, who you think." Everything he said he swallowed in a sob.

He didn't look the kind of man who could afford the rent in my building. Then it occured to me.

"So you might be the new concierge?" The former concierge, "Madame" Bucher, a woman near sixty who'd actually never married, had moved to Provence to tend an elder sister.

"Yeah, I might be, if I can get these keys out. You live here?"

"Third floor, left."

Kneading his coat, he looked me over. A face as sad as his one saw only at a zoo or circus. He had an iridescent clump of lining in his fist now, bouquet style, the keys inside pushing to get through. The other hand had the knife.

"Is that necessary?"

"My wife can sew it." He slit the clump and extracted the keys. "If she'd sewed the pocket right to begin with, this wouldn've happened." I must've raised my eyebrows, though I'm not sure at what. "Yeah, she'll be along. Tomorrow. If not, the next day or the next. I always go ahead, she follows." He unlocked the door, picked up his suitcase and entered before me. He looked around the lobby. "Too much glass," he said. "Though my wife's good on glass." There were three sets of glass-paned doors. One to the front stairs and elevator, one to the back stairs, meant for servants once but now used by students who rented maids' rooms in the mansard roof; the middle set of doors were the concierge's. "There?"

"That's it," I said. Madame Bucher's sheer curtains still hung in the windows.

"Like living in a goddam fishbowl." And he was right, but it was the fish who watched the people. By ancient law—as consequential now as the law back in some states forbidding the bathing of a horse in your hotel room—a concierge's first duty was to watch comings and goings, at whatever hour, and to detect plotters against the republic. Madame Bucher had never had anyone pulled in. This man here—who knew? Didn't he seem anxious to report that missing street sign?

"Not my idea of a job," he sighed. "Heursault. She lined it up. Wife's second cousin. Last one in the family will even talk to my wife." He opened the door. Madame Bucher's furniture remained— maybe it belonged to the building. "Oh, I'm Monsieur Frederico." He went in and closed the door before I could say nice to meet you.

He spared me the lie. He seemed a man so willing to cut himself open and bare his sadness—as if doing so gave him an edge—I found him repugnant.

The next day at the bureau I was translating copy on the Barbie trial down in Lyon. I covered southern Europe, Avril the north. Our two empires we told each other. Before flying to Dublin, she'd just finished translating a series of articles on the deer in Finland after Chernobyl. She had Scandinavian, German, and Dutch feeds. I had Italian, Spanish, French and Portuguese—the romance lines.

As I was trying to recall the word for *caserne*—"barracks" it turned out—in breezed Wild Bill. That is, William J. Steed III. Wild Bill was an anachronism. He'd missed his seat in the great train of human events by about three cars. He had a black mane of hair at least two feet in diameter, a thick beard he ceaselessly massaged, and wire rim glasses. His favorite music came from the Doors. Some of us ghoulishly speculated that Wild Bill was in Paris because Jim Morrison was here, buried over at *Pere Lachaise*, having died in a Paris bathtub some years back. Raised in Amarillo, Wild Bill spoke French with a Texas accent.

"What is the man's problem?" Wild Bill said, the man no doubt our boss, a nervous Frenchman we simply called JP—"gee-pay." "We just don't want to make contact." Wild Bill had a habit of saying "we" when it wasn't clear who that was. "We should have no interest in an oyster truck slipping its brake and rolling down a hill and smashing into a trailer and igniting a butane gas tank and everyone thinking the man and woman inside are fried—along with a few thousand oysters—when all of a sudden they come walking up. And where'd they been?—in town eating oysters!"

"Where was this?" I asked.

"Outside of Meulan. I just got back."

"Do you think anyone Stateside ever heard of Meulan?"

"How'll anyone know what we don't tell 'em?" Just then, seeing the empty seat next to mine, he must've realized Avril was absent and not merely away from her desk. "Where's Little Red?" His pet name for her the past seven months, though never to her face.

"Little Red's in Dublin, visiting mum."

"Uh." He squinched his eyes in astonishment. The sad part about Wild Bill was, he loved Little Red. Born too late again. I watched him droop, his youthful strength gone out of him—replaced by who knew what? Dreaming? Desire? "Avril," I once joked, "you're indeed Wild Bill's cruelest month."

"I'll speak to JP about the oysters, okay?"

"Please do." He'd recovered. "We just do not plug into anything providential these days, do we?" And off he went.

When I confronted JP with the oysters he explained it to me. We're a fledgling service sticking with certifiable reading—radiation, Nazi trials, bombings. News of retribution is especially good, for it adds a sense of follow-up. Now if this oyster truck had been part of a murder attempt by some terrorist group in retaliation for arrests—made in Meulan last month in fact—then Wild Bill might have a story.

Four days after Monsieur Frederico had arrived, his wife showed up. I'd begun to think she wasn't coming. I'd also begun to think I'd been hasty to judge him. He acted slow and sad, like a bear scrounging peanuts, but there could be no crime or harm in this. Then, Monday morning, on my way out to work, I saw his wife for the first time. The husband was on the floor of the lobby sorting mail. She was behind the glass doors of their little apartment, standing on a chair, taking down the sheers. Since taking up with Avril I'd not paid attention to other women. My God, I loved Avril and intended to marry her. Yet, seeing Frederico's wife, I felt my pulse pick up. I may have blushed or perspired. I may have emitted a gust of musky odor capable of penetrating glass. Glancing down at me, she suddenly smiled so deeply, so intimately, it were as if we'd been lovers once and were just now seeing each other after many years. This wasn't me.

Years ago, I had stood with the woman who would become my first wife, both of us naked and joyous, in the rain and mud of Woodstock. But since then, I had come to believe, like the rest of my generation, in the value of properly installed sublimation devices. Besides, there'd been an innocence oozing up out of the mud that was unavailable now in the marble floor of the lobby. Shouldn't what struck me at that moment be reserved for the first time seeing Winged Victory or Venus de Milo or Monet's water lilies—and not my concierge's wife? This seemed impossible. What's more, she on that chair, her bearish husband hunched over on the floor, all my initial repulsion toward him resurfaced full force. Her union with him seemed that improbable, that impossible.

Leaving a curtain half hanging, she came down off her chair and stepped out into the lobby. She had no sad and tired face like her husband. Brown hair, hazel eyes, tan skin all radiated expectantly. She held out her hand for me to shake.

"You must be Madame Frederico. Glad to meet you. Welcome to Paris." I said this in Portuguese.

"Don't bother," said her husband, looking up from his mail. "She doesn't speak it, no matter how I teach her."

I told her my name and she said glad to meet me. Our hands let go. She had smooth, muscular arms. She must've been a dozen years younger than her husband.

"She's French. She thinks Portuguese are stupid."

"I don't at all," she said to me. Then I saw, where her jawbone turned sharply away from just below her ear, a bruise. Balanced there like a small plum, now turning brown, it seemed maybe a week old. Realizing I'd seen it, she turned her face aside. "It's only that my husband would rather blame all his own people than admit personal failure."

He rose like a giant from sleep. I expected him to swing at her. "We chop up our hearts like tomatoes," he said in Portuguese and lumbered into the apartment. The radiance in his wife's face changed to sardonic satisfaction. Venus de Milo sprouting fangs.

"My paper," I said softly, bending down and picking it out of the pile of mail. "If I could have it at my door by eight-fifteen. I know the mail arrives by eight. So eight-fifteen isn't unreasonable. Madame Bucher used to—"

"I will bring it myself. You'll have your paper by eight-fifteen, Monsieur." She smiled—the first smile again.

And so my paper arrived by eight-fifteen all that week, neatly folded and centered perfectly it seemed on my doormat. But something odd had been happening. Each of those days there lay on the paper a strand of brown hair. No doubt from the head of Madame Frederico. Each day I picked up the paper like a salver with the evidence upon it—but evidence of what? All I could gather from each hair was a perverse sense of being flattered. The other thing was, what to do with it. The first time I merely let it fall to the floor in the hall. For it seemed fortuitous. But with each succeeding time, as it became more obvious the strand wasn't accidental—that she meant for me to have it—it became difficult to walk over to the waste can and merely tilt the paper. In fact, the last strand I picked up and held to the light before laughing out loud and shaking it from my fingertips.

On Saturday I opened the door and bent to pick up the paper and saw nothing lay upon it, definitely no long strand of brown hair. The phone rang. It was Avril. She told me her mum was good. Then she reminded me we had tickets for the *Fantastic Symphony*, by Berlioz (our favorite French composer), on Wednesday. And not to forget that my Dordogne piece was due in the mail Thursday. Travel articles were something on the side Avril had talked me into doing. I told her I was going to the office and work on it that afternoon. (The Dordogne was our favorite river.) And also, she wanted to know if I still planned to plant the impatiens tomorrow, Sunday. Absolutely. (Impatiens were our favorite flowers.)

(We had lots of favorites. Maybe it was a nonsense game we'd invented like children. Or maybe we were actually trying to trick destiny into giving us its blessing. The first time I asked Avril to dinner, I mentioned a certain restaurant in the town of Barbizon, outside of Paris. My favorite, I said. Really? Mine, too, she said. So we discovered we had something in common. But then it became uncanny. As months passed, every time one of us mentioned that just such and such was a favorite, so it happened that it was a favorite of the other as well. Then one night in Barbizon—by this time we had our favorite hotel in town, even our favorite room—we lay in bed in the darkness. We took turns naming a favorite holiday, a favorite color, a favorite cathedral, artist, bridge, number, river, mountain, breed of dog, opera, aria, constellation, and movie, to each of which the other answered, "Mine, too," like so many amens. "It's a sign, Avril. It's a sign, sure as burning bushes! Let's spend life together, Avril." "Okay," she said. "Let's.")

Eating toasted muffins in the kitchen after Avril's call (she said she'd take a cab home from Charles de Gaulle Sunday night, for me not to bother picking her up, that she'd see me at work Monday morning), I wondered why Frederico's wife had stopped the strands. Because I hadn't responded to her offerings? But what was I even thinking!

The kitchen window opened on a courtyard. So regal a word, you expect fountains, urns, a carriage drawn by two horses, impatient hooves clacking on cobblestone. But this courtyard had leaking downspouts and two trash barrels—which happened this day to be overflowing with blue bags—standing grimly on cracked asphalt. Directly outside the window was a peculiar contraption: vertical cables on which ran the counterweight to the elevator, a stack of weights actually, perhaps as tall as myself. Two cables acted as guides so the weight couldn't swing like a pendulum. A thicker middle cable did the actual raising and lowering. As I ate my second muffin I realized this weight had been going up and down steadily, some seven or eight times now. I also saw that grease or oil had splashed from the cables onto my window. I'd never known this to happen. I pulled open the window and peered out as best I could without sticking my head in the path of the counterweight. Don't think incidentally that French elevator installers are careless people, aligning a counterweight where it could do most damage to an unsuspecting head thrust out to greet the morning. The entire bank of kitchen windows had been sealed tightly when the elevator had been installed in the Fifties. So Madame Bucher had explained, somewhat in horror, the day she discovered me prying open the window. "Just like a guillotine!" She cried. My desire for ventilation in the kitchen exceeded my fear of decapitation, I told her, assuring her as well that I would be extremely careful and that, should I move out, I would gladly reseal it.

I glanced down, bowing my head into an invisible though certain margin of safety just beyond the sill.

"Get back!" Came a scream as the weight dropped before my

eyes.

"It's okay, Monsieur Frederico. I see it."

"That window should be shut forever!"

"I need air in the kitchen."

"You need a head to breathe with!"

"I know what I'm doing. The question is, what are you doing?" I could see him clearly at the bottom of my margin of safety. He had on a red flannel shirt. In his hand a can, I think brass, with a spout.

"I'm oiling the wires."

"Madame Bucher never did that."

"Don't you think I can see that?"

"Is it necessary?"

"Watch out!" The weight swept upward across my vision. "Monsieur, first—be very, very careful there. Next—I have worked many times and places around trains, cable cars, trams, lifts, to know that moving metal needs oil."

"But it's splashing my window. Maybe you need something more viscous." *Visqueux* was the word in French. He didn't seem to understand and I didn't know the Portuguese word.

"Monsieur, I have worked many times with moving metal and I assure you—"

"Yes, yes. But my window, the oil is splashing my window."

"Watch out!" This time the weight came down just past my nose. I jerked my head back. My nostrils filled with the odor of oil. "See! See! Didn't I say be careful!"

"It's okay, Monsieur Frederico! A miss is a miss! Now what about my window! And what makes that damn elevator keep going up and down!"

"First," he replied calmly, acting as if he had won a point of contention, "my wife is good on glass, and she will clean your window. Next—I put my wife inside the elevator pushing buttons." He beamed, no doubt proud of the procedure he'd devised.

"Very well," I said in a tone of concession, though I couldn't say why. "Maybe tomorrow she can do the window."

On my way out to the office I took the stairs. The elevator had been installed to run in the middle of the staircase which wrapped around it. I heard it coming up. Thinking to say hello to Madame Frederico—and yes, admittedly, hoping to catch a glance that might somehow corroborate the strands of hair—I stopped on the landing of the second floor. The elevator passed upward. It was no more than a black wire cage that barely accommodated two thin passengers. Now I saw, ascending before my eyes, Frederico's wife, and I shuddered at the sight. Her eyes swelled, her lips puffed, and I couldn't be certain, for the elevator light was so dim, but one of her cheeks appeared bruised. Most startling, even in the dim light, was her hair—full and radiant when last I'd seen it, it now had been chopped off, hacked away, if with an adze wouldn't be surprising. She saw me, saw my speechlessness, and she as well said nothing, but looked deeply into my eyes as she was rising.

I tried to work. Castles clung to cliffs along the Dordogne. Richard the Lionhearted captured Beynac. A panorama of pastures spread out below Domme, a view Henry Miller was especially fond of. In a cozy restaurant, *foie gras* and truffles waited. Frederico's wife rose before my eyes.

I'd struck my first wife once. Her name was Pam. It was the one and only time. She'd let a tuna casserole burn in the oven. That I did it so casually, without violence or anger, probably stunned Pam the most. But then, we did everything in life with such casualness, as if fortune would drift our way if we'd only be quiet and sit tight. I felt the same in our rowboat on Sundays, waiting for a bass to strike.

"In the chancel," I wrote to a reader I imagined at the dentist's, "take time to note the capitals depicting Daniel and the lion, Jonah and the whale, and—in a curiously secular vein—a showman taming his performing monkeys."

That evening the weather turned, for Marches in Paris are

so unpredictable. Walking home in a cold wind, I decided I'd go down to the basement where I stored some wine in a bin and grab a bottle. Drinking alone was something I didn't do, but the sight of Frederico's wife still left a rough edge maybe the wine would smooth off. I puzzled over what odd chemistry of the heart had brought them together. But why speculate? For the heart seemed an organ several notches below the brain. If people chose to chop up each other's hearts—like tomatoes, Frederico had said—what could anyone do about it anyway?

Entering the lobby, I saw that a television was throwing its ghostly fluttering light up on the sheer curtains of the Fredericos' apartment. Otherwise the place was completely dark. I could see no one, but I wondered if they were watching me. Also, I wondered when they'd gotten a TV. Maybe I hadn't noticed it before. Quickly passing through the door leading to the back steps, I went down into the cellar.

Parisian cellars are cryptic in the most literal, I mean, physical, sense. No nicely painted cinderblocks or simulated paneling. No linoleum floors. In our cellar, a passage made an "S" beneath the building. Cracked wooden doors lined it, opening into bins, or *caves*, as the French say. Soot clung like black moss to rough hewn limestone. The floor was dirt, and over the years people had thrown pieces of rug and carpet along the winding passage, some of the pieces now as shredded as mulch. Bare light bulbs in bare sockets hung fixtureless by their wires. At each bend of the passage, on the floor, was a little hill of pink rat poison that looked like something meant for sprinkling on a cake. Strangely enough, I always felt content being here.

Turning the first bend, I heard a sound I recognized. Someone was shoveling coal and chucking it into the furnace. Sturdy as she was, Madame Bucher had never done this job herself but had a nephew who'd come around as needed to perform this task. I turned another corner and peeked into the furnace room, half expecting to see the nephew. There was Frederico shoveling away.

"Hey, the directions man! How're you tonight?" He seemed

unusually happy. He paused from his work, holding the long handle of the shovel and leaning into it as though he were about to push off in a gondola.

"Good. How are you?"

"Good, good."

Against all instinct, I then asked, "And your wife?"

"Terrific. I bought her a new TV today, remote and all. She is in heaven. She had been feeling so low lately."

"She didn't look well this morning."

"No, no. What with all that happened. First—this Madame Bucher must have had a cat." She did in fact, a huge orange cat named Clementine. "So my wife is allergic, swells up like a blowfish. Two days we vacuum and scrub and maybe got rid of the cat. Next—she falls off her chair hanging a shower curtain and catches here"—he patted his cheekbone. "On the tub edge. A mess. Next—she decides in Paris she must have a new hairdo and clips off the beautiful waves. She looks like a punk now and regrets it."

"I see." Lying bastard, I thought. Maybe sensing my disbelief, he became serious.

"I see you are not married and at your age I am surprised."

"I was once. It didn't work out."

"You don't believe then. For better or for worse?"

"Two people can never be absolutely sure."

He smiled at the heresy in this.

"That's why it's belief, isn't it?" He pulled the shovel up straight and rested its blade on his shoe. "Still, it is a hard thing to wake one day to the news your wife married you not for love but because you made a good tool to spite someone else."

"Nothing can justify abusing your wife."

"What?" He broke out laughing. He scooped up some coal and tossed it in the furnace.

I walked away. He was still laughing, shoveling harder now. "You have it wrong, Monsieur! You don't see what caused what here!"

Early the next day, I went out and bought pink, purple, salmon and red impatiens, and potting soil. I retrieved window boxes and their hangers from the cellar. There was no sign of the Fredericos. I worried it was too cold yet, too soon to plant. Back in the States, Pam had surrounded us with plants, indoors and out. She talked to them, bathed and fed them, sprayed for aphids, but they always went scraggly and yellow before her eyes. The day she burned the tuna casserole she was out back feeding the azaleas she'd just planted along the fence. She was filling a bucket from a hose she left running, and adding powder that turned the water blue. She poured it at the base of each plant. There were two dozen, all white-budded. I'd been watching from the upstairs bedroom window. I could see she was simply dumping the powder in, unmeasured, haphazardly. Around the twentieth bucket I smelled the casserole. It was beside the azalea bushes, standing in soggy grass, that I slapped her. My final regret about Pam is I never apologized for hitting her. Never begged her to forgive me—though I know begging would not've been necessary.

Around eleven o'clock, I heard a knock at the door. I left the impatiens on newspapers on the floor where'd I'd just begun to put them in window boxes. It was Frederico's wife. I was surprised she'd come.

"I'm here for the window." She had a rag and a bottle of cleaner.

"Yes, yes. Come in."

"You have a beautiful life here," she said, looking around. "Yes, it is beautiful and orderly."

I stared at her, searching for clues. She looked better, remarkably so. Her hair had been curled, all signs of ravaging sculpted away. It seemed brassier now. Her eyes were bright and showed no puffiness. But a bruise on her cheek, slightly rouged over, still lingered, if not in color, in shape.

In the kitchen she went right to work, opening the window and cleaning it. Unable to reach the upper parts of the glass, she began to pull up a chair from the kitchen table.

"No, no! I have a stepstool. Chairs can be unsafe, can't they?"

She didn't respond. I got the stepstool for her and placed it at the window. She stepped up on it and worked with ease, not looking like the kind of woman who could lose her balance. She wore a black skirt and yellow canvas loafers. Her legs were strong and smooth, and I ached to test them, as if to run my hand along the frame of a harp.

"So, you're allergic to cats?"

"Am I ever."

She finished, got down and closed the window.

"Let me give you something for that—" I started to reach for my back pocket.

"No, no. I wouldn't think of it. After all, it was my husband's oil." She scurried into the living room toward the door.

"Wait a minute." She stopped in front of the door and turned to look at me as I approached. "Listen to me. You're not accountable for any mess your husband makes." She said nothing but kept looking into my eyes. "I have to ask you. Did you fall off a chair this past week?" Still she didn't speak, but kept looking into my eyes. "If there is a problem, if, if something isn't right, there are people who can help. People who care. Compassionate people—" She suddenly wrapped her arms around me and pulled herself to me. She put her head to my chest. And even as I held her, I told myself I was confusing emotions here, both hers and mine. She may indeed have needed help from some compassionate person, but that was not me, not at that moment. I do not know what I was at that moment.

"The strands of hair. Why did you leave them on the paper?"

"Who knows?" She laughed. "Maybe because you remind me of someone I once tried to give myself to, too hard and all at once. And with you I wanted to give something of me a strand at a time." She'd made me a shadow of a memory, but I felt honored, not slighted. "Then my husband made me cut it all off. Maybe because he knew." The whole sequence of events seemed to warp in my mind.

"How could he know?"

"Because he is crazy."

She looked at me. Then she kissed me, and I kissed her back.

I wanted never to stop, content in a whirl of bewilderment.

Just then a knock fell fast and hard on the door.

She backed away. I paused a moment, then opened the door. It was Wild Bill.

We exchanged looks all around. Bewilderment doubled, recoiled, then flattened out into absurdity. I saw her lips, actually quivering at first, now curl in amusement. Wild Bill had that effect.

"Wild Bill, what're you doing here?"

"Ah, man, it's too far out. You wouldn't believe what's going down. JP told me to swing by and pick you up. I'll explain in the car." The whole time he said this he was looking at Frederico's wife and raking his beard with his fingers. His eyes squinched.

"Oh, this is Madame Frederico, the concierge's wife."

"Yeah, *enchanté*. Your old man let me in."

"Yes, all of them. I'm going to wash all the windows, aren't I?"

I was surprised, at what she said, yes, but more so because she had said it all in English.

"Yes, they need it badly."

"Maybe you have an extra key so I can go out if I needed something and can get back in."

I looked at her. She was asking me something I didn't understand. "Yes." I got her a key. "Just keep track of how long you work and we'll settle up later."

In the car Wild Bill told me we were going to Versailles to meet a man at a fountain, the one, I happened to know, that had a statue in it of four horses pulling Apollo in his chariot, all rising out of the water and bringing sunlight to the earth. This man apparently knew something about a Monet painting that had been stolen from the Marmottan museum in Paris the fall before. The man had called JP early in the morning. JP, caught without a coat in yesterday's sudden cold and deathly ill, couldn't make it but had two men he could send over.

"Everyone knows that painting's in Japan," I said.

"Never made it out of Paris according to the dude."

"Well, this is just a little too much intrigue for me, thank you."

There wasn't much traffic heading out of town as we hit the A 13.

"That concierge's wife is a hot looking chick."

"She is a fine looking woman." I still tasted her lips.

"You plan to hang horns on her man?"

"I swear, I translate four languages, and half the time I can't understand a word you say." But I knew exactly what he meant.

"How 'bout, you thrash around the pasture before takin' the yoke?"

"No chance. Look, you see her cheekbone? I think her husband hit her. I'm concerned. But what can anyone do about it anyway?" I'd broadened his disquietude, from Little Red to humanity. He squinched.

"We just don't make contact these days." That "we" of his.

"Well, he apparently did!"

"So maybe we should do something."

"So maybe I'll put her in touch with proper authorities. — Dammit, Wild Bill, you're the reporter. I'm just a translator. Why the hell am I going off on this wild goose chase?"

"Guess JP thinks I'll blow the story of the decade. Ever noticed he has trouble taking me seriously?" His car was a Peugeot 504, the tank of France's auto industry, but he was driving like it was one of their Mirage jets. I saw the speedometer nudging 150 K, which translated into 90 MPH.

"You like the Doors?" He asked.

"The Doors? Yeah, I guess I did."

"Did! Jim Morrison was a visionary! You had all the visionaries." I didn't know who "you" was but it must have been something opposite of "we." "Hendrix. Lennon."

"Why is it all our visionaries are dead rock stars?"

"Simple. Something inside knew life would be cut short. So they concentrated their energy into a shorter span of time. Concentration yields vision."

I saw the speedometer nudge 160 K.

"Tell me, Wild Bill, are you visionary?"

"Not me. I'll live to a hundred."

"I'm glad."

He flicked on a tape deck and off we flew—to the tune of the Doors singing "Break on Through"—toward the Apollo fountain at Versailles to meet a man who'd tell us about a stolen Monet. I couldn't even think of Frederico's wife anymore and what I may have let myself in for.

I guess I should've figured it out long before we got there, but I didn't. I should've when we were walking along what's called the Tapis Vert, flanked by rows of statues and vases, but I didn't. I should've when I saw a table, in front of the fountain, set with a white linen cloth, food, and silver buckets and glasses. I should've when I saw people I knew, JP and others from the office, popping open champagne. I finally did when I saw Avril, for she made things happen.

"What's this?" I said coyly to Avril. "Someone gettin' hitched?"

"Ain'tcha ever had no engagement party?"

"Nope. You s'pose it kin make a dif'rence?"

"I shorely hope so."

"If we peasants had been allowed this to begin with," Wild Bill was saying, "we never woulda had a revolution!" Everyone laughed.

"Wild Bill," I said. "We are not peasants. And we were not alive two hundred years ago." There must've been acid in my voice, for eleven pairs of eyes turned on me. Then I blurted—" 'Cept maybe JP!" Everyone laughed again.

When Avril and I were alone, I asked her, "Why here?"

"JP asked me was there someplace special. I said here because you once told me it's your favorite fountain. It's mine too."

I couldn't remember ever telling her that. By this time the fountain had been turned on. Drenched in spray, the bronze-painted horses glistened.

"I was thinking August," she said.

"I don't know. August is my least favorite month."

"Mine, too." She smiled. "Honestly."

(Pam and I had had things in common, too. We were of an age, a generation, a geography. She was from the next town over. We graduated from the same college the same day. My father bought shingles from her father when we replaced the roof. Our mothers went to the same hairdresser, shopped at the same Penny's. But this was commonality given us. We hadn't sought it. That Avril and I loved the same wine that had a flavor of cedar pencils, that we loved the same moment in *Turandot* when Calaf, the Unknown Prince, sings he shall be victorious, that we both loved roan horses—didn't these speak of dovetailing choices? Weren't these choices small eurcharists celebrating a common destiny? Or had I become a pretentious fraud?)

The party seemed a lot of trouble to go through. But that was Avril. She'd flown back the day before—right after talking to me on the phone—gone shopping, prepared food. That night on the phone, she and Wild Bill, no doubt tickled, concocted the stolen Monet. She'd gotten to Versailles by ten. By noon she had everything set up. Now we all were in the spirit of things. It was warmer that day, for the fellow in the fountain had done a good job getting the sunshine out, but it was blustery. Napkins kept flying off. I avoided Wild Bill, and who knew if that confirmed or disproved suspicions he may have had about Frederico's wife and me. Finally Avril said she was going home, did I care to join her? Claiming I'd drunk too much I opted for my own apartment. Wild Bill gave me a ride, driving slower than I thought possible. He didn't play music or talk and the Peugeot ballooned with silence. When I was getting out he said, "I hope your windows are clean, man." I didn't say anything.

Looking up, I saw the impatiens. They'd been planted in boxes and hung on the iron railings outside my windows. In the lobby I could see the Fredericos' apartment was dim. I saw no one, but then I heard the eruption of snoring. Monsieur Frederico was sleeping.

In my apartment, I discovered everything had been cleaned and polished. All the windows, all the glass doors, the mirrors over the fireplaces in the living room and dining room—there is so much glass in a turn-of-the-century French apartment! And all my oak furniture as well—burnished to a deep sheen. I went into my bedroom. Frederico's wife stood at the fireplace mantle. She was polishing a small marble statue, black with gold veins. That it was a statue of a porpoise probably held no significance. That it was a present Avril had bought me on a weekend excursion we'd taken in Italy, that this small sea-side town had instantly become our favorite town of all the towns on the face of the earth—that had to be significant. Frederico's wife set the statue and a dust rag on the mantle.

"I guess I got carried away." She spoke English. I wished she were speaking French. "You have so many wonderful things. What a joy to rub them all and make them shine! So many, many wonderful things!"

She walked over to me. She ran her hand along the lapels of my sport coat, and along the collar of my shirt, as though to smooth away wrinkles. "Is that champagne I smell?" She breathed in the air around my lips. "What a life!" She kissed me, and again, as I had that morning, I kissed her back. In the face of sweet destiny, I kissed her back. I could feel her tipping, tipping us, and we were about to fall over as if off a wobbly chair.

She pulled away. Her lips parted, but her teeth pressed together. "Take me down to the cellar." I didn't think I'd heard that. I stepped toward her. She stepped back. "Take me down to the cellar." The words escaped like gas.

I gestured at the bed with my hand, as if to plead, we have this and you want the cellar?

She looked, but only saw the quilt. It was an old goose-down quilt I'd brought from the States four years ago. The last remnant of a life I'd been so deliberate at shucking off. But the quilt remained, coming apart even where I'd sewn it, and thinning out feather by feather.

"Such a raggy thing! It doesn't become you." She started pulling it up, gathering it in her arms. "Let's take this raggy, raggy quilt and lay it on the dirt in the cellar."

The cellar was the other side of the earth. I shook my head in disbelief.

"What's a short trip down the steps?" She hugged the quilt to herself. She laughed. "What's wrong, champagne breath and coal dust don't mix?"

"I want you here and now."

"You want . . . I want. I want, I want. How much I want."

"Here . . . now—"

"But not in three minutes? Not in two? One?—We could run."

"Why go to goddam basement?"

"Where else could we go in a minute?"

"Here, here ..." I grabbed the quilt and pulled, as if hauling in a net full of fish. It ripped wide open. Feathers flew and floated. I let go. Feathers settled around us.

"That would be too easy, wouldn't it." I didn't answer. She dropped the quilt on the bed, then picked up her rag from the mantle and left quickly.

In the morning I knocked on their door. Monsieur Frederico answered. Eyes slit, hair awry, he slid hands into flannel-robe pockets.

"First of all," I said, "this is for your wife." I held out money. He yawned and took it and put it in his pocket. "She worked five hours yesterday. We didn't specify beforehand, but I assume a hundred francs an hour is fair. Next, I believe you are abusing your wife, and I'm contacting authorities who will shelter her. If she wants to press charges and push for a termination of the marriage, I will help there as well in any way I can."

He rubbed an eye sleepily. "I don't know why you won't believe me."

I was watching over his shoulder, expecting to see her any moment. They only had the two small rooms. She must've heard me. We are a rational people, I was trying to tell her. There are ways of slowly untangling the ragged growth, no matter how much we ball it up. Yes, we have painstaking, legitimate procedures for doing this.

"Let me tell you about my wife—No, she is not here, so don't look. Come in." I stepped in, the place was a mess. "You see she cleans others' but not her own home. Except of course when we were trying to get rid of the cat." He sat down. I didn't. His legs were unexpectedly thin and white. He wore no slippers. "She is seeing another man. I say this man to man for perhaps you know what pain this can be. She says she is going to the market for mussels—that I love so much—but may be with him this very moment. I told you, I always go ahead, and she follows. What I didn't tell you was that he then follows. He always shows up—usually a month, two months later. This time he was so very quick about it. Perhaps he craves my wife more than I realize. Yes, I always go first—just as I will likely go from this place shortly. Then she follows, always. Then he follows, always. It is a hell of a life, no?" He began to cry. "Sometimes I wish that he would just take her. Take her for good!" Another shadow had trudged onstage. Whether cast by a living person or by his mind's own machinery—which he no doubt over oiled—I will never know. His sorrow seemed real enough—but appalled me.

I walked out, wanting only to get to work. I couldn't bare thinking about the Fredericos any longer.

At ten-thirty, Avril said, "August nineteenth. It's a Saturday. Favorite day."

"Saturday? Sunday's my favorite day."

"Saturday's been your favorite day as long as I've known you."

"Favorites aren't carved in stone."

"I carve mine in stone."

"Amen."

"You're acting strange. Yesterday, too." Obviously, I had been. "Distant. Distracted. People noticed. So if it's cold feet, let me know quick. I won't be waking one morning to you saying all's a mistake." She left, without saying for where, and I didn't see her the rest of the day.

At 11:20 I got a phone call from Madame Heursault, the manager of my apartment building. She said she was calling all the residents of the building over matters concerning the new concierge. It seems, first of all, that he had written a check, on an account meant for building supplies, to buy a TV. "Was he crazy enough to think we wouldn't know or wouldn't care!" Yes, I thought, he was. Next, as some residents had reported, his service to the building was deficient—hallways, stairwells, brass doorpulls, were not being properly cleaned, and even the garbage had not been put at the curb for three days straight. Yes, I thought, this is true, isn't it. Finally, and this was the most disturbing thing-—because maybe the TV matter and the service matter could be corrected but this, this—he and his wife had had a terrible fight last Friday afternoon. Though most of the residents were at work—yes, I was, too, I knew—those few at home shuddered at what they heard. Violent screaming and swearing. "Yes," I lied, "I had to run home for some important papers that afternoon. I have to tell you how deeply disturbing it was to hear." It's pretty well settled then, she went on, that the man has to go. Yes, he has to go. She admitted she felt personally responsible. For in fact, Madame Frederico was a second cousin. And though most of the family had nothing to do with her, she, Madame Heursault, had taken pity when her second cousin called several weeks ago to say her husband needed work.

"It is strange and sad, and how she got mixed up with such a man, none of us will ever understand."

"How long have they been married?"

"Twelve or thirteen years. It is incredible."

"She seems lost."

"Lost! Let me tell you, Monsieur. She had every opportunity. Her family owns a great vineyard in Beaujolais. She was sent to study in Geneva, Vienna, London. Anything she could want she could have."

"But what you say seems impossible."

"Listen to me. At eighteen she was engaged to marry the son of an owner of a neighboring vineyard. It was all planned. Like out of a fairytale. Okay, this young man, her fiancé, did something stupid, it isn't entirely clear, but he went away, some say to another woman. But the point is he came back. He admitted his fault. He wanted desperately to make up for his error. But by then it was too late, she had run off with this Frederico—some foreman laying the high-speed train lines."

"That truly is strange and sad, Madame Heursault."

"So now I have the dirty task of going over there this afternoon and expelling the two of them."

"Her as well?"

"If she asked me for refuge, I'd give it. But she will no doubt choose to go with him. What a life she has thrown away for the sake of this man! I'll give him two-week severance—for her sake. I'm wary of him, so likely I will take a policeman with me."

This story of Madame Heursault's told of events that led to events, but ultimately explained nothing.

I worked at my computer the rest of the day, buried in the unchanging news of the world. At last, at dusk, I headed home.

At the concierge's door I looked in. The apartment was empty. That is, the furniture, including the television, all building property, remained. But all personal effects were gone. It was as though a wind had blown through the place and swept away anything not heavy enough to stay put.

Did I really believe that Frederico's wife would remain? She had always followed before. Did I for a moment want her to remain?

She still had the key to my apartment.

I went upstairs and walked in. I looked in every room. Then looked again.

Several months later, Madame Bucher, the first concierge, was back on the job. Her sister in Provence was much, much better. The orange cat, Clementine, slept daily on the cool smooth marble of the lobby, just like she used to do. Upstairs, Avril and I were packing up glasses and dishes. Wild Bill was helping while informing us that in two thousand years—the year two thousand?—no, no, no—in two thousand years, we would all be speaking the same language. Avril's job and mine would be obsolete except in the way that we now have translators of hieroglyphics. We laughed, wondering aloud about unemployment benefits. In the kitchen I began to seal up the window that opened on the dangerous counterweight, for Avril and I were to marry on a Saturday in August, and we'd decided on giving up the apartments we had and moving into a bigger place. The impatiens spilled out in bright colors. We would move them by car rather than have the movers handle them.

I look daily among items coming across my screen for a hint of the Fredericos. For I expect them to make the news one of these days. Till then, I imagine them wandering, he like a bear in front, she behind, dodging—not always successfully—the occasional backward swipe of a paw. It's unclear if he drags her along or she drives him forward. Behind the two of them a shadow follows. Perhaps many shadows.

Oh sweet, wonderful Avril, can we endure, as these two have, for better or for worse?

PLAYING ABOVE THE RIM

The court beneath St. Malachy's American Church of Paris had hoops with chain nets, and when someone canned a good, clean shot, the ball went *chunk.* We called our court The Pit because its walls were but two feet beyond the boundaries. Around three of those walls, about ten feet up, ran a mezzanine, and you had to descend a steep, narrow-treaded set of steps, more like a ladder, to get down on the floor, which itself had spongy spots, dead wood that old veterans like Petey Calisher and I instinctively avoided. There were no windows and no ventilation, the odor and humidity so thick at times you gasped like a person drowning.

Come September people showed up on Tuesday nights and shot fouls to make up sides. Come July vacations depleted the ranks. His fourth year in The Pit—my eighth—Calisher decided to create a team and enter us in the Paris Basketball League. I'd seen dozens of players come and go, such a hodgepodge of age, talent, jobs, education, politics—you name it—I doubted any handful of us could ever hold together. The only thing we probably had in common was the love of a basketball going *chunk.* But Calisher, who worked for the Commerce Department, was in the business of bringing people together, though in the interest of setting trade policy—not a pick or screen—and usually at the best Parisian restaurants—not in The Pit.

As soon as I arrived on court that first Tuesday night, Calisher pulled me aside to tell me about a newcomer he'd spoken with by phone. "Name's Quincy Dobbs and he paints. Graduated Beaux Arts." I chuckled. "My first sentiment, too, Dick," he said. "Except then he asks me—get this—do we have collapsible rims? No, I say. Why? Because, he says, the last time I played—six years ago—I brought down a backboard and put three people in the hospital. Did they survive? I ask. Oh, yeah, he says. Good, I say. Be at Malachy's at eight. He sounds black." For a born diplomat like Calisher to make such distinctions startled me. Now I heard him coo once and go, "Oh-la-la, looky here." Walking in along the mezzanine was Quincy Dobbs.

Though only about six foot—I can say *only* because I'm six-four—he looked big, strong and fast, bursting with coil springs. I stood wondering how anyone who literally crashed backboards could also set a paintbrush to a canvas. I had to be thinking also—though I don't recall consciously doing so—that the person being black compounded the anomaly. I saw Calisher narrow his eyes. Dobbs would be no Bucky Smith, the black Marine who for two years now had played perfectly average ball. Then, when Dobbs had to turn around and back down the steep steps because his calves were so big they scraped on the treads, Calisher whispered, "Now there's a man who plays above the rim."

"Easy does it, Calisher," I whispered back, but he'd already trotted away to welcome Dobbs to the fold.

Despite any six-year layoff, play above the rim Dobbs did indeed. I tried to cover him, ungracefully, in a game of three-on-three, catching glimpses of Calisher on the sideline rocking on his heels and smacking his lips.

"You play in college?" I asked when we broke for a rest.

"No. Too busy."

"How long you been in Paris?"

"Feels like a lifetime."

"How come you never showed up here before?"

"Too busy. But my psychotherapist thinks physical exercise will help my work. I saw the notice at the American bookstore." He had a copper face, thick-browed with wide set eyes, and apparently couldn't care less if I knew who he got advice from.

"I hear you paint."

"You hear correctly." I sensed it bothered him I should have heard anything at all about him.

"Not houses, I assume." I tried to joke.

"I'm sure Mr. Calisher already told you what I paint."

"I guess he did. Quincy Dobbs, isn't it?"

"Well, that's two things you know about me."

"My name's Dick D'Arata and I'm in wine imports. Now we're even." I'd at first thought his terse, no nonsense style, with both words and a basketball, refreshing. No bluster or showboating. But now his voice seemed a bit too chilled, and I judged his handshake too wrenchlike for an artist's—though I'd no other artist's to compare it with. His searching eyes—inquisitive? sensitive to detail?—made me uncomfortable.

Fortunately Marcia Rather walked onto the mezzanine, giving me cause to look away. Long-limbed and taut-muscled, she was a perfect concoction of athlete, woman, and professional. A deadly outside shooter on court, she was a patent lawyer off.

"You mean women play here?" Dobbs asked.

"This woman does. She'll surprise you."

"Well, let us not forejudge," he said, walking away.

Except maybe for the Marines, few of us got to know each other off court. Marcia and I tried, in June, for about a week, during which she did most of the talking, and left me to do most of the drinking. Dreaming of the places where her sinew met soft flesh, I endured her talk of whales, South Africa, the ozone, and Perigordian geese force-fed to plump their livers. Besides a patent lawyer, she was a cause-monger. In Paris, where you can lose yourself for years—maybe a lifetime—in sweet, heady folds, all perfume and saxophone, word of the foundering world glances off honeyed ears. And mine were full of honey then, so I didn't hear much of what Marcia was saying.

No surprise, she was a vegetarian, and I had her to my place for chili, substituting bulgur wheat for beef. After dinner, we stood in long silence at my window. Off court she wore blinding lipstick, her mouth becoming two fire-engine red leeches. Now, on the square below, trees with heart-shaped leaves seemed to conspire with my determination to perform the miracle of springing butterflies from leeches. I kissed her. As she was so preoccupied—with something other than the green hearts, I conclude—she never saw me coming. Unmoved, unperturbed, she pulled her head back. "Dick, I'm not in the frame of mind." Then she added. "Do you always drink so much?" I hadn't noticed. We'd had one bottle, though refills for her could be measured in sips and for me in full glasses.

"Well, I am in the wine business."

"Yes. I guess you are." She excused herself.

I looked in a mirror and, seeing my mouth bloodied up with her lipstick, snatched a napkin off the table and wiped it clean. I took her home on the Metro, Marcia gabbling about Brigitte Bardot's animal rights movement, and all I could imagine was Bardot—with her wonderful lips—running along a beach at Saint Tropez, in a black-and-white movie. Marcia and I didn't stand a chance. Back in my apartment, on the bathroom sink, I found a steel tube of lipstick I never bothered returning.

Marcia descended the stairs onto the court, some preoccupation or other still stuck to her blue eyes. "It's about time, Rather," Calisher cracked, decidedly a coach who wouldn't bide slackness. I watched her pull back her raven hair and fasten it. Sitting on the floor, she pushed a pair of sweatpants down to her knees and pulled off both legs at once with one hand. In June I had concluded she was a bore, which somehow reinforced the sense of my own zest. She probably summed me up the same way. Now we were part of a team.

"Hi, Marcia."

"Oh. Hi." For a second she'd forgotten my name. "Hi, Dick."

Leadership goes to him who seizes it, and no one seemed to mind if that was Calisher. He'd been doing the work to get us into the Paris Basketball League, having already secured sponsorship from Rosa's New York Pizza, off the Champs Elysees. He chose up sides for four-on-four, putting Dobbs and Marcia in the backcourt on one team. Apparently Dobbs decided to give Marcia her chance. Shredding the defense, he unselfishly fed her the ball and she canned the open shot. Her glazed, preoccupied eyes had no trouble sighting the hoop. *Chunk. Chunk. Chunk.* She very nearly smiled. Indeed, Dobbs' presence injected everyone with an energy I'd never seen in The Pit. At the end of the night, when Calisher wanted ideas for a team name, we were too tired to think about it. Surprise us, we told him.

The day before filing the papers with league officials, Calisher found out the Commerce Department was transferring him to Japan. The news changed him forever, and what I'd perceived in him since our first meeting as blind chauvinism worsened into maudlin patriotism. I can picture Calisher staring at the blank on the application form after *Team Name,* his heart athump with the desire to leave a mark on France unknown since D-Day, and suddenly seeing *Little America* go off like a bomb bursting in air.

The second Tuesday, in the silence that followed his announcement of the team's name, Calisher barked, "You told me to surprise you." Then he started firing the new uniforms at us. The jerseys sported *Rosa's* in tomato red above the numbers on the backs. Finally, Martinez, who worked for IBM, sang out, "Yes, yes. Little America." Sincerely. "Yeah, man, that's very excellent."

Newly christened, Little America spent three hours running and memorizing plays, Calisher driving us like a man obsessed. With him at the wheel and Dobbs supplying a magic fuel, we might mesh after all—not merely a team, but an unstoppable machine.

A few weeks into the season, we were clobbering a team from the west side of Paris in The Pit. Bucky Smith had gone in for me, and I climbed the steps to take a seat beside Calisher in the mezzanine. "Jesus, Dick," he said out of nowhere a minute later, "Japan doesn't know what a basketball looks like."

"So be Johnny Appleseed, plant backboards wherever you go."

"I couldn't slip a backboard in, the country's so goddam crowded. We'll be lucky to get a four-room apartment." I'd been to a party at Calisher's. He was used to space. He had five kids and at least that many bedrooms, and his living room itself was the size of a b-ball court, with marble fireplaces and gilt-framed mirrors, not to mention a chandelier a maid spent entire days on a ladder cleaning—so Calisher informed a circle of us standing beneath it with upturned faces.

I saw Bucky try a lob into Dobbs, the ball overthrown and out of bounds. Calisher growled.

A moment later he asked, "You ever *seen* Tokyo?" I hadn't. "The buildings look like boxes. Power lines are everywhere, like the man upstairs dropped a bowl of black spaghetti. And the Japs scurry around in perfect files. Like ants."

"*Japs*, Petey? *Ants*?"

"Dick, believe me, they think *we're* some lower form of life." Maudlin patriotism was worsening into something else. "I'll need a boatload of your insipid wine to wash down that insipid food they eat."

"Stop bashing Japan, Petey—and stop bashing my wine."

I imported California wines, which was at first as hard as selling dandelions to a florist. Now I supplied some thirty bars and restaurants, and several supermarket import aisles. My savior was Zinfandel, a variety the French had never cultivated. Maybe with good reason. "No body, no personality," Calisher always chided, bored by my offerings. Ostensibly pushing US trade causes, his real vocation—one he'd have a sorry time pursuing in Tokyo—was sampling and purchasing wines for the Embassy. "Buy American, Calisher."

"Dick, you are what you drink. Not how much you drink," he'd advised at his party.

Smith was wide open for a three pointer when he tried another lob into Dobbs. Errant again.

"Hit the open bucket, Buck!" Calisher shouted.

"Give him hell, Petey. We're only up thirty-two points."

"You get a couple of these guys together and all of a sudden they think they're the L.A. Lakers."

"*These guys*, Calisher?"

But he was too intent on the game, and next time Smith brought the ball down court and tried yet another lob to Dobbs, this one sailing clear over the backboard, Petey exploded. "Buck up, Bucky! Go to the bucket, Buck-key!"

The words spit forth in a spray. Maybe Smith the Marine was accustomed to getting chewed out, for he just nodded, yes, yes, yes. But the look I saw Quincy fire our way made the mezzanine feel like a shooting gallery.

Calisher's wife and kids, sitting a few feet away, had come to every game to cheer Little America. His two oldest—pretty girls, thirteen and sixteen—were giggling now. Calisher went and stood before them. "Do you think this is a laughing matter?" The girls sat up straight. "Do you?" They shook their heads.

His wife, Linda, stood up. "Petey! Enough already!" They were eyeball to eyeball, and I'd never imagined Calisher's face could look so washed out. He was the grinner, the winer and diner, unimpeachable in belief and method. If Linda didn't always understand him, America, with a firm hand on his shoulder, certainly did. At that party of his, the *hors d'oeuvres* had toothpicks flying tiny Old Glories. His maid probably had orders to collect them all afterward and give them a proper burial. "Come on, kids," Linda said. They rose in unison, our entire cheering section, and left, not to return until the last game of the season.

Afterward Calisher said sorry to Smith, who didn't seem to understand what the apology was for. I invited Calisher out for a quick beer. Malachy's was on the river, and we crossed the bridge to a bar overlooking the Seine. He talked about the transfer.

"I don't know if it's a betrayal or a challenge, Dick." He was completely despondent. "Okay, so I do my duty, and I'm outta there in three years, maybe two."

"It's a shame the Japanese don't shoot hoop like they swing a baseball bat. You'd probably feel a whole lot better."

"It so happens I like baseball better than hoop. But you won't catch me in a stadium full of Japs."

"Jesus, Calisher, cut it already."

"Look, D'Arata, don't tell me. I've been to Tokyo three times, I walk around those streets and my skin actually crawls."

"Ants, Calisher. You told me. The Japanese beat up on your father or something during the last world war?"

"The old man sat it out with a heart murmur."

"So maybe it's your girls. Maybe you worry who they'll bring home."

"Yeah, I've thought about that. But it's something else, Dick. Look, I lived in Caracas for three years, Nairobi for four, and I loved 'em both, and I loved the people. And they loved me."

"So they called you Bwana and the Japanese won't, that it?"

"D'Arata, sometimes people can be too different. *Capiche?*"

"No, Petey, *no capiche*."

"Too distant. Too strange. Impossible to really know. Don't you see?" The spotlights from a passing tour boat illuminated Malachy's green-coppered steeple. Maybe Calisher took it as a sign. "Look, I attend that church, and I know way down inside we're all supposed to be made of the same stuff."

"That's a pretty bleak thought."

"I'm serious. It tears at me here to say it"—he thumped a fist on his chest—"but what if we're *not* made of the same stuff?"

"Petey, I think you got a batch of bad sushi and haven't recovered." Now the boat's light was in our faces and I saw Calisher paralyzed with fright, like a hedgehog when you catch him in your headlights. I laid a twenty-franc bill on the table and bid *au'voir*.

Whatever tore at his insides he took it out on us. Halfway through the schedule, having played each team in the league once, we were 8-0, an unstoppable machine—maybe. The fact is, the French were fairly inept at this game. They did a lot of shakin' and bakin', but not much cookin'. And they didn't play defense. "The Maginot line all over again," Calisher often cackled, calling us into a huddle—something the team tacitly took now as dancing around the crazy man. Then he'd bludgeon us with what we were doing wrong. Though we were averaging twenty-one point wins, he'd send his slow self in to play only when nothing short of divine intervention could reverse our victory. He'd throw up his lazily arching shots and always hit the middle of three attempts. A crowning ritual he looked so happy performing.

On a bright Sunday in November, Marcia Rather and Quincy Dobbs were sitting on a bench on rue des Rosiers eating falafel sandwiches when I turned the corner and spotted them. I was with a woman, wispy-haired, curvaceous and smiley, named Veronique. I'd met her at a nightclub near the Arc de Triomphe a week earlier. She was taking me to see a leather clothing boutique she owned on Rosiers, a bent street in the old Jewish quarter, now undergoing the beginnings of gentrification. Marcia was coming out of a deep laugh about something, her face filled with such expression—such happiness—I didn't recognize her for a moment. Quincy, too, was emerging from the same spot of delight. Though Marcia and I had unequivocally proven an impossible match, I felt a stab of jealousy and an impulse to about-face. But they'd seen us. We walked over and made introductions. It was before noon and, maybe because there was something in that Sunday light, I knew they'd spent the night together. I'm sure they knew Veronique and I had done the same and, as we stupidly talked about the weather, I attempted to convey what Marcia's look certainly conveyed: no dull times now, you see.

I thought we were about to get away when Veronique said, "Oh, here." From her giant purse she easily withdrew two business cards, as if it contained a few thousand, and handed them to Little America's backcourt. "I'm right down the street." Then to Quincy she said, "You would look splendid in leather pants."

Marcia blew a gasket and, holding the card before her, seemed to read a list of charges. Why was Veronique contaminating the neighborhood with a boutique? And weren't belts and shoes about the limit of leather a person needed? And did she mean leather pants somehow suited black males better than others? Seeming not to believe in what Marcia was saying, Quincy had a wry look, and that relieved me, like suddenly we were buddies watching women wrestlers. Marcia's falafel had fallen apart in her hand, half its ingredients on the sidewalk. Veronique's moulage smile never broke.

"My dear," she said, "how wonderful to see such conviction in these days of cynicism and self-indulgence." Then she sashayed off. I nodded to Quincy and he nodded back, but the wryness was gone, replaced by something decisive, as if the girl his money was on had won the match. Walking away, I realized Marcia wasn't wearing lipstick. I almost turned to double check, but didn't dare.

"Self-righteous bitch," Veronique said, unlocking her shop. Even if that were Marcia in a nutshell, I couldn't help feeling twinges the next few games anytime she and Quincy combined to score a basket. One had to marvel at their play-making, harmonizing all the more with each game, and as the rest of the team hadn't seen them on Rosiers, there was nothing else they thought to attach to it. Absurdly, I found myself feeding Marcia passes at the most strategically inopportune moments.

Then a poster appeared in the lobby of the American Church advertising an exhibit of Quincy Dobbs' work at a gallery on the Left Bank. I went, determined to refute any talent he might have other than playing above a rim. It was not until I saw what was actually there that I realized I'd been expecting to see tortured shapes, angry graffiti-like strokes, struggle, dispossession. What I saw was the exact opposite. I don't know a great deal about art—I'm an ad and marketing man, after all. But I enjoy museums, looking at paintings and stating my likes or dislikes, even if I can't explain why.

Quincy's paintings surprised and uplifted. He had no landscapes, no still-lifes. His work depicted people, candidly seized in bold brushstrokes. Some black, some white, they seemed to move in and out of the canvas, carrying something invisible as they went, sometimes catching you eye-to-eye with an offer, unexpectedly serene. There was one painting I returned to several times. It suggested movement, action, a little story: a woman, naked, is rising from a chair at a window, where no doubt she's been gazing, waiting. Now you've entered the room and she is moving to greet you. Out the window the trees are autumnal, and on her face and in her eyes is quiet, knowing joy.

The gallery bubbled with people. I'd scarcely been able to give Quincy a handshake, but I hoped he knew I was congratulating him for something special. I was about to leave, taking a last look at the woman rising from the chair, and taking a last glass of wine, a meaty Cote du Rhone, when Marcia came up alongside me. She'd ignored me before that. I turned to her, and she looked all around me.

"Couldn't your friend make it?"

"She's out—" I almost said skinning calves. "She's out of town." I looked at the painting. "That's you, isn't it?"

"Yes." She sounded defiant, for there she was, against her will, naked before me.

"It's a wonderful painting, Marcia."

"I don't know."

"Yes, it is."

"Maybe."

I left her standing before the painting. Taped to the gallery's front door, I saw, was a poster that hadn't been there when I arrived. Something about a demonstration against racism. I knew Marcia put it there, and I knew I wouldn't attend. Racial peace was made between individuals, I must have thought, not groups. I walked out into the night, feeling lighter on my feet than I had anytime since the morning on Rosiers.

Come late December, three days before Christmas, all was not well in Little America's backcourt.

Calisher sensed it first. At a gym in the eleventh arrondissement we were playing a group of Africans we'd already beaten in The Pit by thirty-one points. They were lanky, angular and awkward. Some of them, perhaps all, might have been among those Africans you saw on the terraces of Trocadero or Montmartre, spreading out blankets and arranging meager trinkets to sell to tourists. You had to wonder how they survived. In the first game they ganged up on Dobbs, and time after time he drove the lane, drew a crowd, then fed it back to Marcia, who canned shots from the top of the key that night as easily as dropping fruit in a basket. About ten minutes into this second game I twisted an ankle. I came out and sat next to Calisher, who wanted an instant answer to the question, "What the hell's Quincy's problem, why's he not dishing it back?"

"They're not collapsing on him tonight. Two guys're hanging back at the foul line. So how can he dish it back?"

"No, no. Somethin's wrong out there."

"He's scoring points, isn't he?"

"He's endangering the whole mechanism."

"Calisher, they adjust, we adjust, right? They adapt, we adapt." I slipped off a sneaker and started taping the ankle.

"You know what I read yesterday?" He asked.

"I don't know, what, *War and Peace*?"

"Tape it from the arch up, funny guy. They're going underground."

"What?"

"The plans are on the board. Sixty stories deep. Entire cities. They're bringing sunlight in with fiber optics. Ants, I'm telling you."

"I didn't know ants had fiber optics."

"My ass in a pit crawling with ants."

"My advice to you, Calisher, is skip the entomology and pick up some books on Japanese art and cuisine."

"I don't like their art, and I don't like their food." He was beyond advice. Finishing the ankle, I looked up in time to see Dobbs flying in for a dunk, something in his face I'd later decide was pure anger.

Calisher exclaimed, "Sweet lightning!" and an instant later there was a zipping, ripping sound, like a tree falling at high speed, and an instant after that Dobbs was sprawled on the floor. The rim lay beside him, a chunk of backboard still attached. The referee, an African himself, assessed things quickly, and then, as if in a boxing ring after a KO, raised the closest African player's hand. "*Defaut! Vous gagnez!*"

Calisher stomped onto the court, ranted and swore in French, and got nowhere. He threatened the ref with an official protest, though he must've known the Paris Basketball League, as amateur as it was, would meet such a protest with confusion or yawns.

Finally, he turned on Dobbs, pleading in French, "Talk to him, will you!" And the implication in that—*He's one of your people*—made those of us who understood the language blink. Apparently Smith did not. Dobbs meanwhile walked over to Marcia, still standing at the top of the key, where she'd been waiting all night for passes that never came.

"Wouldn't it be great if they beat us," Dobbs said to her, obviously mimicking something Marcia had told him. Things became even clearer when he added, "Anything else you want to hand these poor boys?" The rest of Little America, sensing something, began to pack up.

"What kinda crap you bringin' on the court?" Smith said. But Dobbs was already headed for a drinking fountain in the corner of the gym. No one but me followed him over, and I waited for him to finish his turn. Whatever jealousy I thought I'd squelched, I still found myself delighting over puzzle pieces the rest of the team lacked. As I stepped up to take a drink, Dobbs and I exchanged the slightest nods—mine the one both wry and decisive this time. After gulping away for a few seconds, I twisted around and faced the man I'd been playing center against.

"We beat you." He smiled. His skin was so black it had a sheen like brushed aluminum.

"Yes," I said calmly, but I felt my legs turn to pudding and my face drain. I must've wobbled.

"What the hell's the matter with you, D'Arata?" Dobbs asked.

"I hate to lose, Quincy. I simply hate to lose."

What was the matter was this: back when I was learning marketing, how to ferret out consumers' needs—or create those needs—I sometimes played ball with a fellow named Matt Showalter; people called him *Showboat.* He was a solid player, and on Saturdays we'd drive over to a black section of Albany in his Firebird to shoot what we considered real hoop. I was idealistic or naive enough then to believe I was somehow building bridges. Not Showalter. He just loved to bang bodies. Unfortunately, though solid, he had a loose mouth. "Action talks, bullshit walks." "In your face." That kind of stuff. Or "Nuthin'!" as soon as his opponent let go a shot.

One day he came up against a black guy with the same kind of mouth, and they went at each other like tigers, bounding and roaring. Showboat's team needed one hoop to win the game. The black guy all over him, Matt took the ball to the basket, faking a lay-up on the right and swooping under for a reverse on the left. Bingo. It was a beauty of a move. But Showboat didn't leave it at that. "In your goddam face!" The black guy made a move at him, but his buddies pulled him back, and Matt strolled away.

Now, there was a fountain at this playground, and Showalter and I went to get drinks. Me first, then Matt. The black guy walked up behind him, seemingly cooled off. Matt bent over the fountain. The black guy reached out his hand, gripped Showalter's head like a grapefruit, and smashed it down. "In your motherfuckin' face!" I heard something. It was another kind of *chunk,* an ax in a dead tree stump. Showalter stood up straight, dazed, the blood pouring from his mouth. I put my arm around him and led him away as everyone watched silently. Then he began crying like a baby. I drove him to a hospital. All the way there he kept spitting out pieces of teeth and cupping them in his hand, saving them, like he thought they could glue everything back together.

After that whenever I tried to drink at a fountain, no matter how thirsty, I felt the spigot was a chisel coming at me and quickly backed off. In France, drinking fountains are rare, and I'd not be surprised to learn the bottled-water companies hold a lobby against them. Living in Paris so long, I'd forgotten everything about drinking fountains. Until I turned and saw the African standing behind me.

We nearly lost our next game because of the US Secretary of State. He was on his way to Warsaw and decided last minute to stop in Paris and dine with the French Minister of Foreign Affairs. "Probably thought a square meal before kielbasa city was in order," Calisher told me on the phone the day after Christmas. Maybe it was spending holidays alone (though I had given myself a superb Chateau Haut-Brion, '70), or a call I'd gotten before Calisher's, but

I was in little mood for him.

Turns out he'd been invited to the meal. Buck Smith and two other of our players, also Marines, would be on duty to beef up security. The dinner fell on the same night as our basketball game.

"That means we've got four players, Dick. Now, nowhere in the rule book does it say you have to have five players on the court. I also spoke to the league president, the same clown who said, 'You broke rim, you lose game,' and he sees nothing wrong with us a player short. He probably thinks this is great for parity. *Egalité, n'est-ce pas?"*

"What if we only have three players?"

"What?"

"Dobbs called. He quit the team."

There was a litany of curses, then, "Why didn't he call me?"

"He said to pass the word to Coach Bigot."

"Bigot!"

"It was your *talk to him* apparently."

"Dobbs assumes I meant something other than I meant."

"What did you mean?"

"Talk to him! Dobbs graduated Beaux Arts, so he must be able to *parlez-vous* pretty good. That so difficult?" A shock of the obvious. I wanted to believe him. "And the problem's not me, it's Dobbs and Rather. I figured it out, they're sleeping together or somethin', and the well's dryin' up."

"Does that bother you, Petey? The thought of him all over that sweet white babe?"

"Look, D'Arata, I know what you're trying to do, but it ain't that way. I was interested in the man's French because mine sucks. Got it?"

"Well, Petey, it's good to find a man like yourself who's so discriminating in his discrimination."

"You gonna go see Dobbs or not, Dick?"

"Sure, Calisher, I'll spare you getting his door slammed in your face." He gave me Dobbs' address.

"Now, if he refuses to come back I'll skip the dinner and play myself. I think we can handle these squirts, Dobbs or no Dobbs."

"Petey, do you think, possibly, this basketball thing has gotten out of perspective? You'd miss dinner with the Secretary of State?"

"You're right. Maybe I can corner him and get some answers on the Tokyo transfer."

"Wish me luck, Coach."

"Good luck, Dick."

The next day I went to Dobbs' place. He lived in Montparnasse at the end of a *cul-de-sac*, more country lane than city street, with trees and houses, most of which had tall-windowed ateliers. I thought I'd left Paris and stepped into an artists' colony in Provence.

When he opened the door Quincy's first words were, "Coach is sorry and takes back what he said—even swears not to tell nigger jokes in the Embassy bathroom."

"You think people tell nigger jokes in the Embassy bathroom?"

"He'd probably like to. And he surely wanted me to talk to the African ref because he thought I had an in."

"I believe Coach had your language abilities in mind. Now I know Petey—"

"Look, before you waste your own language abilities, I've decided to continue playing. I need the exercise. Exercise'll be good for my work." Hadn't he told me the same thing three months ago? "Come in." My mission aborted, I nonetheless entered.

"Drink?"

"Red wine is fine."

It was a neat, one-room living space, with fine clean touches in the decor and many wall-hangings, masks and statues I assume were African. But no paintings. I strolled about, exploring. Off the one room was his studio. I started to step in. "Sorry, no one's allowed in there uninvited." He walked over and closed the door.

"Will Marcia be sitting for you anymore?"

"No."

"Didn't you two look exceptionally happy that Sunday on rue des Rosiers?"

"We were happy. Now we're not."

"There'll be no more problems playing ball with her?"

"I'm gonna puke in a second, D'Arata. The *problem* as you well know is she turns buying a loaf of bread into The Human Struggle. You can only take that drivel for so long."

"Right, but—don't tell me—getting laid on a steady basis is good for one's work."

"Look, D'Arata, whatever your reasons, if you're trying to insult me, don't bother, and if you're trying to exonerate her, you'd better know she doesn't think a whole lot of you."

"I bet. And every word she said is true." I finished my wine. "May I have some more?" Encouragingly, he kept up glass for glass, well into three bottles. There we were, basketball teammates, bonding.

At one point I remarked how bright his apartment was. He said he'd taken it precisely for the light coming through the studio window. "But more, I need the isolation of the street." Without stating the price, he said the rent wasn't that steep. "I don't come from money exactly—I guess that's relative—but it's something I've never had to worry about." His father was one of the best ear-nose-throat doctors in Macon, Georgia, peering into the holes in the heads of white and black patients alike.

"Everybody's pink inside," I joked.

"So says the gynecologist," he replied, humorless as ever. "When it comes to ears and noses, that's not true. But I'll pass it on to my father. He's not opposed to bending the truth if it'll get a laugh."

I asked him straight out, "Where'd you learn such good hoop?" Almost bashfully, he said he'd been All-State in high school. Passing up twenty-eight basketball scholarships, Quincy went to NYU, pre-med, briefly following—as Van Gogh had in theology, he noted—his father's footsteps. Spending more time in art museums than labs, he heard a calling beyond medicine. "I made my choice." I wondered if *calling*, by definition, can be chosen. Yes or no, he later completed studies at Beaux Arts, "the only American black at the time," and for the last six years worked methodically ten hours a day.

"Till five months ago, when the big slump hit," he said. "Those paintings you saw were from before, except for the one of Marcia. I hoped the show would pull me out, but it didn't." *Just like Marcia didn't,* I thought. "Nothing did."

"Why not? I read some reviews. Very good." I had concurred.

"My paintings sell. But people's approval—it's beside the point. Now, having got a taste of approval, something inside has let up. False satisfaction. I shot my wad before getting way down in, where the real fecundity is."

"You talk funny, Quincy. Look, appreciate the kudos." The copper in his face was turning molten.

"You want to see what my struggle is, D'Arata?" He plodded into the studio and returned carrying a canvas in such a way I could only see the back of it. It was maybe two feet by three.

"Here is my struggle." He flipped it around. It was empty. A white surface full of nothing. He seemed desperate to get from me the very thing he'd a moment ago declared anathema—approval. "You don't know, you can't even imagine, what struggle is." I didn't counter with selling California wine in France, but I did ask if Marcia knew.

"She thinks so. Only she doesn't have a struggle unless there's someone to struggle against, see. Whereas, it's me against this."

I rose from the sofa and went to the door to let myself out. I resented his patent on struggle. I turned around to look at him, the canvas squarely clamped before him. "Well, you're always good enough to play in the European pros."

He smiled for the first time that afternoon. "D'Arata, quick—name a famous black painter." I couldn't. He let the canvas drop a little. "I told you, I need the exercise."

"I'm glad." Mutual advantageousness. "Incidentally, Quincy. I get this ringing in my ears lately. Any chance it's the alcohol?"

"There's a simple test for that. Stop drinking."

"Okay, promise. Not another drop till after the season. I'll be so shitfaced sober no one'll know me."

Then he asked me suddenly, "D'Arata, what was the look on

your face that night at the drinking fountain?"

I didn't even hesitate. "Because I once saw an ugly, mean son of a bitch smash another ugly, mean son of a bitch's face in a drinking fountain. So I get nervous when someone stands too close behind me."

"Especially if that someone is black?"

"Who said anything about black? Hey, this fountain was whites only."

He smiled again. "*Touché*, D'Arata. Oh, and by the way, you didn't miss much as far as Marcia goes. That woman talks the joy out of everything."

Now it was mine turn to smile. I think I did, then closed the door. At whatever cost, we had our star back. Calisher whooped when I phoned in the news.

With difficulties, we won the shorthanded game, as well as our next, the second-to-last. I found out Calisher actually shook the Secretary of State's hand. But that's it.

"I'm not high enough on the ladder for him to fuss with."

"Chickenheart. Why didn't you tell him how you feel about Japs?"

"Get outta here. Besides he's State Department, not Commerce." In both games Quincy simply refused to shoot the ball. He wouldn't even drive the lane and pretend he might shoot. He'd left Little America with pure anger and returned a cheerleader. Good, good this, good, good that, for anything anyone did. We were 14-1 and tied with the Montmartre Aigles. The Paris Basketball League, no doubt remembering who invented this game, arranged the schedule so Little America would meet Montmartre, last year's champion, in the final game. We'd barely beaten the Aigles the first time out. They had a legitimate ballplayer, formerly of the French national team, in one Marcel Gault—pronounced *Go*—who had given Quincy everything he could handle.

"I hope you're just saving yourself for the championship, Quincy," Marcia said as we were packing up to leave.

"There's even a trophy, Quincy," Calisher added.

"Calisher, this team'll win the trophy, with or without me."

"You gotta go after Gault, Quince. Be all over him. That's all I ask."

"Don't you worry. I'll go for Gault." A laugh reeled out.

"I know you will, Quince. I know you will."

Each was *Gault-ing,* going, gone—over his own edge, and they were talking through a glass wall. Seeing it, I hated Quincy's returning. Why had he bothered when he knew he didn't belong among us clowns?

I walked out with Calisher. He gave me a ride to the nearest Metro. He told me in Japan there are shrines full of small statues, dolls made out of stone, draped in red and white linens. "The souls of aborted babies. Population control. Barbaric." He put on his windshield washers.

"So tell the goddam Secretary of State next time you see him."

"What is it, Dick? Championship jitters?"

I had to smile. "Yeah, Petey. I got the jitters real bad." Perhaps I'd become intolerant, ornery, having not had a drink in two weeks.

It was nearly midnight when I dragged myself out of the Metro. About a block away was a vacant lot, and right along the sidewalk were two small billboards, that very morning plastered with new ads, for detergent. Most of my higher education way back when had been devoted to marketing and advertising, and on my way to work I had paused with admiration before the signs. Each showed a painting of wash on a line, the caption under one reading *Madame Van Gogh's Wash* and under the other *Madame Picasso's Wash.* Mimicking the styles of the artists, the colors were eye-catchingly bright, not like the gravy-stained stuff you see in the Louvre, and I had to commend the detergent folks for tapping right into the collective unconscious of the French. Now, this night, I found two kids making graffiti on the wash of Mesdames Van Gogh and Picasso. They were North African I think. Graffiti didn't exist in France when I arrived eight years earlier. Lately it sprouted up furiously, rampant but fruitless vegetation.

"Why don't you learn something constructive," I said in

French. They continued working with impunity, brandishing big, wide-tipped magic markers I don't imagine were marketed but for this one purpose. I couldn't at all make out what they were writing or drawing. "I said, learn something constructive!" I whacked the taller of the two in the shoulder with the heel of my hand. He shifted the marker and yanked something from his pocket. A fingernail file.

"You don't scare anyone with a nail file. Or with that!" I glared at the graffiti. When I looked back his eyes amazed me with their derision. Didn't they understand I was thinking of them?

"Don't tell me what I don't do." He wagged the file. "Next time maybe, no joke."

He and his friend walked away, as I did too, once I watched them disappear around the first available corner. A few minutes later I unlocked my liquor cabinet and stared at the bottles. Looking at the world with a clear head only left me disgusted. But the thought of breaking a promise to Quincy, as meager a promise as it was, disgusted me more, and I locked the cabinet.

We played for the championship of the Paris Basketball League in The Pit. The mezzanine was pretty crowded. The Calisher clan had returned, plus Embassy people had come, and the Montmartre Aigles brought their own fans. There was a table with a blue velvet cloth on it, apparently for the trophy, though I didn't see it anywhere.

Two hours before tip-off Dobbs called. "I won't be there tonight, D'Arata. Inspiration has returned. I can't let it go for a minute. I'm even working by halogen lights."

Something in me rose up high and happy. "That's great news, Quincy. Don't let go of it."

"I won't let go of it if it won't let go of me."

"Let's get together sometime."

"Sure, D'Arata." But I suspected he'd had enough of anyone connected with Little America.

When I told Calisher Quincy was home busy painting pictures, he slammed a basketball against the wall. He called the team around him and announced Quincy had better things to do than to be there when we needed him most. "Well, the hell with the bastard!" How obsequiously Little America concurred.

Marcia began rallying the team—"We don't need 'im! We don't need 'im!" As if we had become the underdog. But if we really didn't need him, then why were we the underdog? I wanted to walk out, but didn't. I never could turn my back on the prospect of a good game of hoop.

Smith ended up covering Gault—jabbering at him the whole game —and held him to sixteen points. The real star turned out to be Dan Star, a model from California. Normally waltzing around a court like it was a ramp at a fashion show, he literally bounced off the walls of The Pit that night, unmindful of limb or pretty face. What transformations a championship match inspires! Even I, feeling I belonged somewhere else though I had nowhere else to be, turned into the Rebound-Eater, nothing escaping my grasp on either board. With ten seconds left we were ahead by two points when Gault hit a three-pointer. Instead of calling time out, Calisher jumped up and down in the mezzanine, flapping his hands with a "push-it-up-the-court."

We widened out quickly, and rather than going back tight to the hoop, the Aigles came out after us. Suddenly there was a gaping hole in the middle. I went in wide open, the Marine Syzmanski fed me a pass, and the sure, victory-clinching lay-up was mine. But a funny thing happened.

In the high speed of it all, I still had time to think about things, to assess and make adjustments, to apply the right spin. Little America had no business winning. I put up the shot and the ball rolled, as clumsily as an egg, off the rim. Beautiful. Defeat was ours.

Then Star flew in, took the rebound and flicked it up and in before his feet touched the floor. The buzzer sounded. We'd won.

The team broke out in cheers and high-fives. Marcia went around hugging everybody, including me. Little America's happiness was not to be denied. Were there any snag at all in the celebration, it had to be the chain nets, since no one, not even Calisher, thought to bring metal snips, and we couldn't, in the tradition of victory, cut them down.

Up in the mezzanine Calisher accepted the trophy, which, it turns out, was right there all along. The league president flipped up the velvet and picked up a hoop. It was a brass, polished ring, a perfect hoop. Leave it to the French to come up with that. Monsieur President, surrender in his eyes, handed it over. Calisher raised it high with both hands, priestlike. Then, rotating it, he made a halo. He had gone to heaven. He paid sloppy homage to teamwork. Then said he was sorry he'd no longer be part of this great team. He announced that duty called and the Calishers were off to Tokyo. Finally he announced there was a party back at his place.

"Let's drink!" I shouted. Victory would be good for something.

There were little backboards on Calisher's gilt-framed mirrors, and the maid went around handing out little foam-rubber basketballs which turned out perfect for sopping up the champagne we spilled. Petey soon had the hoop around his neck, which might have been a noose, had my sabotage worked. But of course he knew we couldn't lose. Everyone decided he should keep the trophy. More corks popped, and even Marcia put away her share of bubbly. It was getting late, and I walked over thinking to ask if I could see her home on the Metro. There would always be something about a woman who played basketball. I heard her addressing Linda Calisher on the need for women's rights in Japan, Marcia's glass ringed with lipstick, and I decided she'd never, ever require an escort.

Maybe a month later, late at night, I was coming back from a party thrown to celebrate the opening of a pet shop by a woman named Hugette. She had done things like put out *foie gras* in pet dishes and fill glass bottles with metal spouts—I think meant for thirsty hamsters—with cognac. It was a wild time, and I got good and drunk. A few blocks from home, leaving the Metro and looking up the street, I made out someone working on the billboards. I thought it might be the North African kids. I'd prepared a speech for them, part apology, part lecture, if I could remember it in my condition, and I wasn't really afraid of a nail file turning into a knife. Then, as I got closer and saw arms making swabbing motions, I thought it might be the men who pasted up new ads. So soon? Even a good billboard in the right place, I remembered from somewhere, needs at least three months before its message sticks to the target's brainpan. Finally, at their sides, I saw they were indeed boys, but not the North African boys. Hardly. These two were as white as white can be.

It took me a minute to absorb what it was they were posting. Over the graffiti that was over the wash of Mesdames Van Gogh and Picasso they'd now plastered pictures of the perfect French family. *Pere, mere, fils et filles.* Something like painted photographs. Their eyes were full of *esperances* and *reves*, and the smallest hint of worry. There were eight of these posters, all identical. The slogan along the bottoms said, *France for the French.* Smaller print beneath said, *Sponsored by the National Front.* The National Front was a party of extremists that had gained remarkable popularity over the past year, solely by blaming immigrants in general and Africans in particular for whatever woes befell France, from crime to high taxes to AIDS. Blacks were the insidious culprits, their seed pestilent, their contamination ruinous.

Though I'd considered myself a liberal, fair-minded person since as long as I could remember, I never marched a step in a protest, never sang a song about overcoming, for I thought that a kind of bandwagon mentality. Yet now, alone and soused, I felt outrage. In French, I began yelling, indeed bellowing, "That's vile! That's hateful! Sick! Disgusting!" I clawed at the poster they'd just put up, all wet, and pulled, tearing the perfect French family in half.

One of the boys chanted, "Go home! Go Home! Go home!" In English. I ranted about fear and racism. The other boy stepped to the side and pulled something from his pocket. A walkie-talkie.

I heard him say, *"Rouge! rouge!"* In a minute men came out of nowhere, approaching cautiously. I counted six, all so white, and saw them circle me.

There was one man who said, "You misunderstand us," in English. Strangely, I continued to rage in French.

"I understand perfectly what you're doing!"

"You misunderstand us," he repeated calmly. Seeing the circle beginning to close, I nodded—nearly bowed—to his unctuousness, and slipped away.

At home I put some things in a bag. A few brushes and a can of black paint I'd used to re-do my balcony railings. Some yellow as well from the kitchen, and some woodwork white. Oxford shoe polish. Some blue magic markers I used to number boxes of wine. Finally, from the bottom of a little basket I kept extra aspirin and the like in, Marcia's tube of lipstick. I waited an hour, fixing a cup of instant coffee to sober me, then returned to the posters. They'd replaced the one I'd torn in half.

I smiled once at all those faces gazing into a future free of Africans and went to work. Whatever statement I was trying to make, more than anything I had a rollicking time. When I finished it looked like the Sunday funnies. Different members of the multiple perfect French family came away with different features: black helmets, big red lips, thickly-veined eyes the size of cue balls, buck teeth, bomb-shaped boobs, hair like coil springs, houseflies on the tips of noses, cherry-size freckles. They were a goofy bunch. My artistic abilities weren't much, and I regretted not having more materials to work with, but you got the idea. My mind now clear and sharp, I put on the last touches, delighting over every dab and stroke.

Then I saw the six men and two boys were back. This time the circle formed and closed as quickly as a pack of hounds on a rabbit. I never had a chance to run. They were all over me, kicking and punching. I flailed away enough to create a brief opening for making a break. Just as I did, something hit squarely at the base of my head, and as I was going down, before hitting the sidewalk and passing out cold, I did something I must always wonder about. I clamped my hands to my mouth to protect my teeth.

I woke up in a hospital the next morning. If it were possible for me to observe the scene from across the room, I would've imagined I was watching some anointment of the dead. A nurse had a bottle of baby oil, and with cotton was dabbing my arms and chest, followed by the gentle wipes of a soft towel. The pack, no doubt meaning to show me my true color, had smeared me with black paint, and the nurse had been busy through the night reclaiming my whiteness. When I finally began to gather where I was and what had happened, she said she was almost done, my skin back to normal. I looked at my arms. The color was murky. She said my face was pulp—I could feel it. She had cleaned it first to get the paint out of the wounds, some of which were then stitched. A good thing I was still unconscious, I thought. Later that day, the doctor said I had two broken ribs and a mild concussion, not too bad. I'd even managed to keep all my teeth. He reiterated what the nurse asked—wasn't there anyone I wanted to call? No, no. There really wasn't.

I listened to the man in the bed next to me, a contractor for the Department of Autoroutes with intestinal polyps, who charmed me with visions of dazzling highways spanning France. At some point the police came. I remembered the time with Showalter, how police had come then, too, with an edge to the voice suggesting one's own stupidity was to blame. The French cops had seen my art work and had the same edge. They asked for descriptions, and I told them to find some of those lovely posters—not mine, *theirs*. On the second day Marcia came to see me, entering the room with her arm thrust out, clutching a bouquet of tiger lilies like an Olympic torch. I'd made the papers, at least the one she read, and she was anxious to know if I'd want to join some group or another. I laughed out loud, and she left before the nurse put the flowers in water.

On the third day Calisher came to see me. Word was floating around the Embassy about the American named D'Arata who got bashed by fascists. He made it sound like I was a hero. I asked what he was doing in Paris. The move to Japan was still on, he told me, but he'd been able to delay the inevitable a while longer. He brought the trophy—the hoop—in a plastic shopping bag and wanted me to have it. I absolutely refused, adding, "Be sure and hang it right side up on your office wall in Tokyo."

"You know what I've decided, Dick—I'm gonna buy all the goddam Zinfandel you've got. I'll drown the bastards in Zinfandel."

"Petey, you absolutely have to stop thinking like that." Though I meant what I said there flashed in my mind the picture of a little kid pouring Coke over an ant hole, maybe some forgotten stunt from my own childhood. Why does such nonsense stick to the brainpan? "Besides, the Japanese have simpler access to California wine than by way of Paris."

"Not for them, Dick. The Embassy. You'd be surprised how many of those creeps can't contain their delight over the thought of my departure. I've got a few thousand left in the wine budget. A fair and equitable parting gesture, I figure." I never did sell him the wine.

He also wanted me to take charge of Little America. I didn't absolutely refuse. In fact, despite months of telling myself I had better things to do, I took over in September as organizer and coach. Some players didn't return, and new players arrived. I finally phoned Quincy Dobbs, though not about basketball. When I had lain in the hospital, on the fourth or fifth day, his work's serenity and light, that I had once thought to appreciate, resurfaced, and continued to play on my mind through spring and summer. By fall, whether he cared to hear from me or not, I needed to know how he was doing.

I dialed, and from the receiver came a disconnect recording, with no new number. I never heard any more about Quincy Dobbs the painter. Whether that meant the dealers who make art available to the public gave up on him, or if it meant he had utterly retreated, like a spider into its solitary corner, I feared few would ever know the exquisite gift he held for us.

WILSON'S LAST GARDENER

Carefully training his manicure scissors, Francois Tabet snipped a hair—no bigger than an eyelash—from the wart that stood out on his left ear like a tiny blood sausage. As he had no sink, the hair fell into an enamel pan, and he smiled in the mirror. Thirty-two and not bad looking, he had a tawny beard and skin ruddy from working outdoors. The wart had come in his early twenties, and he never heeded the common advice to have it removed. When it seemed it could grow no more, he measured it. One-point-six centimeters. A wart like that distinguished Francois, and he liked watching people try not to notice it. Snipping off hairs that came in the night, he groomed it faithfully. Even during the time he spent in jail.

The heat of August had boiled over into September. He put on a black T-shirt with a pocket for cigarettes and green rubber boots. Last night's rain had cooled things, but as he stepped outside and double locked his trailer he could feel the humidity remounting. The trailer sat in the old family orchard west of town, beyond a refuse sight for *Vegetation Only*. So the sign said, yet once in awhile an outsider dumped a stove or a washing machine. The orchard had gone untended six years, since the death of Francois' father, a simple gardener who had taught his son the trade, and whose permanent grin Francois found embarrassing. The trees bore rust-spotted apples and branches choked with mistletoe. Tossed his way like a plate of bones, the orchard was now his, the family intending to keep him at a distance without entirely disowning him. The rest of the people in Merville-sur-Lac simply ignored him.

Steam rose off Lac Leman. He stopped for cigarettes at La

Renardiere Cafe where two men stood drinking coffee at the bar. They were talking about the new American. For a week now the air had buzzed with talk of Monsieur Wilson. He had bought an eight-room lake-front house, east of town, where property values grew more and more wild the further you went toward Evian-les-Bains. Francois couldn't remember the lakeshore ever having an American. Waiting in line for sweetbreads he had heard the butcher tell a woman how Monsieur Wilson, firm on buying the house but having only American checks, told the realtor to hold everything and went racing off to Geneva in his yellow Alfa Romeo. Within an hour the American returned, slapping one-point-two million French francs, cash, on the realtor's desk.

Within an hour of hearing that story, Francois knocked on the American's door, smiling and offering his gardening skills. He paused as a truck arrived with two wooden crates that had to be maneuvered inside. Then the American invited him in and, amidst the weighty Second Empire furniture that had come with the place, they talked salary. It took only a moment. Sensing something in the American's cobalt eyes that didn't bide haggling, the Frenchman agreed on sixty francs an hour. He made no mention of jail and his release three months earlier, and when the American glanced with curiosity and a hint of disdain at his ear wart, Francois turned his head aside. He wasn't about to undermine his find. Then he said, "I'll start tomorrow, *Monsieur Double-Vee*," addressing him as he once did all his clients, using the first letter of the last name. The American smiled and shook his head. "Tomorrow, then."

The men drinking coffee spotted Francois Tabet at the cigarette counter. Never able to live down the fact his sister Nicole had slept with this felon, the one man, a mason, stayed back, as the other, a carpenter, walked over.

"So, you got in real quick with the American, didn't you."

"You mean, Monsieur W? Just being my charming self."

Now the mason called over. "A lot of work at that place, Earwart. A lot of money. Mess it up for the rest of us and you'll see if your trailer floats."

Francois paid for his cigarettes, winking at the young woman behind the counter.

"Be sure and check first to see if Nicole's inside."

Even the carpenter snorted a laugh. The mason shouted obscenely, but Francois, on probation, was out the door.

The American's house, lavish next to anything in the town proper, had been built by the local doctor, Jean Ricard. A lifelong bachelor now retired to the Cote d'Azur, he'd done all his own gardening. An admirable job at that, Francois pointed out the first day. But Monsieur Wilson had his own ideas how things should look. Francois saw the American turning into a person who, because he had money, thought he knew better. He wanted the magnolias and rhododendrons cut so far back it was slaughter, and Francois pleaded to save the green buds, next spring's flowers.

"The branches block the view of the lake," the American said. He spoke an impeccable French that Francois found unnatural and irritating. He also wanted a rose-arbored terrace near the water's edge, and Francois warned him of the *seiche*, the word for the strange way Lac Leman could start rolling back and forth.

"Then the mason will have to build a wall. I want to be able to sit and read my paper under the roses and look out over the lake." The American had something about looking out over the lake, like he'd never seen water before.

Francois arrived for his second day of work right at ten o'clock. The American made clear he didn't wish to be disturbed before that. A truck arrived with flat stones and sand for where the arbored terrace would be. Monsieur Wilson had said to use any tools on the property. Convenient, since Francois had sold off most of his own to raise money for a lawyer. Though once the police ripped open the door to his hiding place and found everything he'd stolen, a defense was futile.

The Frenchman scraped away sod, pounded down soil with a heavy iron tamp, laid sand and leveled it. At one o'clock Monsieur Wilson called him up to the house for ham sandwiches and beer he set on the outside white table with the wrought iron chairs. Collars of fat hung from the bread. Monsieur Wilson ate the same, but inside at the dining room table. Francois saw him through the window reading his peach-colored newspaper. He knew it was the *Financial Times* from the ones he'd seen in the garbage pail.

Some time after lunch Monsieur Wilson came out. In the sun Francois still couldn't tell if the American's crewcut was blond or grey. He was at least ten years older than Francois, a head shorter and medium weight. His tan pants had a sharp crease, his black shoes a deep glaze. He told Francois to prune the roses that afternoon and mow the lawn.

"I was planning to lay the terrace stone."

The American smiled and shook his head, already a habit that made Francois feel he wasn't being taken seriously.

"Yes, I'd like the terrace done, soon as possible. But look at this grass, and those bushes. I can't stand the sight of them." Twenty ragged bushes or so bordered each side of the yard, and the grass was ankle deep. "While you're at it, why don't you prune that hideous thing on the side of your head." The American continued smiling.

Francois gave his wart a stroke with his fingertip and smiled himself. "I've grown attached to it, Monsieur W."

"I hear you like being different. Contrary."

Anger bubbled in Francois' chest. He waited for it to pass.

"I'm a good gardener, Monsieur W. So I guess I can cultivate anything." The American chuckled, turned and walked off, saying he was going for his afternoon stroll. Francois said he'd get right to the lawn and roses.

Trying to start Doctor Ricard's tractor mower, he wondered how it must be, spending one's days free and easy. Then pulling a sparkplug he barked his knuckles, and with the pain flared the thought, *once a drudge, always a drudge. Just like your father.* But unlike his father, Francois agonized over inequity as if it were a personal plague. He alone realized the curse it was to be born in Merville-sur-Lac. A drab village, it survived since the days of the

Savoy dukes by serving those who were better off. Nowadays that meant Lyonaise, Parisians and Brits in secondary residences—and one permanent American—their gates admitting the have-nots like Francois only in daylight. He hated it, though to leave this town never occurred to him.

The sparkplugs filed clean, the mower sputtered to life in a burst of smoke. Francois cut a swathe down the middle of the yard, riding high as a Savoy duke. By four-thirty he was raking clippings into piles. His fingers were sore. He had gloves, but the stitching was split and he'd pricked himself on thorns. He saw Monsieur Wilson walk down the slope of the yard with a fishing pole and a box. He had put on tennis shoes. By now Francois' boots had puddles inside. The American cast a line out into the lake. The Frenchman leaned his rake against the rail fence and walked down.

"Need a license for that, Monsieur W."

The American smiled. "Just limbering up the arm. I'll get a license soon enough."

Francois' eyes fastened on the box. It opened like a book, green felt on each side with an assortment of things that looked like baubles and earrings attached to the felt by hooks.

"You a fisherman, Monsieur Tabet?"

"No, I'm a hunter."

"Hunting's nothing like fishing. Fishing, you can't see the prey under the water. It's a great feeling when the invisible fish bites."

"This is a long way from America to come fishing."

"When we were kids my brother and I fished this lake. The family had a summer house on the Swiss side. Great view of Mont Blanc. Our father was a hot shot then. This box belonged to him. We fished and water-skied and rode bikes around the lake." He droned on with all the enthusiasm of a snail. Far off a passenger boat streamed silently toward Montreux. "Isn't that a sight. This has to be one of the most peaceful spots on earth."

"A little too peaceful."

"Sometimes you have to slow down. Forgo excitement. At least that's what doctors in three different countries tell me." He put his hand to his chest and patted slowly.

"Ah," said Francois, taking the hand to mean heart troubles. For all he had going, the American acted like a broken down man. "Well, no worry about excitement in Merville-sur-Lac."

The American inhaled deeply. "Don't you love the smell of fresh mown grass." Francois couldn't say he did, his nose too used to it. Monsieur Wilson glanced around. "You *are* going to pick up those piles, aren't you?

"I was thinking in the morning."

"I hate to see things put off. You haven't even cleaned up the branches from yesterday. And what about those clumps of sod?" He looked at the sky. "There's plenty of daylight left."

"It's hot, and I have to take everything away by wheelbarrow. It'll take thirty trips. Maybe tomorrow I could borrow a wagon and hitch it to the tractor."

The American laughed. "Now who around here is going to lend you a wagon?" Francois figured people had blabbed all that had happened—and a few things that hadn't.

"People know I'm clean now, Monsieur W."

"They want nothing to do with you. They say you won't change. They say you stole from everyone you ever worked for. What am I to believe? Just today I heard about that funny closet you had with the second door inside."

It wasn't until Francois underestimated the value of a ruby ring that someone called the police. They questioned his other clients, and suddenly everyone seemed to be missing things, things thought mislaid, not stolen. As good a gardener as Francois was, people now had "suspicions all along" about that dirt digger with the thing on his ear. Accusations filled the sky like swallows, and Francois, indignant and outraged, threatened to sue everyone between Evian-les-Bains and Geneva for defamation of character. By now, from a Lalique goblet some child may have chipped and hidden in fear, to the violin an alcoholic uncle likely had pawned, all losses, great or small, were neatly blamed on "Earwart Tabet."

On their third search of his apartment the police spotted the tattletale tongue of a red shoelace sticking through what seemed a seamless wall in the back of the bedroom closet. They pried their way in, to what amounted to a second closet. Though no Lalique goblets, no Amatis, there was, along with a single red and white golfer's shoe, a simple yet odd assortment. A silver ladle, an oar, a cut-glass ashtray, a silk scarf, a ricer, keys to a Mercedes attached to a miniature riding crop. Forty-three pieces of evidence, set neatly on shelves or hung on hooks. Items Francois obviously hadn't intended to wear, use or sell. People called him foolish or sick, and Francois didn't attempt explanations. Not on their servile minds. A golfer's shoe—two-tone, spiked—or an ashtray with all those perfect facets, a silk scarf he kept in a plastic bag to preserve its scent—these were amulets, charms. They warded off the inequity. At least for awhile. Glass turned this way and that made light from the closet's bare bulb prismatic, silk or leather emitted arcane aromas, metals hummed with power—transfixing Francois in moments of exaltation. Exaltation this flat-minded town wouldn't understand. All they understood was a sullied reputation. Rancorous mail reached Francois' cell. "Shouldn't you be proud! Now that old employers hesitate to hire help from a thief's town!" And that from the mayor.

"I did my time, Monsieur W. I'm not about to throw away a second chance."

"It's just I know some habits are hard to break," Monsieur Wilson said, suddenly setting down the pole and unbuttoning his white short-sleeved shirt. He had muscles, but like his French too perfect and unnatural. Francois had seen through a window an exercise machine with chrome weights. The American pulled one side of his shirt back. Spilled over the ball of the shoulder, like icing, was a scar.

"See that? Solid as steel. I had to build it back up. Put me out of work for months. It got blown apart because I used to be hardheaded. Like you." From what he'd seen hunting, Francois guessed a gunshot wound. "I know about second chances. You can't be choosy. People with sway don't allow you the option."

Who ever had sway over Monsieur Wilson? Francois wondered.

"Did you ever steal, Monsieur W?"

"You might say that."

"Gamble maybe?"

"Oh, I like gambling. But your concern's my garden, not my past."

"You know enough about mine."

"Boss's privilege." He buttoned his shirt and picked up the pole.

It was hard to get a fix on the American, speaking one minute like a broken man, and the next like a mysterious stranger, scar and all, right out of a late-night movie. "Maybe we've got things in common," Francois ventured.

"What you did sounds like insolent mischief," Monsieur Wilson said, cranking the reel slowly. "What I did was business. Though after awhile I suppose it got to be an addiction. Was it like that with you?"

"Yes, I suppose it was."

"You start to prickle with heat, just thinking about doing it. Then, after all the anticipation, when you actually go to do it, the heat is eating you up."

"Yes, yes," Francois said. "Like a fever."

"Well, you take that fever of yours and multiply it. Fifty, a hundred times. That's the kind of fever I used to get."

Even with what they had in common, be it a form of illness or thrill, there came comparisons and airs. "And what makes your fever so big?"

The American snickered. "Let me simply say it didn't come from stealing a lady's bifocals."

Francois felt his face burn. He could remember that woman's eyes, swimming with condescension behind those glasses. Now the American looked at him with eyes that said, *We'll never let you forget*, as if he shared more with the town than Francois. The fishing pole suddenly jerked and Monsieur Wilson pulled back on it till it bowed. Then the line snapped.

"I've lost my touch." He sighed and reeled in the loose line. "So Monsieur Tabet, the choice is simple. You want to keep an honest job, you'll pick up those piles." There were the eyes. *This is how it is from now on.*

"I don't have a choice, Monsieur W, and you know it."

Francois walked to the shed, pulled out the wheelbarrow and loaded it. Then, doing what he knew he'd hate doing, he pushed it through town. Trip after trip. His boots, aflood with sweat, made soggy, sucking noises at each step. People watched, but Francois, his blood molten, refused to acknowledge their stares. Yet maybe seeing him work, with dusk coming on, they'd think better of him. Maybe Monsieur Wilson, giving him a second chance, had that intention. More and more people came to doors and windows. Witnesses to penance. After two hours he was done, his nostrils pungent with the dump's rot. He figured if people weren't willing to forget, then he'd really give them something to remember. Trundling the wheelbarrow back through town he grew dizzy wondering what. Bank job? Arson? Kidnapping? Then he heard prison laughter. Stopping in the square he settled on pulling off his boots and emptying them in the public cistern. By now people had settled in for dinner, not a face at a window to watch.

He returned to Monsieur Wilson's shed, then went to the kitchen and knocked. The door opened and the American stood there in a white tuxedo and a gold bow tie.

It took a second for the words to come out. "I'm finished."

"Good, good," Wilson said cheerfully. "That wasn't so bad, was it." He pulled out his wallet—it was packed—and handed Francois seven crisp hundred-franc notes. He'd gotten five yesterday.

"This is too much, Monsieur W."

"You earned it. Maybe you could put it toward a new wagon." Francois folded the money and slid it in his pocket behind his smokes. "I have to run, Monsieur Tabet. Over to Geneva, visit some Swiss friends." Francois thought the Swiss as smug and dull as their clockwork. "I've got Swiss blood on my mother's side."

Figures, Francois thought. "You want to take a shower? I know you haven't a water hook-up." Francois didn't tell him that. Someone from town must have.

"It's nice out. I'll dive in the lake."

The American was staring at his ear wart.

"Tell me, do you have a girl who likes to nibble on that?"

"Not lately."

"Seriously, you should have it removed."

"I told you, I've grown attached to it."

"Somehow an ear wart doesn't become a gardener."

"You don't like it, maybe you should find another gardener."

"You're my gardener, Monsieur Tabet."

"You can't just make me your gardener."

"Sure I can. You need the money. Winter's coming and you'll need a real apartment. Can't jump in the lake in January. Most of your equipment has to be replaced. You need money all around, and I can provide it." He stepped close, his eyes focusing on Francois' ear. "You know, the more I look at it, the more I realize that wart is the root of your troubles."

"Who do you think you are? You can't come in here and start rearranging my life."

"I would think you'd be pleased having someone take a personal interest. I can fix you up."

"I don't need fixing up! Especially by some outsider, some know-it-all American."

"Outsider? American? I thought you said we had something in common."

"I don't go around trying to act superior."

"Don't you?"

Francois turned, about to stomp off, but his feet were too sore. He practically limped.

"We'll have to get you some new footwear. Well, hard day's work, good night's sleep! See you in the morning!"

He sounded like a jolly priest giving absolution. Or the judge.

"Nothing a year in prison won't cure!"—then a horselaugh. They reveled in dressing him down. Francois kept walking, burning. A new wagon. New footwear. Made him sound like a child—or a pet. Money or no money, he wouldn't take treats for playing the dog. About a block away he stopped and lit a cigarette, waiting for complete darkness, deciding. There was something in that house, more than money, Francois did want. He didn't know what exactly. A little piece of the American himself, something to start a new collection with.

Too hot to sleep, his body no longer cool from his dip in the lake, he lay naked in bed, sipping whiskey and thinking about a sunny day two years ago, when he won the Merville-sur-Lac *boules* championship. He saw heavy metal balls arcing lazily through the air. Then he saw Nicole, her face bright with excitement, and heard her rapid, clapping hands. Afterward she invited him to her place and fixed him a champion's dinner. How good it would feel having her again. He believed he had a chance. He'd seen her around town, and though they didn't speak, they exchanged a certain look.

He didn't hear anyone walk up, but now, in the middle of the night, there was a knock at his trailer door. He had a wild thought it might be her. Then his heart skipped at the other possibility, though it was equally improbable. He lay still, thinking maybe he'd heard nothing at all. The knock came again, unhurried.

"Open up, Monsieur Tabet. I know you're there. I can smell my aftershave." Francois had sprinkled some in a paper towel to wipe under his arms after the lake.

He swirled the whiskey in the bottom of his glass and wondered what would happen if he didn't answer. If he did answer, wouldn't the American understand a forgivable moment of the fever. Hell, it hadn't even been satisfying, the old feeling wasn't there. On the other hand, maybe the American could only understand a fist to the face, like they did in jail. At the very least, a man with heart troubles shouldn't come looking for fights.

"Hold on," he yelled. "Hold on." He turned the kerosene lamp up bright, slipped on jeans and opened the door.

Monsieur Wilson stood there, in his tuxedo and tie, a mist of perspiration across his forehead, the blue in his eyes electric. Leveled at Francois' nose was a gun, chrome, like the weights in the exercise room.

"*Merde*, are you crazy!" Francois backpedaled and fell on his cot. "There's no reason for this!"

"Where is it?"

Francois thought a second. "Where's what?"

The American pushed the gun so close Francois could smell oil. The gun had recently been cleaned.

"No one will miss you. No one will care. Not even your own relatives. That's why they stuck you out here. Now, where is it?"

Not taking his eyes off the barrel, Francois groped at the table next to the cot, pushing a magazine aside and revealing a fishing lure.

"Hand it to me, please."

Francois picked the lure up gingerly and held it out. Monsieur Wilson took and studied it. Then, as though it naturally belonged there, he hooked it in the slit of his lapel. He pulled up a wooden chair and sat down, his eyes taking in the cramped trailer. The whiskey. The magazine with the *boules* players. The can of cassoulet with the spoon sticking out. The blackened propane burner. He relaxed the gun, resting it flat on his thigh.

"I didn't mean to take it, Monsieur W."

"You didn't mean to take it?"

"It was the way you made me feel like dirt."

"I made you feel like dirt?"

"And you left a window wide open."

"Did I?"

"And that box right on the dining room table."

The American shook his head but didn't smile.

"Lures, no less" Wilson said. "It was so obvious it was pathetic. But you bit, like a big, stupid fish."

Francois sat up straight on the bed.

"You set me up."

"It was your decision to go back."

"What gives you the right!"

"I was testing my gardener's loyalty."

"I told you, I'm not *your* gardener!"

"Not anymore, you're not." The American grimaced, closed his eyes hard and opened them. He rose and turned his back. "I gave you a job, good money, a second chance, and you broke into my house. You stole from me." He turned to face Tabet. His eyes seemed watery.

"We're talking about a fishhook, Monsieur W."

"You never know what you steal might mean to a person."

"It was the fever, Monsieur W. The fever."

"Oh, I know, I know." He parted a curtain with the gun and Francois saw the darkness outside. "We share an affliction, Monsieur Tabet. But when I get the fever it's because I'm about to shoot someone." He turned the gun sideways, looking along it and squinting, as if reading fine print. He heaved a breath as though exhausted.

Suddenly, though he dare not speak it, a word uncoiled and hissed in Francois' brain. *Assassin!*

"You're crazy, you and your gun! All you Americans are gun crazy!"

"Maybe. But when I use a gun, I do so with control."

"I don't care how unpopular I am—you can't kill me!"

"Sure I can." The American clicked his front teeth. Once, twice. His face hardened into marble, the perspiration like a band of diamonds above his eyes, themselves shining gems. Francois stared, amazed, and watched the gun rise, when something inside startled him, rustling and darting out. "What do you want, I'm just a gardener!"

The intense eyes blinked, fluttered, like lightbulbs about to expire, the marble softened, and then, with one long stride, the American was bent over the cot, tucking the gun under Francois' jaw.

"Let me tell you, Monsieur Tabet. I was something of a gardener myself. I worked in the most beautiful, the most exquisite gardens. When a thistle or a nettle sprang up, I was called in. And I removed it." With his free hand he slapped the shoulder of the arm with the gun at the end of it. Francois remembered the scar. "Being hardheaded is one thing, but where would I be if I were ever disloyal?" Now Francois caught the misty scent of gin. The fishhook in the lapel quivered.

"Did someone hire you to do this?"

"Do what?"

"Kill me!"

"Hire me? You stupid man! There's not money enough in this town—!" The American swung the gun back, and came around full, fast, smashing the can of cassoulet. Beans sprayed like buckshot, the can bounced and rattled, then wobbled to rest.

Francois' face was buried in his hands. After a long silent moment, he removed them. The American stood there, looking baffled, like he had entered a room and forgotten why.

"There's been a terrible mistake here, Monsieur Tabet." His voice was calm, even. He straightened up, put the gun somewhere inside his tux, pulled down his shirt cuffs, and ran a hand over his crewcut. "You have no idea how sorry I am." He glanced about, squaring his white shoulders. He worked his cheeks like they held mouthwash. "Really, Monsieur Tabet, is this any way for a man to live?" He snapped the handkerchief from his breast pocket and dabbed at something on his sleeve.

With no thought to elegance, Francois took his bedsheet and mopped away the beans and bits of pork spattered over his arms and midsection. Suddenly Monsieur Wilson was at the door, leaving. Francois searched quickly, saw his manicure scissors, snatched them up and sprang. "Wait! Wait!" The American stopped short of the doorway and turned. "I'll show you! I'll cut it off!" Francois put the scissors to his ear. "Just say the word."

The American looked at him blankly. "Please, Monsieur Tabet. See a doctor. It's more sanitary." He turned to leave.

"You can't walk away now!"

Francois picked up the lantern, brushed past the American and stepped from the trailer. He raised the light, making Wilson squint, and held out the scissors.

"Maybe you'd like to do it." He saw the American had to think about this. "Hell, were you *that* sure I'd break into your house!"

"Frankly, yes."

"Well, excuse me. I'm not as good as you at hiding my affliction. Garden—roses—a terrace by the lake! The whole time you were drooling inside like a dog." He flung the scissors aside. "Maybe you'd prefer chewing my wart off!"

"We both had our lapses today, Monsieur Tabet. Let's leave it at that."

"No, let's not leave it. Let's see who's got the guts to make amends." Francois pointed toward town. "They say I can't change. But I can. Question is, can you?" He marched toward a tree. There he hung the lantern on a branch stub. "I mentioned I hunt. Well, I'm a very good shot. You, too, no doubt. But tell me, Monsieur Wilson, can you hit an ear wart, say, at fifteen meters?"

The American stared.

"I'm an excellent shot, Monsieur Tabet. But do you really want me pointing a gun at you again?"

"If I trust you, then you'll have to trust me. I want to be your gardener." The American seemed lost over some complexity of the proposition. "Your own loyal gardener."

"Tonight at blackjack I lost twenty thousand francs, Monsieur Tabet. Swiss, not French. I never did believe in holding at seventeen. I see you don't either. I like that."

Francois, good at cards, smiled.

"I'll see you have the most beautiful garden on the lake, Monsieur Wilson." Words unfurled and snapped in Francois' head. *The Assassin's Gardener.*

"Your resolve inspires," Monsieur Wilson said, but his voice, flat and humorless, did not inspire in turn. "Some changes are so hard to make." He withdrew the gun and let it hang heavily at his side. "Let's hope I don't kill you."

Francois' heart cringed, a dog who wanted to be loyal afraid his master would just as soon kick him in the teeth. To confuse matters, rain began to fall. He watched the American lift both hands, aiming, his eyes balanced above the barrel. The raindrops, though few, pricked Francois' skin like rose thorns. Monsieur Wilson looked skyward. "Is this place like Camelot, where it only rains at night?"

Francois didn't understand. "What's a little rain, Monsieur Wilson? I once brought down a boar in a thunderstorm!" He looked up. The kerosene light made the tree choked with mistletoe seem a ghost of itself. Forcing his body to stand straight, Francois cocked his ear, as if to hear something faraway. Rather, a small voice inside his warted ear said, *What have you done, you stupid man?* Francois imagined the answer: the bullet would miss—to the wrong side. Then, shrugging off his inaccuracy like a bad *boule* shot, the assassin would drag away the body and dump it next to the *Vegetation Only* sign. No one would care. Better Francois than a washing machine. He shuddered.

"Please, Monsieur," the American said. "You must hold still for this to work."

Francois readjusted his stance, his bare, blistered foot squishing a rotted apple. His stomach wobbled violently. "This is our chance at fresh starts, Monsieur Wilson. Don't let anything nudge your hand!"

"I'm trying, Monsieur. It was always a rule with me, never to kill someone I didn't feel totally indifferent to."

"The best garden on the lake, Monsieur Wilson. Don't forget."

"I can appreciate that, Monsieur Tabet."

The rain came down harder, and Francois was grateful, for he realized he had begun to cry. In the hot white kerosene light, through tears and needles of rain, he looked at this foreigner in the glowing tuxedo and gold tie, pointing a gun. So perfectly alien and incongruous. Should this be the last vision for a gardener? A gardener's son? Were the people of Merville-sur-Lac, keeping to humbler choices, led to clearer ends, more comforting sights? Did they walk peacefully across the lake?

The American paused and ran a finger along the top of the barrel like a squeegee. Francois felt about to faint. The small voice now reared up and clamored furiously. *Dirt digger! Earwart! He will miss—he wants to miss! Apologize, and go back to bed!*

Francois squelched it, beat it down. No to humble choices! Let the lake swallow me! He closed his eyes and tried to think of Nicole. But she wouldn't quite come. Opening them, he saw the American wince, as if with indigestion.

"You know, Monsieur Tabet, they say they can take this heart out and put another one in. Like I was the Tin Man." His pain seemed enormous, insurmountable, as he aimed a final time. The sky burst. Rain shattered on the ground.

"Shoot, Monsieur Wilson!" All in an instant, Francois saw the flash, heard the crack, and fell. Proving the voice right, the bullet erred some.

It seemed for a long time his senses were shut off, except to the rhythm of rain. Enough to convince himself he wasn't dead. Finally he moved a hand to head, expecting a hole. There was no pain. He hadn't heard or felt the metal, but now, as fingers found ear, he knew, unmistakably, half the wart was gone. Cool and hard as a pencil eraser, half remained. He covered it with his hand.

"I'm sorry, Monsieur Tabet. The weather's thrown me off. I got some of it, didn't I?" The words above Francois were a fluttery mix of hope and regret. "Maybe we could try again. But in the morning, if that's all right. See, my only white tux is ruined." Wilson sneezed hard.

Francois turned his face from the sod and cracked his eyes. The tux, he saw, was drenched, limp, the fishhook missing from the lapel. The gun hanging loose in the hand looked too shiny to be anything but a toy, and the blue eyes were vacant and perplexed.

"You didn't kill me."

"There was an instant there, Monsieur Tabet, I . . ."

"Maybe I'll let a doctor get the rest."

"That would be easier." Another sneeze. "Tomorrow, then. Ten o'clock. Don't catch cold."

Francois closed his eyes as the rain began to ease. Already, where a moment ago there was the blackest water, he was filling in a future. He watched it emerge, sharpen, then heard a voice—bold, uplifting—call his name. *Francois Tabet. The Assassin's Gardener, Francois Tabet.* His wart gone, his beard trim and clothes sharp, he'd idly converse at the cafe, promenade through town, play Sunday *boules* in the square. A show for the dolts. They'd be dumb enough to think he'd become one of them, but little would they know. It was better than a secret door. He'd get Nicole back, if not someone prettier. Maybe he'd marry. Could he let his wife in on it? *The Assassin's Gardener*. Ah, who along the lake could say that! He smiled.

Then, as the rain stopped, he heard the second gunshot. Somewhere up in the middle of town. Close by, it would have been the crack of a clean *boule* shot, knocking out an opponent. But at that distance it was clearly Monsieur Wilson's gun. Lying on the acrid ground in this orchard he hated, Francois raised his head, the dread of what it meant upon him.

CHATEAU D'AUMONIER

Despite everything else she collected, Mother Larue was not fond of collecting papers, especially those of an official nature, and when she died there was no document to govern the disposition of her many antiques. Mother Larue must have had the foreknowledge that her daughters, Ilene and Eleanor, could work out the details peaceably. However, having no testament to direct them, Ilene and Eleanor were soon entrenched in what many residents of Cape May, even some who only summered there, dubbed The Antiques War. Studied intently, it lasted five months short of twenty-five years and, like Verdun, saw the stingiest reversals.

Ilene, with her husband Bob Lindley and two daughters of their own, lived in a rather large house, while Eleanor had a small house, a rental, trapped ingloriously between Sam Fuller's Sunoco station and the entrance of the Aurora Drive-in Movie Theatre. According to no pattern, Eleanor at any moment would phone Ilene and demand delivery—for example—of the second-empire sofa. "And where in hell will you put it, El!" "Where the sideboard is, Leeny, which you may take back!" Whenever time came for another exchange Mr. Lindley retrieved a truck from the lot of the car dealership he owned—fortunately or unfortunately. Through the streets of Cape May, like armaments, rolled sideboards, wingchairs, highboys, etageres, an anvil, Depression glassware, a three-leaf dining table, chiffoniers—one begins to understand why Mother Larue didn't attempt a will—in ever newer models of Ford pick-ups. Mr. Fuller, "Sunoco Sam," who was as well Eleanor's landlord, always gave Bob a hand. For two-and-a-half decades, squeezing and maneuvering, their knuckles scraping on doorjambs, the men heard Eleanor's singular war cry. Competing with nearby pneumatic growls, the *achoo* of a grease gun and the clang of bells announcing customers, the cry was always, "I will not be denied my share for lack of space!"

At age sixty-one, Mr. Lindley sold his Ford dealership, and he and Ilene, fifty-seven, debated retiring to France. Her roots, as coated as they were with Jersey soil, were French, and, beginning with their honeymoon, they'd been to Paris four times. They knew the bus and metro lines, and enough French to humor the French. Their daughters, Jenny and Cheryl, seldom visited, and no grandchild was in sight. Inevitably, Cape May paled alongside that vision of life pinned to the earth by the Eiffel Tower.

"Not a stick of that junk goes to Paris," Bob said when they were decided. Ilene surrendered all—nearly all—with an acquiescence that signaled her final weariness with things she found ugly, cumbersome and a riddle to polish, and which she coveted for no other reason than to defy Eleanor's perpetual declaration not to be denied her share. As if anyone had ever denied her that.

Of all of Mother Larue's possessions, Ilene kept but one—a bottle of rare French wine called Chateau d'Aumonier. That is, "Chateau of the chaplain." According to an enologist the Lindleys once questioned in Manhattan, its first vines were planted by a chaplain returned home to Paulliac after Napoleon's defeat in 1815. He planted the vines in thanksgiving because the man who had led France in bloody imperial pursuit had been whipped forever.

"It's a wine commemorating the end of stupid wars. Let Eleanor have it," Mr. Lindley said. "Take that bottle and even with an ocean between, you two'll still be squirming against each other like piglets at sore tits."

"Why? She's never shown any interest in it." In fact, the bottle was the sole item that Eleanor not once insisted on borrowing. "For godsake, Bob, she doesn't know the difference between Bordeaux and Boone's Farm." Ilene then wrapped the Chateau d'Aumonier, year 1855, in the Cape May *Pennysaver* for its return to France.

Facing the prospect of their mother's things going into storage,

Eleanor miraculously made room. Sam Fuller swore aloud he felt her floor lurch like the deck of a ship. It was a breezy, clear April day, as Eleanor straddled the stoop of her house, its clapboards ready to explode, and waved goodbye, promising on their mother's soul she'd take good care of everything.

In November, after the Lindleys had been six months in Paris, their daughter Jenny made plans to visit at Christmas. Then, when she received a sudden invitation to speak at a conference in Denver, she insisted on giving Eleanor her plane ticket. A psychologist, married to a lawyer, Jenny said on the phone, "Defuse your emotions, Mother," as if Ilene and Eleanor were part of an experiment—white mice removing blasting caps from TNT. "Aunt El needs a vacation."

"Did she tell you again she was always on the short end?"

"Yes."

"I think our mother did a very fair job raising two daughters, almost on her own," Ilene said.

"I think Grandmother was a horror show."

"Jenny, you hardly knew the woman!"

"Mother, it seems impossible to me that parents love their children equally." Jenny broached the most emotional subjects with no emotion at all.

"Oh? Haven't your father and I loved you and Cheryl equally?" Cheryl was the wild, younger daughter, who at thirty-two still bounced from job to job, boyfriend to boyfriend. Last anyone heard, she'd run off to Aruba with a swimming instructor.

"In all honesty," Jenny answered, "despite what I may think on the job, yes. You and Father have been perfectly fair. Though I know Cheryl would say otherwise."

Ilene took a deep, silent breath. "Okay, give Aunt El the ticket."

A few weeks later, Ilene started getting pains. Several days into December, at The American Hospital, during an *echographie abdominale*, she watched on a monitor what looked like a weather-satellite picture. A ball of cholesterol, not your normal stone, the doctor said, was finishing its journey from the gallbladder to the intestine, discharging pain like lightning. He pointed at something

Ilene couldn't quite see. Much clearer was the thought of Eleanor, an approaching tornado.

"Any family history of gallbladder, liver, pancreas problems?"

"They took my mother's gallbladder out, twenty-six years ago." She didn't mention that when they had her open they missed something, inexplicably, as if like an insect it scooted for cover, and Mother Larue died within a year of cancer.

"Watch your cholesterol," the doctor said. "French food can shock the uninitiated system. Avoiding stress goes without saying. The pain'll pass in a day or so." To Ilene's surprise, it did. More surprising, the pain didn't return, even as Eleanor's arrival drew near.

Exactly on schedule, at 9:43 AM, three days before Christmas, Eleanor touched down at Charles de Gaulle. The sisters seemed genuinely happy to see each other, but every time Mr. Lindley lifted Eleanor's old leather suitcase, it creaked ominously. From the back seat of a car the Lindleys had borrowed to go pick her up, Eleanor chortled away. "The plane was so rocky I pulled out a rosary and prayed. That and watched the movie. Three dollars for a headset! Tuh! Lucky I'm good at movies without sound." Back in Cape May, out the bedroom window, Eleanor's small house had a view of the Aurora Drive-in's screen. For nearly thirty years she critiqued films she had seen but not heard. "Oh, I'll still make a bowl of popcorn and watch from the Lincoln bed." Proudly, Eleanor often said the bed was an exact replica of the President's. Mr. Lindley had seen pictures of the original and knew the one at Cape May was less ornate.

They arrived at the Lindley apartment, and Eleanor, no sooner through the door, declared, "This is something else, isn't it." She didn't know what to make of it. If Ilene had battled tooth and nail for their mother's antiques, it certainly wasn't from a taste for fine furniture. She and Bob had set up house in Paris, France in rubbish.

"French kitsch," Mr. Lindley told her.

Eleanor turned and turned, nodding, considering, strangely

smiling upon marred tables, sofas and chairs with leaky ticking, a pair of lamps with bases built from an Erector Set to look like Eiffel Towers, dingy prints in chipped frames, glass vases decorated with decals of kicking cabaret dancers—it nearly seemed pathetic. Suddenly she froze.

"So, you still keep that on display, I see." It was the Chateau d'Aumonier, cradled in its wicker basket on the bookcase. Eleanor approached it, warily, reached out a hand, paused, then brushed her fingers up and down the bottle, as if summoning a genie.

"El, please," Ilene said. "The label is fragile."

"Why don't you drink this, Leeny?"

"Don't you know, it's so old it would taste like castor oil."

"Then why save it?"

"Because you can't drink it!" Bob laughed. Eleanor looked pensive. "It's an ancestral curiosity, El. That's all."

"Yes, I know. Great-great-great grandfather Daniel Larue brought it to the USA during the Civil War," she rattled off. "Oh, I know all about that wine!" Her expression became pained, her denied-my-share look, Ilene thought. "I'd like to take a nap."

Mr. Lindley showed Eleanor to the spare bedroom and returned. Ilene sighed. "Here five minutes and already the deprived act."

"Avoid stress, remember?" Bob Lindley hugged his wife. "What did she mean, she knows all about that wine?" By way of the Manhattan enologist, the Lindleys knew things about the wine they couldn't imagine Eleanor knew, not that they thought to hide anything from her. In 1855 Chateau d'Aumonier had been named, along with Haut Brion, Margaux, Latour, and Lafite-Rothschild, to Bordeaux's illustrious first rank of growths. Devastation by phylloxera in 1878 spelled the end of d'Aumonier vineyards, and its first-rank position would not be refilled until 1973, by Mouton Rothschild. So a bottle of Chateau d'Aumonier, year 1855, might bring a price for historical value. As the enologist held the bottle before a light Bob and Ilene could see it was the brown of chestnuts. "As much as seven, eight, thousand dollars at auction. Unthinkable to drink, though." They could not take the man seriously. That was fourteen years ago. Today, its structure entirely lost, sediment thick on the bottle's bottom, the wine approached the color of an orange brick. Might it still fetch a price?

The next day a low but warm winter sun caught surfaces in such a way as to make everything glow. Ilene felt like an image in a French film, the light shining through her. Since April, everything she imagined Paris could be,it had become. The radiance, however, wasn't reaching Eleanor, who slumped beside her on a bench in the Luxembourg gardens. They watched as kids pushed sailboats around the fountain with sticks. Eleanor kept fidgeting and picking her nails. Her cuticles reminded Ilene of the shredded mozarella she'd used making spinach lasagna that morning.

"Dammit, El, we're not going another step till you tell me what's wrong."

Eleanor, not about to do so unless invited, opened herself up.

"Oh, Leeny, I don't know where to start."

"El, just say it."

"Sam is selling his Sunoco to Qwik-Fil."

Ilene sensed the roundabout urgency in this. "To do what?"

"Retire to Florida, for crissakes."

"Sam?"

"All of a sudden he wants to golf and deep-sea fish. Do you know what he did? He asked me to go with him."

Ilene brightened. "Oh, Eleanor—go! It's a chance for a whole new life."

"Leeny, I can't simply up my roots."

"What roots? A move like that is wonderful. Bob and I are so happy. Do you know, everyday we walk to French lessons through these very gardens. We hold hands. In class we sit in the front row. We make love now in French."

"Well, Sam and I aren't the kind to hold hands."

"Why can't you for once be out in the open about Sam?"

"Sunoco Sam means nothing. He always smells like that stuff he cleans the grease off his hands with. Like vanilla extract."

"I remember times you sneaked vanilla extract because mother said you were too young for perfume."

"Oh, Leeny, Sam has nothing to do with anything."

"Come on, El, it's you and me on some park bench in France—you've been sleeping with the man for thirty years!"

"That's not true!"

Years back, the first time he and Mr. Lindley had set up the Lincoln bed in Eleanor's, Sam smiled and said, "Yes, a man might feel real presidential in a bed such as that," as if very soon he'd show up like a satyr in a stovepipe hat.

"Okay, El, if Sam means nothing, then what's the problem?"

"My house. Sam has to sell my house in the deal. Qwik-Fil wants to put a Qwik-Lube right where I live." Eleanor's throat clicked. "That means I've got to move. Do you know how high rent is! Sam certainly spoiled me rentwise. So I found a small place for sale. It's one of those mobile homes actually. After the down payment my monthly won't be too overwhelming."

"That's great, El. A place of your own."

"Leeny, I need to sell some things, to raise the down payment." Eleanor had worked most her life as a seamstress in their mother's dress shop, Cape May's most fashionable, but the money Eleanor took in hadn't plumped her savings much. "I had a lady come by to look at the Windsor chairs. All of a sudden there's scratches on one of the rear legs. Did you and Bob take up lion taming?" In fact, a neighborhood cat had gotten at it.

"We tried a chair on Cheryl." The joke missed Eleanor. "So how much can the Windsors bring?"

"The lady came by to look at the chairs—was only curious—and offered a hundred dollars each. And nine hundred for the sideboard with the marble counter. Then she happened to see the Lincoln bed and offered twenty-eight hundred."

Ilene wondered how the lady happened from Eleanor's dining room to the bedroom. "El, go ahead. If you need the money, you need the money. Sell whatever—all of it. I feel a million miles away."

"You and I could never think of selling mother's prizes."

"They were a royal headache. Geezus, El."

"Tuh! You battled like a hun for them!"

"You made me. You were always—after everything."

"Why do you think I was 'after' everything? Because you didn't show the care, the respect."

"The stuff's not a memorial, El. It never was."

"Sure, for you and Bob it was a convenience, not having to spend money on furniture."

"Don't you dare, El."

"It's the truth, God knows." Their mother, sinking more and more money into antiques, had let her insurance lapse. After she died, even the sale of the dress shop, where Eleanor stayed on in a back room sewing, and the sale of Mother Larue's house, didn't cover the hospital bills. It was Eleanor who paid them off by taking out a loan. "Maybe you and Bob were struggling, raising the girls, but you had money enough for trips to Paris. And that thing in Detroit."

"God, El! For the thousandth time—Ford paid for that trip!"

Ilene had gone with her husband to Detroit, which had invited him to a kick-off gala for the Mustang. It was a giddy time. Silvery emblems of a galloping pony, borrowed from the car's grill, hung all over the hotel. Bob and Ilene couldn't close their eyes without a chrome horse racing across the backs of their eyelids. Mother had told Ilene not to worry and have a good time. In remission, she was staying with Eleanor. The night before the Lindleys were due to fly home, mother hemorrhaged, something bursting like an old sack, and she died before the ambulance arrived. An hour earlier she had sat with Eleanor eating vanilla ice-cream, only to say, "Shouldn't you watch your weight? Maybe if you were thin like your sister you could do better than Sunoco Sam. He smells like this bowl of ice-cream." Eleanor never told anyone the part about Sam.

"Well, let me tell you what," Eleanor said. "I went to the grave last week, and you know what I found in the grass—a four-leaf clover! It was Mother saying, 'Go ahead, El, get your own place!

Good luck!'"

"Oh, El—"

"It's the truth. I've got the four-leaf clover in my wallet, if you want to see it."

"No, El. I don't want to see it."

"It's only fair, mother was saying. 'You were always on the short end, El. Now you get that mobile home!'"

"If you were on the short end," Ilene said, feeling as if she'd walked in on a séance, "it's only because you thought you were."

"I was. I was."

"I told you, sell everything. Go ahead, please, please, please go ahead please ..."

But Eleanor, a weight lifted from her shouders, was up and away.

Halfway through dinner that night, Eleanor excused herself to go to bed, saying she still hadn't adjusted to French time. The Lindleys ate quietly, unusual for them, as though the strange third plate, its unfinished lasagna a mysterious artifact, cast a spell of silence. After dinner, Mr. Lindley dried the dishes while his wife washed. They didn't have a dishwasher here and Ilene enjoyed the simple chore of washing dishes in one side of the double sink and rinsing them in the other.

"So when'll we hear from Cheryl?" Mr. Lindley asked.

"When Mister Swim Instructor dumps her without a lifesaver."

"We did teach her to swim, didn't we?"

"Just like we did Jenny." In fact, if they had overcompensated either daughter, it would have to be Cheryl.

"No one forgets how to swim."

"Maybe it's the Kerr blood." Sweeping a sponge around a dish, Ilene laughed. "He probably forgot how to swim, too!"

The family never talked about Father Kerr. As if he never existed. He'd gone off to fight the war in the Pacific Ocean and gotten himself killed. Too old to be going off to war, he lied about his age. When Ilene and Eleanor's mother got notice of his death, she showed no shock or surprise. She changed the tag on the mail box to her maiden name and began to airbrush him from memory. From the family album she removed any picture with him in it, then rearranged the photos so there weren't any gaps. So they wouldn't be reminded of him at meals, she had the top of the diningroom table refinished where he'd left a cigarette burn. Why a man with two daughters, eleven and sixteen, would go fight a war he wasn't expected to fight, she found impossible to reason, admitting finally he was no more than what Cape May had pegged him for—a brooding, indolent man who, even with a good job as a civil engineer, hated work, preferring his energy go to picking fights on the street. If a Larue woman ever did mention Kerr blood, it was only to explain the inexplicable. Maybe Cheryl was full of it.

Ilene fished around the dishwater for silverware. "Sam's selling his station and moving to Florida."

"Oh?"

"Eleanor's selling off some things and buying a mobile home."

Ilene rinsed the last of the forks.

"I see." Mr. Lindley let what seemed settled alone. "Do you know, Sam once told me Eleanor was the only woman he could ever love. But to keep it secret. *Entre-nous*."

"I bet he didn't even bother telling El."

"Sam's the best transmission man on the Cape, but when it comes to a personal life he leaves out some gears."

"You sure I shouldn't I tag along?"

"Bob, I want to be alone with El. I keep hoping we'll have this extraordinary breakthrough."

"I'll watch for smoke on the horizon."

Along rue Mouffetard Ilene pointed out part of a stone wall that once surrounded the city. "Oh, I see," said Eleanor. Further on, Ilene explained about the churchyard where girls once came, believing the spot holy, to whip themselves into spiritual ecstasy. Eleanor sat down on a bench. "If I did sell everything I bet I could raise a down payment for a real house."

"Well sure you could—"

"But then I'd have nothing to put in it."

They took the metro to Sainte Chapelle. Inside was like standing in a box made of rubies and sapphires, sunlight setting the stained glass on fire. Ilene soaked it up.

"Why did you let me take everything else and not the bottle?" Eleanor suddenly asked.

Ilene had to laugh. How foolish to hope the treasures of Paris might dazzle away old demons. "It's French. We were moving to France."

"Ilene, you've never offered me that bottle."

"You overlooked it for twenty-five years, and that galls you, doesn't it."

Whatever the Lindleys knew about the bottle that Eleanor didn't, Eleanor knew one thing for sure. Shortly before she died, Mother Larue told her elder daughter, "Ilene and Bob should have that bottle. Wine is for couples." Eleanor, for a quarter of a century, had been unable to determine if Bob and Ilene had been told the same. The way they showed that bottle off seemed a cruel indication they had been.

"I'm sorry, El. The wine is one thing you're not going to get."

"Mother told you to keep it, didn't she?"

"I swear she never did that."

"You wouldn't swear right here in a church. You wouldn't lie in a church."

"Even if I did, El, it wouldn't count one way or the other. The place has been desacralized or something, ever since the revolution."

"All I want to know, Leeny, is what's so damn special about that wine."

"It's mine, that's what's so special. And you're not getting it."

"We will see, Leeny. We will see."

In bed that night Ilene told Bob, "Please, take Eleanor tomorrow. Get her out of my sight. She wants the Chateau d'Aumonier—on top of everything, she wants that!"

"Don't get yourself worked up. Tell her how sick you were. That'll make her back off."

"Back off? She'll start coming at me!" Mr. Lindley knew what she meant. How, when Mother Larue was sick in the hospital, her eyes dull with pain, or painkillers, Eleanor hovered about her, a cup of water, cotton swab or tissue always in hand. How Eleanor cranked the bed up, then cranked the bed down. She'd given Mother Larue a real workout. Ilene didn't need that.

"Ilene, give El the bottle for Christmas." Eleanor had said only that morning not to expect presents this year because she hadn't wanted to lug anything extra onto the plane. They'd exchanged enough furniture over the years to fill Invalides, Bob knew, but never presents. He turned off the lamp. "What *is* so special about that wine, Ilene?"

She couldn't say. She stared at hash marks on the wall made by the shutters slicing the light from the street. Her daughter Jenny, the psychologist, might have told her, "Maybe it's the cork, Mother. Maybe the cork bobs on a pool deep in your memory." So Jenny might have said, had she—or anyone else—known what Father Kerr had done to the cork.

He sits at the dining room table, a cigarette going. He takes the bottle of Chateau d'Aumonier and with a razor blade carefully slits the seal at the top. If the cork's dried out and letting in air, then the wine's spoiled. He knows it hasn't been properly stored, in a cool, dark place on its side. He uncorks the cork. Smells it, puts it under Leeny's nose. She winces. He wets his finger enough to taste, makes a sour face. Leeny laughs. "We gotta put in the new cork just the same." He plugs in a wood burning tool with an extra-fine tip. When it's hot he makes designs on the cork, exactly like those on the original, a lion on his hind legs, his paws out, boxer style, the year, 1855, and the name of the chateau. The air smells of smoking cork. He sets the wood burner in its metal cradle and pushes the cork into the neck—for he has immense shoulders and arms—with his bare palm. Leeny, six years old, standing on a chair, leans over the table. "Watch out, sweetheart!" She has hit the cord and tipped the wood burner in its cradle, singeing the table. He rubs the spot. "Nothing serious. If anyone asks, I did it with a cigarette. And Leeny, forget we had this open. Else we gotta tell Mom her wine's as bitter as castor oil." He dabs glue on the end of the bottle with a brush and closes the seal. It would take careful study to find the razor slit. If anyone now asked, fifty-two years later, as Ilene Lindley stared at the hash marks of light, if she remembered the time her father replaced the cork, she would search around her mind and ask, "What?"

As he had the day they picked up Eleanor at the airport, Mr. Lindley borrowed the Quests' car so he could take his sister-in-law to the palace of Versailles. "It's got some nice antiques, El." Ilene told her sister she was more than happy to stay home and cook, and managed to whisper to Bob, "Not a word about the doctor."

The Quests lived upstairs. Catherine and her husband Andre, both retired, made a startling pair. Madame Quest, with steel blue hair she cropped close and combed forward, resembled a Roman emperor. Her eyeliner was as thick as the tracery in a gothic window. Monsieur Quest had a shaved head, which sat atop a bull neck festooned with gold chains. Ilene liked to imagine that they had vision into the essence of things. She had invited them to dinner, wanting Eleanor to meet them, perhaps so she could see, as Ilene did, how the Quests were blazes on bark, marking the distance she and Bob had ventured. Afterward, the Lindleys and Eleanor were going to Notre Dame for midnight mass.

Around three o'clock, Catherine Quest stopped by to ask if she could help with anything. Ilene said no, except to keep her company. She cooked and talked. Without intending to, she let her troubles with Eleanor out. When she told how Eleanor now wanted the last thing of their mother's Ilene had, Catherine exploded furiously—"You are a beloved friend and I will gladly wring your sister's neck!"

"Oh, no!" Ilene exclaimed. "Here I am, blasting away. Forget what I've said. I'm sure our differences are no worse than those of other sisters."

"Indeed. My sister and I haven't spoken in six years."

"You see. At least Eleanor and I speak. Please, Catherine, you must give Eleanor a chance."

That evening, Eleanor strolled from the guestroom drenched in kelly green, her rotund waist girded by a red belt.

"Why, Eleanor, you are Christmas incarnate!"

"Thank you, Bob!" They'd had a friendly time at Versailles.

"Doesn't El look lovely, Ilene."

"Of course." Ilene thought Eleanor, despite being close to fashionable clothes all her life, seldom dressed wisely. Tonight she looked like a pup tent with a ribbon around it. The door bell rang.

The Quests came in, brushstroked with purple, as had been the style in Paris since Fall. Mr. Lindley introduced them to Eleanor. If the Quests had never seen anything like her, it was a cinch she had never seen anything like them. They spoke perfect English, but their accents made them sound even eerier than they looked.

Everyone sat in the living room eating canapés as the Quests embarked on a palavering speech concerning the masses of gypsies one was apt to encounter in the metro these days. The gypsies! Eleanor thought. Do you ever look in the mirror!

When everyone sat down to dinner, Eleanor quickly cut the end off the long loaf of bread, because she liked the heel. When she set the loaf back in the basket she happened to lay it upside down. Madame Quest, seated beside her, flipped the loaf right side up, saying, "Never, dear, never. Witches will come and dance upon bread with the bottom up." When Madame Quest asked Eleanor what she thought of Versailles, Eleanor said she had a bed at home that could rival Marie Antoinette's.

The dinner was superb, and talk circulated the table of favorite dishes to be had at favorite restaurants. For every restaurant someone mentioned in France, Eleanor told of something it sounded like on the Cape, including Captain Jack's and The Bavarian Pantry. During the cheese course, they discovered they'd run out of wine. Catherine Quest said she had a nice Burgundy upstairs.

Eleanor suddenly blurted out, "We could always drink the Chateau Ammonia!"

"Ammonia!" Madame Quest squealed.

"You know what I mean," Eleanor said.

"Ammonia!" Madame Quest was squealing over and over.

"Don't laugh at me," Eleanor said.

"It's just funny, El," Ilene said. "Catherine, you don't mean anything, do you." She saw Madame Quest's blackly circumscribed eyes sharpen with cruelty, and Ilene knew it were as if she had drawn Catherine's face herself, with all she had said about Eleanor earlier in the day.

"Nothing at all, Eleanor," Catherine said flatly. "I suppose with so much sediment on the bottom, we could shake the wine up like a bottle of orange juice."

Eleanor didn't know if Madame Quest was being sarcastic.

"I know you all've been laughing at me tonight."

"No one's been laughing at you, El," Bob said.

"And I'm sorry I'm no wine expert. Excuse me if I'm not all highfalutin. Maybe if I owned Chateau Whatever myself, I could pronounce it. But you see, Leeny here has the only bottle in the family."

"Okay, El," Mr. Lindley said. "We get the idea." My God, he wondered, had everything he'd told her gone right through her head! Despite Ilene's orders, he'd let Eleanor in on the gallbladder.

"Who would want that wine," Catherine said, "I don't know. By this point, of course, it's urine."

"Leeny and Bob seem to be keeping it for their thousandth anniversary or something."

"Dammit, Eleanor, what did I tell you!"

"Actually Bob, if you and Ilene have been hoarding that bottle, you should be aware that it may be cursed," said Madame Quest.

"What did you say?" Eleanor asked.

"The Chateau d'Aumonier may be cursed."

Eleanor leaned back in her chair.

"Where'd you get this nonsense?" Mr. Lindley asked.

"I love a good curse," Andre Quest joked.

"Catherine, what are you doing?" Ilene asked.

"Oh, you will like this. Months ago, when I first saw that bottle, something came to me." She rose and went and got the bottle.

"I looked into it, and as I suspected, there is a legend that accompanies a certain bottle of 1855 Chateau d'Aumonier." She set the bottle in the middle of the table. "I've forgotten till now because, well, frankly, who dwells on such things? But, since Eleanor has brought up the subject of possession of the bottle. . ."

"I'd like to hear this, Leeny."

Ilene, sensing where Catherine was going, looked at Eleanor. Despite her petty, coveting ways, she seemed—plucked from her little house and dropped at this table—pathetic and vulnerable.

"'Leeny'? Eleanor, dear, you must stop that. No one in Paris calls your sister 'Leeny.' Now, as for the curse—"

"Catherine, I'd rather not hear this."

"Ilene," Catherine cajoled, "it's mere entertainment!"

"Sure, yes, go ahead, a laugh," the men said.

"Leeny," said Eleanor, "I mean, Ilene. You don't believe in curses, now do you?"

"None of us does, dear," Madame Quest said, finding Eleanor past pity or humor. "That's why we all are so eager to hear. Well, it seems Chateau d'Aumonier was owned by a man named Victor Hinault, whose wines enjoyed grand success. One day, tragically, his beautiful wife, Veronique, was killed in a freak carriage spill between Paulliac and Saint Estephe. Alongside his wife's casket, at the close of funeral services, Victor laid a bottle of 1855 d'Aumonier. According to legend, the grave tender, who must have thought this a waste of superb wine, waited till the funeral goers had left and then, before laying on the slabs of stone, reached in and stole the bottle. Indeed, when the grave was reopened eighteen years later, and Victor—ever faithful to Veronique's memory—at last returned to his wife's side, the bottle was discovered missing. And so it is said, tremendous ill-fortune will attend who ever possesses the bottle, and that its wine, if drunk, will have the swift effect of poison."

Ilene honestly didn't know if such a legend existed. She thought Catherine capable of spinning it right from her head.

"Bravo, Catherine," Mr. Lindley chuckled. "Now are you

suggesting this bottle is that bottle?"

"Well, if this is that," Ilene interjected, "you now know, El, why Bob and I never drank it." She laughed, but she saw clouds cross her sister's face.

"And this might be that," Catherine quickly continued, "given the name—I'm sure it is only a profound coincidence—of the grave tender, who was also the grave robber—"

"Catherine, enough," Ilene said. She remembered telling Catherine how the bottle had made its way to the United States. "Really. Now, I think we should have dessert and then the three of us must be heading for mass."

"Who was the grave tender?" Eleanor asked blankly.

"El, who cares! It's some silly story."

"So why not say the man's name?"

"The man's name, Eleanor," Catherine said, "was Larue."

"Ilene, that is your maiden name, yes?" Andre Quest asked.

"What the hell's going on here, Ilene?" Bob demanded.

"Nothing—Catherine is making up some story."

"Yes," she said, her eyes slit, for the first time looking into Eleanor's eyes not a foot away, "I whip these things up like mousse—"

"Catherine! Please!"

Even Andre Quest sensed his wife's story, for whatever reason, was meant to spook Eleanor. If it had, this strange lady in green gave no indication. Over dessert, as the men steered the conversation toward the prospects of a tunnel at long last connecting France and England, Ilene still thought she saw clouds obscure her sister's face. She hoped they would pass harmlessly. But beside Madame Quest's glow of satisfaction, Eleanor's darkness looked indelible. Maybe not.

"I can't believe you put that beast of a woman up to that, Leeny," Eleanor said as soon as the Quests had gone.

"I did no such thing!"

"Nice try, but I swear more than ever, I'm not leaving Paris without that bottle."

What sympathy Ilene had felt now turned to raw acid.

"Like hell you will, Eleanor."

Ilene put the bottle back in its basket, and off they went to church.

The temperature had dropped that day, and the inside of Notre Dame was cold. So Eleanor kept her coat on. It, too, was green. Her pillbox hat was red. A thousand burning candles filled the church with the smell of wax. All around the altar, centered in the transept, were silky white poinsettias in brass vases. Beyond the altar were intricately carved wooden screens, beyond them another altar all gold and marble. The whole place was circled with altars. Statues and paintings were everywhere, figures with arms, hands and heads frozen in gestures of agony or supplication. Eleanor had seen Notre Dame on the outside, but here inside she couldn't imagine anything so vast. The floor of black and white squares went on forever like a giant checkerboard. She felt compelled to kneel, but there were no pews or kneelers, only tiny chairs with wicker seats. The congregation either sat or stood.

The Lindleys, not church-going people, had heard how spectacular midnight mass was, especially the music. After the twelve strokes of midnight chimed, the organ erupted, and Ilene felt the nave swell with deep thunder, then on her face felt the angel voices of choirboys sprinkle down. *Hodie Christus Natus Est*, the choirboys sang. When they began *Ave Maria*, the congregation joined in, and Ilene heard her voice rise with the others and fill the high church vaults. Something inside her began to rise as well, weightless. After the reading of the gospel, they sang *Adeste Fideles*, and Ilene thought she was flying, her own voice carrying her away. And as she soared and circled, she decided: she would wrap the bottle tonight and give it to Eleanor in the morning! A gift. The only gift she had given Eleanor since she could remember. Yes, El, you will have what you want and believe you deserve, for whatever reasons, known or unknown to either of us. She turned to smile at her sister. There was Eleanor, in her green and red, shaking and sobbing, tears skittering down a face scalded by enormous and sudden grief. She looked at Ilene and whimpered, "I, Eleanor

Larue, am not descended from a grave robber!" Then she pushed her way out, knocking over her chair and bumping wildly into the people between her and the center aisle. Ilene rushed after her, and Mr. Lindley followed. The peals of the organ couldn't drown out Eleanor's cries as she ran toward the door.

In front of the church, she leaned at the black iron fence, bracing herself with her hands on the bars. Ilene came up behind her.

"How could you let that witch tell such lies, Leeny?"

"Maybe it's all true, El."

"No, no."

"Yes, the things mother left us are full of poison."

Eleanor's agony redoubled and she wailed all the louder.

It had begun to snow. Mr. Lindley looked around and made out a cab whose roof light was off. He went up to it and found the driver asleep. In the passenger seat a dog was asleep, too. Knocking on the window, he woke them up.

"Here's a hundred francs to get us home. Just over at Saint Sulpice."

The driver looked. "She all right?"

"She'll be okay."

Mr. Lindley got the women into the back seat, Eleanor in the middle, still shuddering. He put his arm around her and she pressed her face to his chest. He looked at his wife, who turned away.

"That filthy, filthy witch." The words were muffled in Mr. Lindley's coat.

He got her into the apartment and sat her in the living room.

"I'm better now," Eleanor said.

"Eleanor, I've got a present here for you," Mr. Lindley said. "How would you like to open—"

"I don't want any presents."

"El," Ilene said, getting down on her knees at her sister's chair, "forget what happened tonight. I'm giving you the wine."

Eleanor wouldn't look at Ilene. She'd said she'd get that

bottle. Well, it's hers. She got me good on this one, Ilene thought. She expected Eleanor to burst out laughing, having pulled it off.

"El, El," Ilene said, "you deserve the bottle, like an Oscar! That was one fine performance! Now stop, please."

"I said I don't want any presents."

"Enough, Eleanor. It might be worth good money."

"Who's gonna pay good money for a bottle of castor oil?"

"People are funny. Someone might pay so much you could buy your mobile home straight out."

"And what? Squeeze everything in with a shoehorn?"

"El, I think mother would want you to have that bottle."

Eleanor glared at her, eyes spewing hatred from unthinkable depths, her voice choking on its own words.

"I hope it is cursed and it burns your goddam guts out!"

"Eleanor!" Bob shouted. "Cut it!"

Eleanor's eyes shut tight, her head sunk to her chest, and she slid down in the chair, as though she were melting.

Ilene's heart contracted. In a world where even doctors now and then missed the obvious, she supposed anything was possible.

Despite what Ilene had believed for so long, she saw now that hands dispense fairly only for those who believe them fair, even the same hand. She rose, without emotion, and went and picked up the bottle of Chateau d'Aumonier. She took it into the kitchen and, on the porcelain that divided the two sinks, tapped the neck. Once, twice, three times. On the fourth tap, the neck broke off cleanly right below the cork, and the wine spilled out. She tilted the bottle and watched it empty. Against the white sink the brick orange became amber. There was a sour odor, like cut flowers gone bad, but more piercing, an exact odor she could've sworn she had smelled somewhere before. The wine went down the drain, and she ran the faucet a moment. She didn't bother putting the bottle in with those they took to the recycling bin around the corner, but threw it right in the garbage, along with the neck with the cork in it.

She returned to the living room. The curse at last lifted,

Eleanor sat up, breathed deep, opened her eyes wide and smiled.

"Bob, I'll open a present now. After that, maybe Ilene'll show me how to dial Cape May from here."

Yes, Mr. Lindley thought, Oscars, Oscars all around, and placed a box in his sister-in-law's lap.

AN EASY DAY AT EASY RED

Bill Ivors was getting last minute advice from his wife, Jo Ann, while his father, Ed, and his son, Timmy, were waiting by the car singing "Frere-uh Jacques-uh." She took Bill's arm as they stepped out on the porch of their house in the Paris suburb of Nanterre.

"I mean it now, Bill," she said, "don't go playing the great historian with your father. This is Ed's return to Normandy, not yours."

"Okay, Jo. Really," Bill said. For a few days he could forget that Normandy was the very reason he'd come to France. Forget he taught a course at the American college called "The Greatest Invasion." Forget as well his book in progress, about the Free French before D-Day and their frantic race against time. "No problem, Jo." She walked him to the car and kissed them all goodbye. "My three men," she said. Then in Bill's ear whispered, "Ed's trip."

About an hour into the ride Ed quipped that the scenery didn't look much different from what you saw along the New York State Thruway. Bill gently tried to evoke the wonder of just where they were. "Dad, that's the Seine down there, not the Erie canal. Upstream you got La Roche-Guyon, where Rommel had his headquarters. Downstream you got Rouen, where William the Conqueror died, 1087, and Joan of Arc burned at the stake, 1431. Over some bridge around here you yourself crossed the Seine, 1944. You remember where?"

"Hell, Bill, I wasn't taking notes that day."

Though sure it was the bridge at the Norman town of Vernon, Bill laughed, "No, I guess not." A few miles later, glancing in the rearview mirror, Bill saw Timmy jiggling his one front tooth. Timmy's mother, a nurse, had pulled the first, and Bill was hoping he'd not be called upon to do the same in her absence. "Hands away from tooth, son," he said gently. Ed quickly whipped around in his seat. "I'm gonna yank-yank-yank it!" Timmy clasped his hands to his mouth and gurgled with delight.

Bill had booked a two-room *gite* not far from that section of Omaha Beach code-named "Easy Red." The sun glowed hot now as they drove slowly along the shore. A row of modern beach houses stopped bluntly at a concrete bunker, as though some stubborn owner had delayed the development's progress. The bunker had been painted up to look like a turtle, but from its maw extended a rusted gun barrel. Seeing it, Bill automatically estimated an 88-millimeter.

"Park here." His father's voice sounded weak, and after they got out Bill checked if Ed was burrowing in his pocket for his tablets, but he wasn't. Though the angina was nothing new, Bill still couldn't connect it to any clear trigger.

"I wanna play on the turtle," Timmy shouted.

"Okay," said Bill. "But stay where I can see you."

Ed looked around. "There's the steeple," he said, pointing to the horizon. "There's the blockhouse." It was at the foot of a road that cut up through sandy cliffs. Ed sat on the guardrail. "That's the very road we went up."

To Bill's surprise, the beach was crowded and people were swimming. For the last two years, he'd brought his classes here in late fall, with everything deserted, the way he thought Omaha should be. But now, in the August heat, it was just another beach. "So up that road would've been the henhouse," Bill said.

Not many soldiers first saw action in a henhouse, but as Bill had heard many times, two days into the invasion, Ed had, earning himself forever the nickname "Eggs." Bill might have preferred something like "Sidearm," for the way his father threw a grenade or, in later years, a hardball at the A&P parking lot with Bill and his older brothers. But "Eggs" had stuck, and come each June in

Batavia, New York, on what he dubbed "Henhouse Day," Ed held a barbecue and ceremoniously told the story.

"By the time we hit the beach plentya dead are stacked above the tide line. Nice welcomin' committee. The Germans're pushed back a few miles, and maybe twenty of us make our way up this road that leads onto a farm. We're cuttin' across a field fulla craters and stinkin' dead cows, when this guy, Jack Sturm, says he sees movement in the doorway of an outbuilding. The door itself is layin' on the ground.

"Well, I can hear clucking right off, and out walks a chicken, like for a stroll. We all laugh, 'cept Sturm. He gets jumpy and creepy. Says to chuck in a grenade, 'cause there's snipers about, as if we don't know. I say, 'What! And bust up our breakfast! I'll get the eggs, Jack. You cut up one of those cows for hash!'

"Now, these buildings are stone, and there's no way you're gonna shoot someone from the outside—if in fact there's anyone inside. Next thing I know I'm standin' beside that door, the stone wall in my back, and I'm wonderin' what the hell—lob in a grenade. But I couldn't blow up breakfast! So I take a deep breath—an' turn, dive an' roll! I'm all reaction—turn, dive an' roll!

"Sure enough—there's Jerry. But already I fired a good six shots outta my Thompson. Chickens're flyin' all over the place! Jerry drops flat on his back, and the way his eyes're slightly cracked I know he's dead. So I take my helmet and fill it fulla eggs. I keep glancin' at Jerry, though. He looks as new at this business as I am, and I must say he's about the ugliest kraut I was bound to see the whole war. But what gets my attention is, is damn if he doesn't have yolk all around his kisser. Poor bastard was livin' on raw eggs, waitin' for the noise to stop.

"Finally I walk out and shout, 'Throw your powdered eggs to the wind, boys!' and they start whoopin' and hollerin'. Then we all hear it. The whistlin' in the air. Men scream 'Hit it!' and dive for cover."

Now the crowd on the patio would begin to laugh. Ed in his barbecue apron spattered with sauce would start shaking his head, his smile about to burst.

"Yes, yes, once again, I'm all reaction—I dive in a hole—right alongside a dead cow, no less—and slam on my helmet! When the fireworks end two of our men are dead, and that henhouse is rubble—a pile of stones! But there I am, safe and sound, my head and face drippin' with eggs."

Now Ed would look like a man kissed by luck herself. Bill's mother would serve deviled eggs. The guests would grab them up, holding them as though making a toast, and wisecracking about 'shell shock' and how the yolk was on Ed.

The story of "Eggs" Ivors wasn't exactly about parachuting into the night sky over Sainte Mere Eglise or grappling up the cliffs at Pointe du Hoc. And over the years, as Bill began to take history a lot more seriously than Ed ever did, the idea of a soldier dripping with eggs became downright clownish, especially at Easy Red, D-Days's ugliest irony. For that section of beach was supposed to be easy, but it turned out the hardest, the bloodiest, the reddest. At least on day one. Thankfully, Ed had come ashore on day three. Still, reading late at night in a dormitory how Germany's well polished 352nd Infantry Division happened by a twitch of fate to be on routine maneuvers behind Omaha Beach when the invasion came, Bill got a chill. They cost the Allies plenty. What if one of them had been in the henhouse and not some raw kid? Bill sometimes pictured Ed, himself a raw kid, buried in the rubble, dead for his clowning.

"Dad, you wanna see if we can find the spot where the henhouse was?"

"Not today," Ed said. "Maybe tomorrow." He reached his hand in his pocket, pulled out his amber bottle, then pushed it back.

Just then Timmy came running up, waving a fist.

"Look what I got!" He opened his hand, and there lay his front tooth. He opened his mouth, blood outlining his teeth. "I was sittin' in the turtle and decided to yank-yank-yank it!"

"You put that under your pillow," Ed told him. "See how much the tooth fairy leaves ya." Bill looked over at Ed. There'd been no tooth fairy the first time around.

"Granddad, that's silly."

"Silly! You put that tooth under your pillow. You'll see for yourself."

A beaming Frenchman, Monsieur Poitier, owned the *gite*. He'd built it himself, a small ground-level place with a concrete slab out front with lawn chairs and a table. He must have been eighty. When Bill told him his father had come ashore two days into the invasion, he hugged Ed's hand, freckled and red-haired, with both his own, drawing it to his old lips and kissing the middle knuckle. Then the Frenchman went up to his house and came back with a bottle of calvados, what Americans called applejack, and gave it to Ed.

That night, once Timmy was in bed, Ed and Bill took to the chairs on the concrete slab. The sky was clear and starry, the moon a paring short of full. They looked out over a silver meadow that ended at a jagged black hedgerow. Ed poured the calvados, and Bill took a strong, burning slug. After a moment he could taste apples, smell blossoms.

They jabbered about the past. About the house, the neighbors. About Bill and his brothers. Their feats on the track team. Their green and white '56 Chevy. How they could rev it up to 5000 rpms and stand a nickel on edge on the air cleaner—and it didn't fall over. The engine was that perfectly tuned. They talked about Ed's plumbing parts store, leading, inevitably, to Sister de La Salle. She came in one day seeking a soap dispenser. Ed got going, talking and hypothesizing, and by the time he finished she'd bought a urinal for the convent.

But the store would be history soon. Last Christmas, with the family gathered in Batavia, Ed told everyone he'd decided to sell. His sons were scattered, settled far away, and everyone tacitly knew it would no longer be "Ivors' Plumbing Supplies."

"Bill, I found a buyer," Ed said, polishing off the calvados in his glass.

For months Bill knew this was coming and he still felt bad. To think of all the hours the family had put in for over thirty years. When Bill was six Ed paid him fifty cents a week to make sure the faucets on all the model sinks and tubs near the front window were turned off at the end of each day. Of course they were dry, not hooked up, but Bill believed his father knew if they weren't firmly closed.

"So who is it?"

"Your cousin Mike."

"Mike? Mike Aikers? Are you kidding? Mike!"

Bill and Mike hadn't spoken in nearly twenty years. When they were both eighteen Mike was a plumber's apprentice, and one morning early Bill caught him shoving faucet stems in his lunch pail. They were alone in the store. Mike simply slugged Bill in the gut and sent him sprawling into a rack full of shower curtains. "Tell, and I swear you'll never say 'faucet stem' again." Bill was half-buckled over, draped by the curtains, their vinyl smell in his nose. A week later he was off to college, never having mentioned it.

"I know he's not your favorite person," Ed said, "but at least he's family."

"Family! Dad, there's something I should've told you years ago. He used to steal faucet stems."

"Just that once."

"What, you know about it?"

"Mike told me a couple months after." Ed laughed, waved his empty glass. "Said you ended up in the shower curtains."

Bill was amazed how the memory still smoldered. He wondered if his father knew about the punch in the gut.

"It wasn't funny then, Dad."

"Look, Mike felt terrible and came clean."

"Why didn't you bother to tell me?"

"Why didn't you bother to tell *me*?"

There was silence as both men looked at the sky. Finally Ed refilled their glasses. "So tell me something important. How much you think that tooth is worth?" He pulled out a handful of coins.

Bill appreciated the switch of topic but hesitated just the same. "If the tooth fairy accounts for inflation and exchange rates, I guess that ten-franc piece should do."

Ed got up.

"Dad, look, don't be surprised if nothing's under the pillow."

"Don't you be surprised if something is." And in he went.

Bill could hear the Channel waters breaking out beyond the hedgerow, steady, peaceful. You'd never know there'd been a war here. It was so quiet. Like D-Day in pre-dawn, before four thousand landing craft came out of the darkness, ten thousand planes, a hundred-fifty-six thousand men. *Goddam Mike Aikers*, he thought, *that asshole of a cousin*.

"Hey, take a look."

Bill turned to see his father standing in the doorway, holding up his hand like giving the okay sign. Even in only moonlight, Bill could see, between Ed's thumb and forefinger, the tooth, and at that moment it seemed as enormous as a kitchen sink.

In the morning, Bill and Timmy were washing breakfast dishes. Ed had gone out early without eating. Bill didn't ask where, thinking his father needed time alone and maybe had gone to find the farm where the henhouse was. He doubted there'd be any trace of it, though much in this part of Normandy looked like it had lain untouched for fifty years.

They waited outside. Suddenly Ed appeared at the end of a row of firewood. Around his neck he had an inflated inner tube, maybe from a truck tire.

"Look what I got off Mister Poitier!"

Bill stared, wondering how he'd managed that. Charades?

"What're we gonna do with it, Dad?"

"We're goin' swimming, that's what."

"I thought we were doin' museums today."

"What, you think some museum's gonna tell me somethin' I don't already know?"

Bill thought about it. It meant no run-ins with Ed trying to explain things to Timmy. Guns, mines, artificial harbors, invasion maps, LSTs, Churchill, Eisenhower, Rommel asparagus—it would be endless once they got started. Maybe Ed thought the same. They hadn't brought trunks, but they were wearing shorts. Besides, if Omaha Beach were like other beaches in France—and maybe now it was—going buck naked wouldn't turn an eye either.

"Good," said Bill. "An easy day at Easy Red."

Along the waterfront, his ten francs in hand, Timmy saw a green paratrooper, maybe four inches tall with a white chute, in the window of a shop. Only it cost twelve-and-a-half francs. As Bill shook his head, Ed spotted Timmy the difference. The beach was filling up, so they walked out toward the fringe, where a few people had indeed stripped down buck naked.

"This okay, Dad?"

"Why wouldn't it be, Bill?"

They spread out a blanket, then Ed showed his grandson how to fold the chute. Timmy threw the toy in the air, the chute opened and the man wobbled down, hit the sand and fell over. Timmy retrieved it, refolded the chute and threw again.

"He's got a promising arm," Ed said. He took off his shirt and stretched out, resting his head on the inner tube like a pillow. As Bill lay stomach down, he saw something right in front of him, the pull-tab off some kind of can. He pushed it under the blanket.

"Timmy, make sure you keep your sneakers on."

"Geez, Bill, it's the beach. Let him run around barefoot."

"You never know what's in the sand."

"You think he's gonna hit a landmine?"

What did he have to do, fish out the tab and show him?

"Dad, he's wearing his sneakers."

Ed didn't respond, and Bill regretted being brusque. After a few minutes he said, "Hey, get a load of that." Off to their right was a young couple, maybe eighteen years old, lying on an open sleeping bag, their clothes in a small pile. The boy was skinny as a pipe and wore shiny black trunks. The girl had taken off everything. She was big, still carrying baby fat, but her skin was tight and smooth.

"Well, that's a damn better sight than the last time I saw Easy Red. I gotta hand it to the French, they ain't all hung up on what's God-given natural." It pleased Bill to hear this. The girl lay on her back, a towel neatly across her face. There was a bottle of sun screen beside her and two yellow knapsacks. A portable cassette player was on. His head cradled in his arms, Bill's eyes focused on her pubic hair out over the horizon of his bicep. He heard the couple talking.

"They're not French, Dad. They're German."

Ed cocked his head.

The boy was propped up on bony arms. He had a long pimply face and bags under his eyes. His nose seemed thin as a fish fin. Still, wearing a bracelet and neck chain, he scanned the water with a satisfied air, his lower lip pulling on a moustache that might fill out in a year or two.

"Don't they know where they are?" Ed asked.

"They're kids. To them this beach might as well be at Thermopylae." The volume on the cassette player shot up.

"Hey, can you turn that thing down over there?" Ed called.

The boy looked at him. Maybe he didn't understand English. "I don't like him. He's an arrogant punk."

"He's just a kid, Dad. Forget about it."

"I asked you nicely to turn that down."

"It's a free beach," the boy said.

"Do I have to turn it down for you?"

Then the girl spoke, sharp words coming through her towel. Bill knew enough German to get the gist: "Don't start a fight with an old man. Grow up." The boy didn't listen.

Ed rose and went toward him. Bill scurried up, looked around quickly, and saw Timmy still busy with his paratrooper.

"I'll ask you again. Would you please turn that down?"

Bill tried to intervene, speaking German, and the boy laughed.

"If you don't want to hear it, you can move."

Barefoot, Ed kicked a knapsack. It rolled across the sand.

"Your ass, boy."

"Dad, please." He grabbed Ed's arm. "Not in front of Timmy."

The German raised his hands. "Okay, old man, I surrender!"

Bill felt Ed's arm tense.

"You skinny son of a bitch—"

Suddenly the girl whipped her towel away, riddling the boy in German and shutting off the music. His hands dropped. The girl's face was a frightful shock of peeling sunburn. "I'm sorry," she told Ed. By now, people were staring. She pulled the sleeping bag up between her legs.

Just as she did Timmy's paratrooper wobbled down, glanced off her shoulder and landed in her lap. She squealed, then seeing what it was, jiggled with delight. The paratrooper hid in a recess of the sleeping bag, as if in a ditch, like he was having a smoke and trying to figure out what next. The German boy started hiccupping with laughter. Then everyone was laughing—Timmy, without his front teeth, a man on a nearby blanket, two women in bikinis eating sorbet, Bill. "Com'on, Dad," he said. "You're the one always yucking it up." But as Bill kept laughing his father's eyes went blank. Without a word Ed walked away, picked up his inner tube and slipped an arm through it. The girl wrapped the paratrooper in its chute and handed it to Timmy. Her boyfriend put on a set of headphones. They were still chuckling, and Bill wanted to explain something, but didn't know what.

To Timmy he said, "I told you to get your sneakers on."

"I don't remember where they are."

"Then you sit on the blanket until you do remember."

Out in the water Ed was in the inner tube bobbing softly. Bill waded toward him, the water surprisingly warm, the sand snug.

"I guess we found out why she wears a towel over her face. Her boyfriend could use one too."

"I guess so," Ed answered quietly.

"That surrender business, that was going too far."

"Like I said, an arrogant punk."

Bill looked out toward England, unseeable, felt strangely

invigorated, but happened to yawn. "That soldier in the henhouse," he said.

"Yeah, Bill?"

"I bet he was no uglier than that boy there." He vaguely thought, without wanting to guess too much, that that was it. The soldier in Ed's story looked like this boy on the beach. Maybe he caused it all to come rushing back at Ed—if ugly was the denominator. But this boy wasn't ugly, not really. Just afflicted with youth. Youth. Maybe that was it. On Henhouse Day, you forgot how young they had been. "Was he as young as that, Dad?"

"I suppose he was."

"Hitler was throwing everyone in by then. Even kids. The Russian front had decimated him. Of course he insisted on keeping the Fifteenth Army north of the Seine, still thinking the invasion would come at Calais. He stretched himself thin."

"Bill, shut up." Ed rubbed his hand on his stomach, in the red hair turning gray. "I'm gonna say something here."

"What're ya gonna say?"

"It wasn't a soldier in the henhouse. It was a girl."

Bill looked at his father and locked eyes, saying nothing.

"See, it was a girl in the henhouse. A French girl. She was on the ground before I knew it." Ed turned his eyes away. For a split second Bill thought it was a joke.

"You puttin' me on?"

"No." Ed's fingers drew gently at the hair on his belly.

"Every year you tell that story to twenty-odd people stuffin' their faces with barbecued chicken. You sayin' it's not true?"

"The eggs part is true—I promised the boys breakfast. And the incoming fire—and me jumpin' in with that dead cow—and slammin' the helmet on my head."

Was he saying he filled his helmet full of eggs with a girl he just shot dead lying on the ground?

"Jesus, Dad. Eddie 'Eggs' Ivors? 'Henhouse Day'? I don't get it."

"It's a funny story that really happened."

"Except for one goddam detail!" Bill wiped a handful of water over his face. "Christ, all of Batavia is walking around with this fairy tale in their heads."

"So next Henhouse Day, you come by and tell 'em, Bill." His voice was even as he shifted his weight and the rubber tube squeaked. "See how fast you can break up a barbecue."

Bill stayed silent. *Why tell them anything*? He wanted to know. *Year after year, with a whole goddam ceremony*? He suddenly saw the yolk, as he had so often, "all around his kisser," but now it was caked hard around a girl's mouth. He felt sick. He didn't know what appalled him more, the truth or the lie.

"You ever tell anyone else?"

Not answering, Ed looked up at the sun, squinted, then rubbed his eyes shut with a thumb and forefinger. When his eyes opened, they fluttered at Bill. "Jesus, son, you're supposed to be the historian. You know horrible crap happened. After, you did anything to keep the demons away." That wasn't history to Bill—for him, lies were the demons.

"You tell Tom? Ray?" Those were Bill's brothers.

"What if I did?" Ed paused. "What if I didn't? Hell, Bill, I was never gonna tell anyone anything. Swore that from the start." Ed paused.

You fuckin' told me, Bill thought. But he could not respond. Still, he would have time to reflect. That's what an historian did. One could spend a lifetime reflecting on the horrors of a few years—or a few seconds. Truth's angel dead in the dirt.

Then Ed said, "I remember the goddamn sergeant chewing out my ass for clowning." Bill saw his father smile. "Hmph! Then he winks, thanks me for loosening the boys up. Turned out the rest of that day was easy. No action. 'Cept every time someone looked at me they started laughing. Later I find this water trough and I'm trying to wash the eggs out. My head's down in there. The guys were off chowing down, laughing. God, I was so happy to get my head in that trough, so I could just sob and puke. Get it out, I told myself, once and for all time. No one had to know about that girl.

She just didn't belong."

Bill looked at Ed floating in his tube and seeing a hand pressed to his chest tried not to overreact. "Slow down, Dad. You OK? I'll run get your tablets."

"I've been caught without 'em. I can ride it out." Ed breathed deeply, massaging his chest. Bill wondered if his father's pain was like the constriction he himself now felt.

"Only one person I ever really wanted to tell, but couldn't, and that's your mother. Somehow I think she's always known. Known something. And every year she still makes those eggs. Real reason she wouldn't come on this trip is probably thought I was lookin' for trouble, not that crap about being afraid to fly over the ocean." Ed bobbed on the water, his hand doing hypnotic circles over his heart. He seemed relaxed, serene, as if in the middle of a gentle stream flowing toward a clear sea. He slowly exhaled. "Did I really land here?"

Bill saw people filing down the paths and roads from the plateau behind. Like the invasion in reverse, the colors now infinitely brighter, the beach chiming with laughter, sun drenched and sibilant. "Was the henhouse really flattened?" Bill asked.

"That's for sure."

"So the artillery would've killed her anyway."

"I guess it would've." Bill saw his father had stopped massaging. "I went up there this morning and found the farm. It's all fancy now. There's a lawn surrounded by hollyhocks where the henhouse used to be. I stood on the spot and talked to her." After a second Bill realized he meant the girl. "I told her, 'No, we weren't hungry. I was only showing off. You're right about that. We were scared as you and needed a laugh.' Then I told her, 'If I didn't happen along you'da been blasted to kingdom come all the same. It was your time.'" Bill wondered if the French girl would have understood English.

Then, against every instinct, he asked, "What did she say?"

"The same thing she always says. 'You could've just told me to come out, and I would've.'"

The two men were silent a long time, as if swallowed by an undertow useless to fight. Bill let himself be pulled down, till he thought he might gasp and suck water into his lungs. Finally he heard his father laughing softly.

"Man, that was a beautiful Chevy you boys had. 265 engine, Holly carb, Hurst shifter—"

The Chevy. The Chevy.

Despite himself, Bill could see the parts lying on newspapers, out in front of the garage, beneath the basketball hoop. He saw a fly wheel. Then he and his brothers walked across the yard, under the maples, to hear the story. Their mother yelled for getting grease on the eggs.

After a while Bill heard something else. He focused, looked toward shore. Timmy was on his back, crying in the sand, a foot hiked up in the air.

"I told him his sneakers goddammit. I knew it." Without looking at his father Bill asked, "You all right?"

"I'm OK. You run ahead."

Bill ran ashore. He picked Timmy up by the arm and whacked him on the butt, something he'd never done. Timmy's face stiffened and he abruptly stopped crying. Bill called back, "He cut his foot, Dad! I gotta run him up to a doctor!" Even to Bill it sounded like, See, I warned you about the sand! "It's no big deal, Dad!" Ed started for shore, the inner tube in tow, and waved a hand. Bill lifted his son, running him up the beach, darting between blankets, towels and chairs.

In an hour he returned carrying Timmy. His foot was bandaged and he slurped taffy, the doctor's reward for not so much as a peep when the cut was cleaned and the needle pulled the thread through. Down on the sleeping bag the German girl was in T-shirt and shorts. Ed sat beside her as she rubbed lotion on his back and her boyfriend read quietly. Bill shook his head, filled with the wonder of Eddie "Eggs" Ivors. But he didn't want to reach them, not yet, and he told Timmy to watch for the lost sneakers.

In the doctor's office he had thought about demons. Maybe

his father was right. Anything to keep them away, or at least to yourself. Lift and place the eggs one by one in your helmet. Then go tell the boys to throw the powdered stuff to the wind. That's what they needed, and the girl on the ground didn't change that.

He also thought about this. If only Ed had done what the girl said. Who knew how many times! If only he had told her to come out. Bill saw the girl appear in the doorway, and suddenly he knew what Ed had known for fifty years. Hear the whistling in the air? How simple to sweep her up quickly and dive in a crater, next to a dead cow, and cover her. Even a clown hunting eggs in the middle of the greatest invasion ever known could've handled that.

"There they are!" Timmy shouted in his arms.

THE HOUSE OF HOLY SIGHS

When in Nice, they always stayed in the Old Town, where the names of streets and squares were in both French and its Italian relative, Nissart. Their hotel, on Place Rossetti, was just around the corner from Uncle Giorgio's. The uncle was called Gigo. Sam and Tony guessed that might be short for gigolo. Gigo lived in the old family house at the end of an alleyway they loved walking down. A small 16th century place, it had been built by settlers who'd made the trip west from Genoa. If only Garibaldi had his way, Gigo liked to say, the house would still be in Italy. The three men would sit around the dining room table, listen to Italian opera and play gin rummy. Uncle Gigo, who had never married, tossed in the occasional tale of an unabashed female conquest. Even now with his white hair and cherub face, the uncle was still strikingly handsome. Sam and Tony had to figure strikingly handsome just ran in the family. They could even see it in the oval photos on the gravestones at the cemetery just up the hill from here, where they had laid flowers that morning, something they did every trip.

Gigo had a stock of Italian wine, and Tony enjoyed fetching a bottle from the musty cave. Most of it was Valpolicello, but he also had a row of hearty Barolos, one of which they drank now. *Rigoletto*, on pampered vinyl, played in the background. They passed around plates of *socco*—thin fried pancakes of chick pea flower and olive oil, stuffed zucchini, and *pissaladier*—a kind of pizza smothered in onions, all steamy treats they'd made themselves. Sam had a restaurant back in Philly off Market Street and loved Nice for the food, the blend of French and Italian, and carried a notebook he jotted in. He'd named his place "La Nissa Bella."

Tony, his son, jotted notes too, but on art, and the Cote d'Azur was an endless feast. That afternoon he'd been to the Musee Chagall to gaze at the series inspired by the "Song of Songs." He especially liked number four, the newly wedded lovers soaring on a winged horse above the earthbound masses, the bride's gown trailing like a comet's tail. Tony had been leaning in, his face almost touching theirs, when he heard a voice. "Sir, please, don't breathe on Chagall." Tony stepped back. "Sir, please," he said. "I am only inhaling."

"Based on a book in the Bible," Tony was now telling Uncle Gigo, "which no one really knows who authored, maybe Solomon. A celebration of spicy erotica, a delicious break in a tome full of God's wrath!" Tony waved a fork with an anchovy stuck on the end of it.

"My son the professor," Sam said. "Save it for the book and take your turn."

Tony drew a card, slid it into the middle of his hand, then laid down a seven of clubs. The deck had a bit of oil and crumbs on it by now, as usual, but no one minded.

"I'm no professor," said Gigo."But I enjoy seeing Chagall now and then, like an old friend from my youth."

A buzzer went off in the kitchen and Sam ran and got the dish full of hot fritters he'd made from courgette flowers. He set it on the folded dishtowel, within everyone's reach, then milled on the salt and pepper.

"So Tony," Uncle Gigo said. "You come here every few years and I never hear anything about that someone special, you know what I'm saying?" Sam and Tony looked at each other. They hadn't told Gigo about Tony's eight-month marriage that ended in divorce two years ago. They'd agreed beforehand not to bring it up. So complicated—or maybe so simple— and neither of them would want to see Gigo's cherub face screwing up in confusion.

"Just following your lead, Gigo."

"Yes, well. Hundreds of women, like our lusty Duke of Mantua—" he gestured toward the stereo—"*questa o quella*, and now I am a lonely man." He reached and took a fritter and blew on it. "There was one woman, though, years ago, she was special." His eyes lit up.

"What's the matter, Gigo," Sam said. "Not rich enough for you?"

"Dad, really," said Tony.

"In fact, she was poor. But she was rich in here." He patted his chest. "You know what I'm saying? Like your Angie was, Sam." Gigo had made it to Philly only once, for a week, enough time to pick up a love for cheesesteak sandwiches, gin rummy and Angie. Gigo could make her laugh in a way Sam couldn't. A year later Angie made her one trip ever to Nice and Sam found himself feeling like a chaperone. About a year after that, when Tony was sixteen, his mother died. One day she was making marinara sauce and felt a stab below her ribs. Six months later she was dead from pancreatic cancer. Both Sam and Tony maybe took the swiftness of it all as a sign of a woman's frailty, though neither ever said it. When they called to tell Gigo he cried, too saddened to make the funeral.

"No, Tony, don't wait too long."

Suddenly Gigo smiled, glowed, picking up the jack of hearts Sam had just laid down. He arranged his cards quickly and slapped them on the table.

"Gin! I win" He swept up the cards and started to shuffle. "One more round! Tony, put on some Puccini! Sam, go get the tub from the fridge!" The one containing the oddly delicious tomato and basil gelato. "We must let it soften."

Sam rubbed his hands together, clapped loudly. "*Prego*!" And off he trotted.

"Okay. Just one more," Tony said. He sounded tired. "Tomorrow's our last full day. We should get out early."

"Where to, Tony?"

"The Villa Santo Sospir. Check out Cocteau's murals."

"Oh! Cap Ferrat! Rich stuff! I have a few stories I could tell."

"I bet you do," Tony laughed.

"Hmmm," Gigo got lost in some reverie. The white-haired cherub suddenly looking like an old rascal, a glint of the satyr in his eyes. He leaned over the table. "You know, Tony, there is something very special about a very rich woman's fritter. *Dolce, dolce*." He smiled and chewed luxuriantly.

The excursion to the Villa Santo Sospir had been a last minute addition to the itinerary, a week of plans carefully agreed upon before they boarded the charter in Philly. It was Tony who had suggested it. The father knew about Cap Ferrat, the mansions, the names, and had to suspect what that might stir up. But it was as though his son had laid down the challenge—and maybe Tony had meant to do just that—like saying "one last hand." Sam was in good shape, often biking to work across the Ben Franklin bridge, so didn't mind the long walk from the bus stop out to the tip of Cap Ferrat.

They passed mansion after mansion which they could make out through lush vegetation. White, star bursting flowers exploded on trees and shrubs. The air was heavy with a thick oily fragrance. Tony, allergy prone, might have felt assailed, but the real danger no doubt was the heady odor of intoxicating wealth. Amazingly, they made it all the way to Villa Santo Sospir without discussing anything more than new dishes for Sam's restaurant.

Story had it that Jean Cocteau, just finishing the filming of *Les Enfants Terribles,* had been invited to dine at the villa—with his handsome boyfriend—by Francine Weisweiller. Cocteau ended up staying for twelve years. The artist couldn't resist the mansion's blank white walls throughout, like empty canvasses. Even before he turned his attack toward the ceilings, Cocteau had dubbed the place "the tattooed house."

Tony found it all fanciful, hard to take seriously, especially when the south of France offered the likes of Matisse, Cezanne, Picasso, Van Gogh. But damn, it was fun and uplifting. At least Sam laughed out loud. Yet he had to see it was doing something different to his son. Maybe Tony was thinking of the Villa Louise in Boca Raton where he and Pamela had honeymooned. Named for her mother, it belonged to her father, Ellsworth Chesterton. He'd just had it refurbished. Seven bedrooms, six baths, a foyer rising up two stories to a glass rotunda. The redone walls were bare and maybe Chesterton sought Tony's artistic eye for suggestions. There was enough furniture to get by and the newlyweds joked about roughing it. The old staff remained. A cook cooked, a servant served, a driver drove. Sam had heard about all that. But Tony hadn't told him about the clear night, on the boat at the bottom of the garden. Pam pulled out a chunk of coke – which she swore she wouldn't bring – and they snorted up. Later, staring into the high rotunda where the moon was trapped in the glass dome's web, Tony began to howl with joy.

Now Tony and Sam were standing in a bedroom, looking at a fresco.

"It's Acteon," Tony said. "And those are Diana's nymphs in a grotto spring,"

Sam grinned. "Reminds me of a certain hot tub in the Poconos."

"So, Acteon, a mere mortal, is out hunting when he stumbles upon Diana and her girls naked in the water. She's a goddess, gets pissed off and splashes him. His skin starts turning to hide, he sprouts horns—you can see there—his hands turn to hooves and he loses his voice. He runs, and his own hunting dogs find him and rip him apart." Tony paused. "Maybe the dogs symbolize his desires."

"I prefer the hot tub idea. You're always tryin' to read too much into things."

"Right. Eat, fuck and be merry. Let's get outta here. I need some air."

He hurried to the nearest exit. Outside, he breathed in deeply, exhaled. Sam caught up.

"Cocteau was a frickin' dilettante," Tony said.

"Well, I wouldn't invite him to dinner."

Tony ignored his father and walked off at a fast clip. Sam kept up. After about ten minutes, Tony suddenly stopped at a stone bench and sat down, breathing hard. "Where's my inhaler?" Sam dug it out of his backpack and handed it to him. Tony held it to his mouth and did two quick blasts. He began to breathe easier, and looked around.

"You know, maybe the rich *are* different."

"Tony, Tony, don't . . ."

Now the men looked at each other, with their striking Italian features, classic Roman profiles, *tete-a-tete*. Sam had eyes that sparkled more, crinkled at the edges, seeking humor, which they tried to do now. Tony's eyes always saw something more serious.

"I'll never get it out of my head," Tony said. "No matter how I twist it, how I turn it, I just can't pry it loose."

The script had begun, a play that had opened and closed dozens of times. Usually staged in the restaurant off Market Street or in Sam's house on the other side of the river in Camden. Did Tony think sitting on a stone bench on Rue Princesse Grace on Cap Ferrat would make a difference?

Maybe Sam should have said nothing, let it go after two years, but he followed the script, as always. He laughed, eyes twinkled.

"You were blinded by your wallet and your dick. I don't know which is worse."

"You'll never admit we might actually have been in love."

"Wallet and dick."

"We were in love."

"You were her Roman trophy. Her dago trinket."

"You just had to do it, didn't you."

"Only because I knew I could."

"I will never pry it loose. Never."

Tony suddenly got up and walked away. The opulent stage wouldn't change a line. He'd end up as always coming around to his father's way of thinking. Pamela was Pamela. Sad really, yes. A lost soul. But utterly spoiled. No matter how often she stumbled, fell, she knew the bank account would remain a plump cushion. Besides, she was not our stock. DiGrigorio. Antonio Vincenzo DiGrigorio. Next to that a Chesterton might as well be a chestnut.

They said nothing more and then, before they reached the stop where they'd get a bus back to Nice, they began to hear music. It was old Nissart music, with guitar, fife, and accordion.

"Son, they're playing our song." Off his father started, toward the music. Tony followed, not minding. The musicians, tables and chairs, bar—all seemed makeshift, set up for a day or two, in a small park. It was crowded and they found a spot off to the side, shaded by an umbrella pine. The father happily talked Italian to the waiter who brought chilled white wine for him and pastis, water and a bowl of ice for Tony. The band was singing a song about a girl at a spinning wheel dreaming of her soldier.

A dark-haired woman sat down at the table just next to them. She looked Italian, maybe fifty. The waiter, who obviously knew her, came to her quickly, seemed especially gentle toward her, and suggested a seat closer to the music. She said she was happy sitting in the shade. Tony thought she looked like a woman in mourning. Maybe she was just sad.

The band played more songs, nothing they recognized. But when they did "La Nissa Bella," Sam joined in. Before the song ended, the woman joined in, too. "Viva, viva, La Nissa Bella!"

After a while the father placed his hand on Tony's arm. "There's something I never told you." They looked at each other. The father's ever ready twinkle wasn't quite there.

"No, what?" The son sipped his pastis, could smell licorice on his own breath. "You suddenly going to depart from the script? *Ad lib*?"

"Pamela's old man paid me to do it."

Tony gulped. Ice caught in his throat. He coughed.

"Wait. You saying Ellsworth calls up and says, 'Hey, Sam, old buddy, I got a little job for you '. . ."

"He just said find some way to end it. You really think he wanted his dago in-laws dropping in at the little mansion on the Main Line or at the Villa in Boca? You two had made it eight months. He was beginning to worry."

"So, you weren't just trying to save my dago soul."

How stupid not to put it together! All the new décor at the

restaurant, tufted red leather, murals with scenes of Nice – not a month after the divorce papers had been signed. And two months before that Tony had walked into the kitchen to find his father slicing up slugs, stuffing them into used escargot shells, and slathering them with garlic butter.

"Six minutes under the broiler – who'll know the difference?"

"Palate of the beholder." Tony had answered."But really, Dad, I can lend you money . . ."

"On what? A professor's salary? At best you are an over paid babysitter."

Tony needed to piss. He saw some portable toilets, but they had long lines. Then he saw a few men pissing into the bushes next to the cabins. As he relieved himself he thought: I can't do it anymore. I can't do the script anymore, especially now that the script has gone haywire. He knew he'd always wonder: What if Sam hadn't laid out the temptation? Or Ellsworth? Sins of the fathers. Even cutting up the kids, so each one could prove to himself he was right. What a relief to just stand here pissing in the bushes on a beautiful, sunny day on the Cote d'Azur. Why couldn't he just stay here?

He heard engines flying low and looked up to see a jet adjusting itself for touchdown at the airport on the sea's edge. He loved flying into Nice, watching the shimmering turquoise get nearer, waiting for the strip of land to appear. He loved the anticipation of all the art—the museums, the ateliers.

Tony realized the man next to him was staring down at him. The man was good looking, like him, with dark classic features. This was the last thing Tony needed.

He zipped himself away and walked back to the table. His father had moved, now sitting next to the woman. They laughed. Tony sat alone, poured more pastis and then poured in the melted ice. He thought about Pamela, the first time he'd met her father, right after the old man found out they'd been married on the quick in Camden. The old man had asked him what he did. He didn't mean, how do you intend to support my daughter? Ellsworth took care of his kids, especially Pam, the youngest, most fragile, most shattered by her mother's death in an accident.

"I'm a professor. Art History."

"That's something I suppose." He sniffed. "Seems like a contradiction. Art. History. Like fantasy, reality."

"Picasso said 'Art is the lie that leads to the truth.' "

"I own a couple of Picassos. I'll try to remember that." He sniffed again. "Just keep Pamela off the stuff." And he walked away as if he'd delivered another employee his job description. Tony didn't even have time to ask him, which Picassos?

For nearly six months Tony had kept Pam off the stuff, mostly coke and pot. He busied himself with art research, wrote papers, worked his way up to tenure track. Pam seemed unable to do anything. Though she began dozens of sketches for clothing designs, she never finished one. They had an apartment on the fifth floor in a modern building overlooking the Delaware. One night Tony came home late to find Pam sitting on the balcony in a chilling rain, her eyes glazed. She'd been thinking about her mother. Tony could tell, and he knew how she felt—almost. Pam had a drunk driver crossing a double line to blame. She couldn't get the crash out of her head, the imagining of it. Sometimes he awoke in the middle of the night to the sound of her sobbing. Tony saw a bottle on the little teak table. Quaaludes. Ludes weren't made in the States anymore, but Pam had a former roommate with a South African connection who had turned her on to them. He grabbed the pills, grabbed her, pulled her inside and set her on the sofa, pulling the afghan around her. He stepped back and rattled the bottle.

"Why'd you have to start on this shit?"

She smiled. "I like the afterlude. Get it?" She didn't break out laughing the way he thought she would.

"I'll make a pot of tea."

"I don't want any tea. Just hold me." He sat beside her and hugged her. She was shivering. "I love you so much, Tony." She had wavy blond hair, all damp now as she nuzzled into his neck. "Let's go to bed. Hmmm. My very own Italian stallion."

The musicians continued to play. Suddenly Sam was standing before him with the woman, her arm hooked through his.

"Listen, Tony. Gabriella here has a great collection of Puccini." The woman, who had looked so sad, now beamed. "She says she'll give me a ride back to the hotel."

"What about Uncle Gigo?"

"You explain. He'll be tickled." The woman obviously didn't understand English. She had one thing on her mind, taking her newfound smile to the next level.

"Don't forget, airport by noon."

"I won't forget, son. I won't forget." As they turned away the woman gave him a small wave of her fingers. Every sad woman needed a fix of one thing or another.

The waiter arrived with more pastis, said it was on the lady. Tony smiled ironically. Then thought, why not? He was here in the sunshine, surrounded by laughter, singing. Why leave? He made out lyrics, clapped to the beat, and nodded in unison. Then they played a song about a drunken father trying to diaper a cat. "Why do you cry, my little one, my little one?" The crowd howled back, "*Miou*! *Miou*! *Miou*!" Tony laughed, sipped pastis, warm, without the fresh cubes, as the memory he would never pry loose crawled out of its hiding place. The economy, restaurant hard hit, Tony helping out, even waiting tables, Pam always with an excuse not to join him. After setting up that day, he was in the kitchen chopping onions. To protect his eyes from the vapor he wore goggles that made him look like a bug, a creature from space. Sam walked in. He had the twinkle, like he was about to shout "Gin!"

"Where ya been!" Tony shouted.

"Belleview." That was Tony's apartment building. Sam's mouth squirmed around and he put thumb and forefinger to his lips, like he was going after an olive pit. He plucked something off his tongue and held it up. Tony lifted his goggles. Sam set it on the stainless steel table. "This belongs to Pamela."

Tony's eyes swelled, burned, tears started. "Fuckin' onions." He threw down the goggles, ran out the door, found a cab back to the apartment. By the time he got there Pamela was out front alongside a cab of her own, the driver loading the trunk. He walked up to her.

"You know what he told me?" She said. "'It's what Tony would want you to do.' I don't know what's wrong me, Tony. I really don't. It's not your fault." He found it impossible to speak as he looked at her incredible green eyes for the last time. A lawyer arrived with papers the next day.

"Why do you cry, my little one, my little one?" Tony howled in—"*Miou! Miou! Miou!*"

She was my wife and I was her husband. And Sam fucked her. And tomorrow Sam would be back at the hotel—where they always got separate rooms because, well, you never knew—and they would breakfast on *café au lait* and croissants and maybe wrap a couple in paper napkins for the plane and Sam would share the funnier details about bedding down the Italian woman. They'd pack, check out, get a cab to the airport, which Tony would spring for, buy a few last things in the gift shop, watch movies on tiny screens and be back in Philly in time to have dinner at the restaurant.

If Tony chose to let any of that happen.

A man approached the table. Tony looked at him. It was the man he had been pissing next to, the one who had given him a glance. The man handed him a card.

"There are certain women willing to pay," he said in accented English. "Very wealthy women." Tony looked at the card. It merely said "NICE ESCORT" with a fleur-de-lis on each side and a number at the bottom. When Tony looked up the man was gone, just like that. A flash in a mirror.

Riding the bus back to Nice, going along the coast, he chuckled to himself. A life in Nice. He could imagine it. He knew his uncle would be waiting, knew Gigo worried about who would take the house after he was gone. They would talk, discuss living arrangements, strategy. Yes, they were all so strikingly handsome. Being handsome just ran in the family. Maybe the *handsome* were different. Entitled. A life in Nice. He could feel it. The pure sundrenched beauty of the *Cote' d Azur*, at once earthy and sublime. An endless terrain of art. Now and then he could meet up with old friends. Maybe lunch with Picasso in Antibes, or Cezanne in Aix, or going the few extra miles to Saint Remy, stroll with Van Gogh in the garden of the asylum. He looked out the bus window at the water. At this hour, in this light, an incredible green, like his wife's eyes.

FEAST

Ah, Deana! You came to this azure coast to learn cooking, but here's a quick language lesson: disappointment in French is *deception*. You're not even sure of his name. Renaud? Reynard? Renault? Flying in luscious arcs you simply chanted, Re. Now you're alone in bed, Cap Ferrat out your window, distant, dusky. A shaggy leg in the sea.

You were deck-chaired in the sand when he approached, a stranger worried about the sun, bottle of oil in hand. "Protect yourself." His looks were fiftyish, a decade on yours. "May I?" Before you could speak he was rubbing your neck, shoulder blades, spine, the oil suspiciously hot. "My wife died of melanoma." No ordinary opener, that. Fingers kneaded spirals. "I must confess, I've watched you the past three afternoons. I see by your book you attend *Ecole Bocuse*. I love cooking. As did my wife. She had your structure, face, sharpness. Though she was dark and you light. Her nipples chocolate buttons, yours pink radishes." His melodic voice wavered. "I've not touched another woman since her death, fourteen months, but you I am compelled to kiss. Slowly, slowly, head to toe." You said, "Come with me." Appetite? Pity? Play-acting on an exotic set? Moments later, in this ancient apartment, shutters thrown, to sunlight, salt breeze, his lips commenced, gratefully, childlike, to savor your startled flesh and hair. Endless. "Ah, Re, Re." Ah, Deana. Happily devoured. "Come inside awhile." He did, with joyous ferocity, staying so long the afternoon turned apricot and you could explode no more. He pulled free, liquid moon glow streaming, abundant, like so much sorrow mitigated.

Suddenly he dressed, fled. "The market!"

Well, here you lie, gutted by pleasure. And that's enough. Don't expect him to return with groceries while his seed cakes on your belly, thighs, pelt . . . The door bursts open. He dances in, singing a French song, arms full of peppers, leeks, garlic, olive oil, *herbes de Provence*, lamb and wine. "Ah, Deana, let's feast!"

MY STUNNING WIFE, STUDS

Back in the States, it got so every stranger's glance seemed an accusation. Again and again her husband said, "Honey, you're a beautiful woman. Of course people stare." When that didn't work, he took time from his pharmacy, arranged for the kids to stay at his brother's and booked a trip to Paris, the Alps, and Vienna. Three weeks of anonymity seemed the perfect prescription, and for six days it was. Every time he saw her mind drifting toward the mess back home he hustled her into another Paris landmark.

Then, this morning, in the taxi to the Gare de Lyon, she starts.

"When we were checking out, a man kept staring at me."

"Sweetheart," the pharmacist says, "nobody here knows you from Eve."

"I heard him say he was from Alliance, Nebraska."

The husband grants it isn't clear how far news of "the mess" went. But not Nebraska. His wife has on a silky tan blouse and brown skirt. Though she dresses modestly, she's a stunner. Looks like Grace Kelly he's always thought. He bends over and kisses her temple. "What man from Alliance wouldn't stare?"

She slaps the cab seat. "The son of a bitch was staring 'cause he knows. And don't you dare say 'the mess' again."

Now they're at a cafe in the station waiting for a train to Lausanne. She's sitting at a corner table and he's standing at the bar because he had to get away from her before he screamed.

Well, it is a mess. No other word for it. A mess for her just walking in public, for him at the pharmacy, their two children at school. The worst mess of all sits in the bottom of his heart, where he doesn't know what to believe anymore.

"I wonder where she's going." He hears the words vaguely. Sees two men who weren't there a minute ago drinking beer at the bar. The one man, with red hair, wears a crinkled suit.

The other man says, "You find out and we'll change our tickets." He's got black hair, and his suit's in no better shape. They sound American. They keep looking at the wife and even lick at the foam on their lips. The pharmacist is about to go back to the table when the black hair says, "I think I know her."

"In your dreams, man."

"No, no. I mean, I think I know who she is. She wrote that book. About homeless women—real tear-jerkin'. 'Cept she made it all up."

"Ah, yeah, yeah," says the red hair. "I remember that."

The pharmacist sneaks a peek at his wife. The men's voices are low enough that she can't hear them. Sipping her wine, she suddenly looks her husband in the eye, hits him like a dart. He wants to tell these Americans to back off. Whatever they think they know, it's wrong, incomplete, half-stirred. But how can he talk with his wife watching?

He looks in the mirror behind the bar and sees the cover of the book materialize. A photograph of three street women on a park bench. Behind them is another woman. She's got a comb and scissors. Like Norman Rockwell doing Day at the Beauty Parlor, but down-and-out.

"So how was it the shinola hit the fan?" The red hair asks.

"Book's out a couple months when the bag women go to the publisher. Want to know what they're doing in this book. He says something like these are your stories, but they don't know anything about it."

"Where was this again?"

The pharmacist hears his city's name. A medium-sized, uneventful place.

"So what's the publisher do?"

"Pleads dumb. Maybe he doesn't know it's a sham."

"Or maybe him and Miss Beauty Queen sat around making up sob stories."

"Maybe. One thing for sure. *She's* never been homeless."

"Not in a million years."

His wife's publisher. The pharmacist thinks he's a heart-sleeved charlatan. Knows the wife from college, both liberal arts majors, back when that was popular. Adores her, would do anything for her. But what did he say when she proposed a book of interviews with homeless women? "I don't know. A beautiful author might seem suspect." That made her want to do the book all the more and put her picture on the back cover. My wife the interviewer. The oral historian, like Studs Terkel. My stunning wife, Studs.

"The women get nowhere with the publisher. So they go to the newspapers. They smell fraud, scream publishing stunt and run an ad for anyone who's in fact been interviewed to come forward."

"And no one does."

"You got it, pal."

The pharmacist remembers his wife shouting, "Jesus, do you think they read the papers before wrapping their feet in them!"

She did do interviews. In the mornings. In the afternoon, before the kids came home, she transcribed from a recorder, then wrote a brief physical description, giving age, place of birth. The publisher saw some dozen interviews and said, "This is great stuff. Really great stuff. But we'll need three times what you got."

"Shit," says the red-haired American. "Can you picture her running around with scabby bag women?"

"No way." They order more beer.

In his entire life the pharmacist has never punched a man. He's startled by this realization—and by the urge to haul off now. But he knows his hands are not made for measuring the way a boxer measures. He looks at his wife. She finishes her wine, glances at her watch, then holds the empty glass in the air. This'll be her third, and she catches her husband's disapproving look. Then she stares at the men to his left. Nails them. *If you're going to let them get away with that kind of talk*, she seems to say, *then I'm going to drink!* The waiter's happy to bring more wine, would bring barrels day and night.

"Hey, man," says the red hair, "I think she was just eyeballing you."

"Not me," says the black hair. Then he taps the pharmacist on the shoulder. "Think you got an admirer over there, pal." The pharmacist doesn't look. "You understand English, pal?"

"Yes, I do." For his wife's sake, he grins. No hint of the lava inside. "And I've been standing here listening to you denigrate a woman you don't even know." He shakes his head, laughs, like they're arguing who's the best quarterback ever, Montana or Brady. "I think it stinks."

"The broad's a fraud."

He sees his wife crying after the kids are in bed. That morning she went to do more interviews. She was working the downtown area, where plenty of shoppers walk around. He made her promise, she had to stay out in the open, no alleys or abandoned buildings. His wife approached a woman on the stoop of a boarded up jewelry store. She was middle-aged, his wife says, had on a floral print dress and a navy blue sweater.

His wife leaned down and said, "Hi, what's your name?"

The woman said, "Who wants to know?"

"I want to help you. I thought knowing your name would be a good start."

"How you going to help me?"

"I'm going to ask you to tell me about yourself on this tape machine. Then I'm going to write what you say in a book, along with what other women like yourself say, and we're going to publish that book and people are going to know your stories."

"Then what?"

His wife sat down next to her. "Then maybe we will wake some people up."

"What I say won't wake anyone up."

"Yes, yes. Maybe only a few—"

The woman grabbed his wife's head in her hands and drew her toward her face. "Nobody wakes up." His wife tried to pull back, but the woman rubbed his wife's face with her own face. Up and down both cheeks, around her chin and across her lips. His wife screamed a contracted, startled scream. The woman let go.

"See, none of that beauty rubs off on me."

The pharmacist, still grinning, steps closer to the American.

"You are a narrow bastard. You heap dirt on a beautiful woman, probably because you know you'll never touch a woman like that in your filthy life."

"Hey, hey, hey, pal. Here I am, clueing you in on this number and look at your gratitude."

"Yeah," says the red hair, "and while you're getting all puffed up like a rooster, the chick has flown."

The pharmacist turns and sees his wife is gone, her empty glass on the table. He's a tall man with big bones, make him look stronger than he is. Right now he'd like to load the Americans' beers with diuretics, so they'd spend their trip in the can, bladders shriveling to raisins. As things are, he works with what's available and carefully empties an ashtray, half and half, in each of their glasses.

"You got a real goddamn problem, don't you pal."

"You sure do," the other says.

He simply turns his back on them. They're not the types to jump him, he figures, and he feels better than he has in months. Then he gets it—a tremendous punch in the kidney. He doesn't turn to look, but walks away, the pain spinning in his back like a pinwheel.

Out on the concourse, all the high-speed trains are nosed up like snakes at a trough. His eyes water as he reads the destination board and finds his quay. Then he sees a slow, blunt-nosed train. Sparrows flutter around the front of it, pecking at dead bugs. They don't bother with the sleek bullet trains. Maybe bugs don't stick to them.

He sees his wife next to a car about halfway down. He catches up smiling and they board without a word and find their seats. The pinwheel in his back has slowed.

After his wife told him about the woman on the stoop, he told her to stop the interviews. Stop. It was dangerous. He said what he thought he'd never say, what he'd despise any husband saying. "I forbid you." His wife said, "I have a book to finish." She wasn't afraid of him. But he thinks she was afraid of those women.

He doesn't know how it is possible, but after the woman on the stoop, his wife fabricated the rest of the interviews. Invented them. Made them up. He's not sure how to put it. A ventriloquist doing cries in the air. His wife says she watched the women at a distance, from diners, from library windows, buses, her car. She says she heard their voices. *Heard them*. When he presses her on this point, she only says, "I did. I heard them." With those first dozen, real, interviews, there were thirty-three in all.

The seats in this train car are arranged so that half of them face forward, half backward, all facing the middle. This means, now that they're cruising along at a hundred-and-sixty miles an hour, a woman facing them from several rows away is openly staring at his wife. Who knows why? His wife has her head down, studying a map in the brochure. She says, "Those men in the bar were American, weren't they."

"Yes. So?"

"They were talking about me, weren't they."

"No, no, they were talking football. Trying to tell me Brady, not Montana, was the best quarterback ever."

"They were talking about me. I know they were."

"You're imagining things."

In a low bitter voice he has never heard before, she says, "Don't tell me what I imagine."

And she's right to say that, he realizes, because you can never know what another person imagines or thinks, or for that matter, remembers or plans or intends. You cannot know. It is impossible. He wonders, how do we live with each other? How do we get along at all?

In his wife's lap he sees a large-scale map of a mountain above

Villars where they're renting a chalet. Hiking trails wriggle on the page. The brochure promises serenity, cowbells from mountain meadows the only sound. At night there's a restaurant they can walk to and eat fondue and drink white wine beside a fireplace. He leans over and, without really meaning to, exhales softly, around her ear and down her neck.

She slaps the brochure shut, pressing it in her hands like a prayer book.

There is a rushing concussion of sound as a train, also going a hundred-and-sixty miles an hour, passes the other way. His wife turns her face to the window. Not three feet beyond the glass is an incredible roaring blur, which lasts a few seconds. Then the countryside falls silently back into place.

"Don't make me hate you," she says. "You, at least, have to believe me."

"Yes," he says, "I do," and they stare out at the world. As the sun fades, lights turn on in farmhouse windows, yellow lozenges dotting the earth.

A FUTURE IN FRENCH KISSING

During my fifteenth year, though I didn't know their reasons at first, my parents sent me to Uncle Charlie's in France so they could get divorced without my having to watch. Strange, because by all accounts it was a bloodless, even amiable event, a peaceable end to four years of separation. I had just finished grade school (not at the normal fourteen because I once flunked), and in the Fall I'd begin St. Leo's High, which perennially had the best baseball team— Catholic or public—in the county. Too old that summer to play in our city's Lou Gehrig League, where for the previous three years I had garnered a .402 batting average and MVP honors in our final championship contest, I had no opposition to visiting France and growing worldly.

At the end of World War II, Uncle Charlie married a French woman, Babette, and their's is considered still the romance of the family and fair compensation for the numerous separations and divorces that have plagued our kin. As the story goes, my uncle parachuted into a bog somewhere south of Utah Beach shortly after midnight on June 6, 1944, liberated himself and seventy pounds of gear from the muck, and the next day liberated the small town of Sainte-Mère-Eglise from the Nazis. For much of my boyhood, I imagined him accomplishing the feat single-handedly, and so my disappointment upon seeing *The Longest Day* and discovering he had plenty of help. Babette, picking my uncle from dozens of G.I.s— eyes are love's first compasses, my mother has said—invited him in to lunch, and he managed to sneak away from the 101st Airborne "Screaming Eagles" long enough to allow destiny to play its hand over a dining room table that wobbled slightly on an uneven floor. Charlie and Babette didn't even speak the same language, but as the cider rocked in their glasses something was communicated. For after the war my uncle and Babette married in the town church (in the movie it's the one from which Red Buttons hangs all night by a snagged parachute), my uncle having learned by his wedding day how to say "*Oui*." He and Babette moved to Paris so he could attend an American college there on the G.I. Bill and afterward moved outside the City of Light to Saint Cloud, where Uncle Charlie taught math at The American High School. In time, my aunt and uncle spoke each other's language perfectly. They had a daughter, my cousin Odile, one year my elder. By sixteen—I was more intimidated than impressed to hear—she mastered not only French and English, but was on her way to conquering German and Italian. I guessed a Pentecostal flame had landed on her head around puberty.

My own father hadn't served in the war because of a valve in his heart made faulty by a childhood bout with rheumatic fever. He lived cross-town, and I lived with my mother in an apartment complex, which I anxiously informed new acquaintances should not be confused with The Projects about a mile away, where—as everyone knew—lived the spongers of society. My mother worked four to midnight at the Howard Johnson's as a hostess, and she paid the rent. We accepted no handouts. Every few weeks I saw my father, and he took me to a good many Bison baseball games. The Bisons represented our city in the International League. Each spring we attended the opener, and that involved my mother ruefully writing an excuse for me to take to school the next day avowing I had been ill, her dilemma that it had to sound serious enough to warrant absence but not so serious I couldn't whip it overnight. Whenever our team lost its first home game my father chomped at the chance to make his joke. "Well, they won't be serving beer at the stadium this season." Having learned to go along, I'd ask, "Why's that?" "Because they lost the opener." He'd smile slyly, raising one eyebrow. "Oh, I get it," I'd moan, wiping my face with my hand for effect, and my father would laugh. His habit was to make a noise like a puppy who had to go out, "Hmmn—hmmn—hmmn," high atop his throat, behind his nose.

I guess I should've figured something was up when a week before my departure for Paris, after my father and I had watched the Bisons triumph with surprising ease, 8-2, he sat glumly beside me as the stadium emptied and told me, with a tone of finality I couldn't appreciate in the afterglow of victory, that I should always mind what my mother said, that she was a good, good woman, despite whatever differences she and he might have had. Or maybe I'd already grown used to my father's recent lapses into mawkishness.

My mother bought me a diary for my trip. On the cover was—is, for the book is at my side this night—a drawing of a man in the basket of a hot-air balloon that made me think of Jules Verne's *Around the World in Eighty Days*. He looks through a telescope, pointed not downward at a landing place, but upward and outward, toward stars or mountaintops, a detail I'm sure didn't escape my mother's eye when she made her selection.

The diary reads: "June 11. Jet plane take-off what it must feel like to go for land speed records at Salt Flats. Saw Newfoundland and England out window. Food was wrapped up like mother leaves me before work. Though she wraps everything twice. Arrived Orly 9:12 AM (their time). Uncle Charlie and Aunt Babs waiting. She is smaller than I thought. Odile home with broken foot. Roller skated into a storm drain (very clumsy or fragile or both). Car smelled like someone spilled french fries under the seat last year. Old and greasy. But couldn't see em. Got to UC's and AB's house and realized the smell belongs to UC. Why doesn't AB tell him?"

What impressed me immediately as I entered Uncle Charlie's house—other than the fact of his odor—was its qualities of coordination. Everything matched something else, all things blended together by Aunt Bab's singular hand. Back in our apartment, nothing matched. A squarish, blue sofa had nothing in common with a plump green chair which had, protruding like a hood ornament from each arm, a wooden head of a duck, bill open in mid-quack. The chair, in turn, had little to do with the brown-flowered pattern of our curtains (brown flowers?). On our coffee table, a statuette of an aproned, bonneted peasant girl, hailing from a place I'd never studied in geography, smiled gleefully at a fake-crystal bowl of plastic fruit, the daft girl taking it perhaps for her land's harvest. But here at Uncle Charlie's the floral pattern in the chairs and sofa was picked up in the flowing drapes. Their flowers were yellow and pink on a creamy background. The end tables matched, as did the lamps upon them. Well distributed pieces of Sevres porcelain (the factory was practically around the corner, I'd learn) shone like stars in a constellation. A glass-doored bookcase, reaching almost to the ceiling, held a treasure of hardcover books, those on the top four tiers with English titles running north to south, and those on the bottom four tiers with French titles running south to north. The living room extended from the front of the house to the rear, where grand French windows opened on a patio surrounded by rose bushes—yellow and pink flowered.

As soon as we arrived Aunt Babs called upstairs in French, perhaps announcing Odile's poor provincial cousin. What issued back was an exasperated flurry. "Odile has just had her bath," my aunt interpreted, "and you will meet her in a moment." In the meantime I asked my uncle if they picked up any American stations on the TV I saw in the corner. It was at least three times as big as our Zenith. No, he said, but then they never watched TV, except for an occasional soccer match or opera production. What a waste, I thought. Another cry issued from above, and Aunt Babs said Odile was ready. The three of us ascended the stairs, Uncle Charlie carrying my suitcase. Along the stairwell, at every other step, hung etchings of long-haired men. The kings of France, my uncle noted, from Francois Premier to Louis Seize. I looked at Francois a moment. Then turning up the steps I'm sure I heard him whisper, "A foreigner encroaches—pass it on."

We dropped off my suitcase in the guestroom. The bedspread and curtains were flannel not floral, I was happy to see. At Odile's closed door, my uncle tapped with one finger. "*Entrez*," my cousin sang, her mood improved.

The first entry continues: "Odile's room is so clean I want to turn all her furniture over. Furniture is white with gold pinstripes like Larry's brother Jim's GTO. Blue everywhere else. An Olivetti typewriter on her desk with a blank sheet of paper in it (why?) But what gets me is the frickin puppets. Everywhere! And they don't look like they're ever used. They all just sit around looking at Odile (why? who set them like that?)"

It was true. It didn't take long for me to realize more than just Uncle Charlie's, Aunt Bab's and my eyes were on Odile. From dresser, shelves, windowsill and desk, puppet eyes gazed upon their mistress, as if she were dying. They weren't the kind you put your hand in, but marionettes, and all their strings and the attached wood pieces lay limp. She was sitting up in bed, a satiny blue blanket pulled to right below a chest that hadn't developed much. Her shoulder-length hair, wet with comb lines, was the color of toast. From what I could tell, she wasn't fat, but her face had a plumpness. I guess its rosy glow was her Norman blood. Milkmaid smooth, that skin would never taste foul, metallic pimple cream. I shook her hand, damp and warm from her bath. Protruding from the end of her blanket was a plaster boot, propped on a blue cushion. I wondered how she'd kept it dry. I wondered also why it had no signatures. It was a week old and still white as flour. Crutches leaned against a chair set near the bed for, I guessed, visitors. Maybe she never had any.

But she had one now. My Uncle pushed me down in the chair, and I learned about Odile. From Odile herself I learned she was sorry she wouldn't be able to sightsee me around, but it was Audrey Lennon's fault for bumping her off the sidewalk into the storm drain. From her mother I learned Odile was in the third year of a five-year plan to go through the Louvre, one visit per month. From her father I learned Odile finished second in her class this year (again the fault of Audrey Lennon, who was first). Her mother brought up the puppets: Odile's fascination with them started when she was eight and saw her first puppet show in the Tuileries (whatever that was). Since, she got one each Christmas and birthday. I looked at them and they looked back at me, and I felt as if I were one of their own, set here to watch over Odile. I didn't ask how they got posed that way. From Odile I learned she wouldn't be joining us for dinner because the steps were impossible.

When Uncle Charlie fell in love with Aunt Babs that day in Normandy, it had to be her cooking. Sitting in Odile's place at the table, I feasted on things I could neither recognize nor pronounce. I only knew my mouth had died and gone to heaven. Of course, with my mother working the four-to-midnight shift at Ho-Jo's and leaving things wrapped on the counter to be reheated, that transport of taste buds wasn't difficult. Awaiting dessert I thanked my uncle for the invitation to France, as I understood it was the cause of my being there. "Nothing to it, son," he said. That was the first of endless times he'd call me son, and whenever he did acid dripped in my gut.

At home, on my mother's dresser was a framed picture of her and Uncle Charlie. Today it is on her credenza in a different apartment. They are on a beach near their parents' cottage, leaning in swimsuits against the side of his Packard (which Charlie had bought—from a man who totaled it in an accident—for thirty dollars, and rebuilt the engine, and reshaped and repainted the body, all by himself). They have two other sisters and a brother, but they must be in the water or back at the cottage. Each has an arm around the other. Now, I ask, when does a child first learn, or sense, that the laws of God, man or nature forbid the marriage of brother and sister? As young as six or seven? Not until twelve or thirteen? I only know one morning, age nine, as my own father lay asleep in bed, I studied the picture on the dresser and thought those laws a shame because my mother and her brother looked the perfect couple.

When I saw my aunt loading a tray for Odile, I offered to take it up. My uncle had just retired to a chair where he lit a cigar, sipped a cognac and opened to his place in a book on Hitler. Why anyone should read such a book was beyond me, and in a way still is. It was clear this was reading hour, and to me reading was for school and I was out for the summer. Also clear was they were not about to change habits to accommodate my presence. I saw French magazines awaiting Aunt Babs on a table beside another chair. I couldn't bear to absorb all that silence.

Tray in hand, I mounted the steps past the whispering kings of France and began what would become my daily mission of bringing food to Odile.

I sat in the chair while she ate.

"Too bad about your parents," she said around a mouthful of veal *Normand*. I can identify that dish now, but couldn't then—just as I now know she was refering to the impending divorce I yet knew nothing about, and so could only assume she referred to their four-year separation.

"It's no big deal."

"No big deal! I mean, if my parents—oh . . . sorry."

"Your parents are perfect, according to my mother."

"Thanks." She said it like that made her perfect. Maybe it did.

She asked if I knew what a Chinaman was. I thought it was a joke.

"I give. What's a Chinaman?"

"Don't you play baseball?"

"Do apples grow on trees?"

"Well don't you throw Chinamen?"

"What're you talking about?"

"Chinamen!" It was the exasperated tone of earlier. "I don't know, some kinda throw from the bowler to the batsman. Audrey's brother showed me. They're English."

"It has something to do with baseball?"

"The Lennons call it cricket."

"Cricket isn't anything like baseball."

"If you're going to correct me—! I was only trying to talk about something that might interest you." Her eyes darted about, as if to get a cue from one of her puppets. "You were traumatized when your parents got separated, weren't you."

"Traumatized?"

"Shocked and rendered helpless."

"Yeah. I guess."

"That's why you flunked that year."

How did she know I flunked?

"Well, the only reason I flunked was because I watched television all night instead of studying." True. After my reheated dinner, I sat for hours in that green chair, a finger in each duck bill, and became Beaver, Little Joe, Bat Masterson or Napoleon Solo. The world could not touch me. When I did flunk, my mother asked if I'd be happier living with my father, for if happy I might once again study. I got this picture of my father and me sprawled on the floor watching the tube all night, yucking and yipping. He'd not raise me up, I'd bring him down. It was my life's first moment of decision, for my mother had handed it to me. I stayed with her and got a B average for the rest of grammar school.

"Well, I'd be traumatized, too," Odile sympathized. "Though I don't know about flunking."

I didn't like this at all, comparing parents, comparing educations, comparing cricket and baseball. Then like a godsend something peeked from under her cover.

"What's that?"

"Nothing," she said, pulling the cover up.

"Well it's something."

"You're too young to know."

"You're sixteen, I'm fifteen."

"A year can make all the difference." Then giving me her tray to put aside, she said, "Oh, okay. It's my mother's anthology of erotic poetry." She pulled it out.

I wasn't sure about "anthology" but I knew "erotic." In my closet, behind the box holding my HO car-racing set, were two *Playboys* gotten by way of my pal Larry's brother Jim, who was also letting us read—if he ever finished it (he did that Fall)—his copy of *Candy*, and woe to our hides if we returned it with so much as a page in any way defiled. But suddenly, next to Aunt Bab's Anthology of Erotic Poetry, that all seemed like macaroni-and-cheese alongside veal *Normand*.

"You can look at it if you want," said Odile, handing it over.

I carefully took it and turned pages.

"Are any of these in English?"

"It's *French* poetry."

I could hear the pages moan, but I might as well have been a blind man at a porno flick.

"Oh, give me it. I'll read you one." She grabbed it and flipped a page or two. "This is by Villon. It's written in medieval French. A man speaks to his lover." She cleared her throat of the purple salad she'd last eaten. "'I do not lose the seed I plant in your field, when the fruit resembles me,'" she translated into singsong. "'God wills I plant and fertilize this field, and that is why we are here together.'"

I waited. "That's it?" I certainly was aware of greater printed sexuality than this.

"Are you one of those boys something has to hit you over the head like a board?" She periodically made a hood scoop of her lower lip and blew upward, as she did now. Her hair had dried a sandy blond, and puffy bangs rustled in her own breath.

"Seeds, fields, planting—I get it. But that's not very exciting."

"Exciting? Maybe this is better." She rifled through the book and charged into a passage. "A woman to a man this time. 'Plunge, plunge, plunge your member into my hot quiff, till I quake with pleasure and my dam bursts!'"

If it had been Larry and me down in his cellar, we'd've laughed and wowed and read that passage fifty times. But in this female presence I cringed.

"Does it really say that?"

She shoved the book in my face, and antsy letters crawled before my eyes.

"Your parents let you read that stuff?"

"I got it from the bookcase downstairs. They don't exactly hide it. After all, it's poetry, not smut."

I felt sordid and small, and I sat silently as she read more Villon. Unfortunately she'd read his best stuff first. Finally I pleaded jet lag and said I should get some sleep. She seemed satisfied, maybe the way I used to feel getting our parakeet to do a trick. As I was about to leave with her tray something occurred to me. "I thought you couldn't get up and down the steps."

"Of course I can." She sent a course of air through her bangs.

Maybe I was sordid and small, but not deceitful.

The diary reads: "June 15. What the frick am I doing here? Five days down and fifteen to go. I'll never make it. Odile has taught me cheek kissing. Says it's the proper thing to do. She holds out her mug for me whenever I walk in her room. Right, left, right, on her cheeks. I think she gets off on it. In Paris they do it four times, she says. In suburbs three (Odile). In the country two—unless you both happen to be from Paris, then you go back to four. Did someone really sit down and figure this out, or is Odile full of crap? Hasn't read me more poems, maybe thinks I'm beneath them. Saw Notre Dame today. UC climbed to the top of the south tower with me. I felt woozy. (Do I have a problem with heights?) Looked at gargoyles face to face. There's one gargoyle up there, he's holding a rabbit in his claws and chewing its head off. Catholics had a strange sense of humor back then (1163, UC says). But just like with boat ride and Arc de Triomphe and Montmartre, I get the feeling he'd rather be somewhere else. Maybe I don't show enough excitement. What does he want me to do? Stand on my head? He still smells like french fries and calls me son. Tomorrow he starts teaching summer school, so I gotta go out on my own. AB is always busy, always going shopping or having lunch with someone. Had my first snails tonight. Delicious like everything else. But pulled that first one out of the shell and thought of a slug fried on a hot sidewalk. Really chewy."

The day after writing that, I went to the Saint Cloud indoor pool, where Aunt Babs suggested I go if I didn't want to venture down into Paris by myself, which I didn't. Next to our city back home, Paris was a jar full of grasshoppers crawling all over each other. Any moment I expected to get brown juice spit in my eye.

Aunt Babs had given me a beach towel that smelled of coconut oil and had "Deauville" written across it. I set up in a corner, did ten laps and lay down on my towel. There was a boy about my age within earshot. I say earshot because he was listening to a transistor radio. There was some American flap-jawed disc-jockey playing all the songs I knew. Then there were commercials about how to conduct oneself in a foreign country, how not to sell cigarettes you got from the PX to the locals, and how to complete certain forms when being transferred. In the middle of "You've Lost That Lovin' Feeling" it occured to me what Uncle Charlie's house suffered for lack of. Music. At home I had a stack of forty-fives and a crummy mono record-player. On the tone arm I'd taped a nickel. The needle chiseled away equally at the voices of The Temps, The Tops, Bob Dylan, The Who, and Cream, and I never noticed. At Uncle Charlie's, though a grand looking stereo console sat in the light from the patio doors, no music ever broke the holy silence. Deciding I had to get to know the boy with the music, I walked over.

He had a mop of copper hair and a face riddled with acne, some of which had spilled onto his shoulders.

I asked, "You American?"

"Yeah."

"What's your name?"

"My older brothers call me Wretch." He spoke as if through a fog.

"That's a funny name."

"Not as funny as my real name."

"What's your real name?"

"Cornelius B. MacDougal."

Wretch, I learned, was an army brat, and he was listening to Armed Forces Radio. He knew baseball, cars, and music—was American through and through. Ironic, for he'd been all over the world but had never stepped foot in the United States. His father was a colonel, and they were soon leaving France because de Gaulle had decided to throw out the U.S. Army. Wretch had just finished freshman year at The American High School. I asked if he knew my uncle.

"Oh, you mean Rosebud. That's what my older brother named him, cause of the way he smells." I thought I should rush to my uncle's defense, except that Wretch had voiced an incontestable truth.

Rambling through typical chitchat, we stumbled onto complementary dreams: I was to be a professional ballplayer and he was to be a sports photographer, no less renowned. Before leaving at noon, he gave me his phone number and directions to his house. "Wait till you see my cameras," he proudly piped.

Over dinner, I mentioned I had met this kid named Wretch.

"Corny, the youngest MacDougal boy," my uncle said. "You'd best stay away from him."

"Did he do something wrong?"

"Nothing yet. But his brothers are trouble. If he turns out anything like them."

And I thought, sure, because one of them named you "Rosebud."

"Learn to select friends carefully, son. Your father didn't. Bad company's what started his troubles, getting in with that creep at the mill. Don't you make the same—"

He stopped short. He must have seen me glare as the thought shot up, *You don't even know my father! You never even met him!* Then maybe he realized in the same instant what I did: that he knew things I didn't, that my mother had told him certain things about my father she'd never tell me. No more was said. And I didn't mention that I was going to Wretch's house the next day.

Wretch's room was a welcome mess. Strewn clothes, unmade bed, comic books. I wanted to roll in it like a dog. He had a collection of model cars, which he'd customized and spray-painted pretty well, though he was heavy on the candy-apple red. We went through his baseball cards, all three hundred, imagining perfect teams and ideal trades. He favored the Orioles, as his father was from Baltimore. Then he pulled open the bottom drawer of his dresser and showed me his cameras. Without saying which were which, he said two came from Japan, where he'd been born, two from

Germany, where they'd last been stationed, and one from France. I asked why he needed five, and he said a sports photographer has to have different cameras for different situations. The cameras were covered with dials and levers, and I seriously doubted Wretch knew what they all did. "So sometime you'll take my picture." Wretch looked vaguely at the window and said not today, the sun wasn't out. "I meant at Candlestick Park, Wretch, or Yankee Stadium." "Oh, yeah. I forgot. Let's eat." We had baloney sandwiches on Wonderbread and wolfed down Twinkies, all via the PX. Finally the conversation turned to girls, and he asked me straight out if I'd ever been laid.

"Wretch, I'm fifteen years old."

"Same here. But we're going to the Aleutian Islands next, and my brother says Eskimo chicks put out. So I got high hopes." By now I knew Wretch had two older brothers, though they seemed blended into one omnipotent being. "My brother got laid in Germany when he was fifteen."

"Wow."

"Yeah." Wretch scratched idly at a pimple on his nose. "You ever French kiss?"

"I kissed regular."

"I haven't even kissed regular much. I guess because my skin grosses 'em out. You know, my older brother once hung a lip on your cousin Odile." I found that bulletin unsettling, especially if Wretch's older brother looked like Wretch. "He slipped her some tongue, and she slapped him." I could hear the crack and felt better.

"Odile went out with your brother?"

"She was goo-goo 'cause he's been half around the world."

"He really Frenched her?"

"Tried at least. My older brother says it's something when they let you do it. If you don't mind swappin' spit."

When I arrived at Uncle Charlie's late that afternoon, there were seven men and himself standing on the patio drinking wine. "Drinking" isn't exactly right. They'd each take a swig, then play with the wine in their mouths, some like they thought it was mouthwash, some like they thought it was meant to chew. Uncle Charlie kept sticking his nose deep into his glass, which he held by the base, not the stem. Then they started writing notes, and saying things about "attack" and "depth," "hints" of this and that, like oak or vanilla. They carried on, sometimes bursting into French. When my uncle saw me watching from the livingroom, he looked concerned. I think I know why now, but at the time I thought he was worried my cut-off jeans and tie-dye T-shirt might taint his get-together. He came in, wrapped an arm around me and led me toward the bookcase.

"How're you today, son?"

"Okay."

"My friends and I were sampling some '45 and '47 Latours. Two superb wines."

"I bet they couldn't tell Pabst from a Carling or a Utica Club," I said, maybe because I'd once seen my father win a bet doing just that.

"Probably not. So did you go to the Sevres porcelain museum?" He'd suggested it on the way out the door that morning.

"No."

"Oh. What did you do then?"

I considered lying. "I spent the day with my friend Wretch."

"I see. He's your friend now."

"There's nothing wrong with him."

"His brothers are trouble—"

"Whatever they did"—tag you 'Rosebud,' stick a tongue in your precious daughter's mouth (did my uncle know about either?)— "that doesn't make him bad."

"Son, if you hang around a barnyard, you're liable to get shit on your shoes."

"I don't have shit on my shoes. And neither does my father."

I turned and went up the steps, half expecting a reprimand, but it didn't come. That evening I asked my aunt if I could eat with Odile in her room. My uncle and I exchanged a glance that confirmed a meal apart might be for the best.

During dinner Odile complained her broken foot was "mucking up" her Louvre schedule. She was stalled in the middle of the Dutch wing at something called "The Tattoo Lesson" by someone named de Grebber. I'd grown used to her arcane details, for in fact how much she knew about so many different things always astonished me. I seldom talked. What after all could I possibly reveal to her, Ty Cobb's lifetime batting average? Yet this night, after returning our trays to the kitchen—and dodging my uncle's glance over his Hitler book—I ventured onto ground I thought had to be common, asking Odile if Audrey Lennon was any relation to the Beatles. The way she said no, I got the feeling she didn't know the Beatles had a Lennon. When I asked if she ever listened to music she responded, "Of course. The Sunday evening productions on TV are superb." Like her father's wine, I supposed.

"What was with the men in ties gargling wine today?"

"Silly, they were conducting a wine tasting." Over the week Odile's exasperated flurries had disappeared, as if familiarity with my provincial ways had begotten patience and solicitude.

"It looked pretty funny."

"Have you ever tasted really good wine, I mean the very best wine?"

"No." Except for communion, I'd never tasted any.

"Well, wonderful things happen in your mouth, this whole big production." I guessed she meant something like an opera.

"But your father was a soldier. He usta rebuild cars. I heard he ran the hundred in ten-three in high school. Why doesn't he drink beer?"

"Oh, that's all he used to drink, before my mother Frenchified him." For an instant I thought she said french-fried, which would have explained a good deal.

"And why does he always have to call me son?"

"It's subconscious."

"Meaning?"

"Meaning his psyche wants something so badly he doesn't even realize it."

"His psyche wants a son?"

"Of course."

"So why don't they try'n have one?"

"Because when I was born I broke the equipment. Mother can't have more children."

Wasn't that Odile, I thought, to get in to something good, then louse up the works so no one else could get in.

"So let 'im adopt someone. But not me, okay."

"You're certainly prickly tonight."

"I am not . . . prickly."

"Ah!" Odile gasped at the edge of some discovery. "Oh, I understand now. My father must've told you."

It was forever like the Chinaman thing with her. "Okay, Odile, what did he tell me?"

"It's over, it's official."

"What's official?"

"The divorce."

"What divorce?"

"Your parents', silly. Who else is getting divorced?"

"Odile, my parents aren't getting divorced."

"Of course they are—they did. You're the one who said it's no big deal."

"Divorced?"

"Oh, Jesus. Denial. You're not gonna be traumatized, are you?"

"My parents are divorced?" Life passed out of me, though I couldn't've been dead because the pain was too great. I sat down on the edge of her bed.

"My God, are you saying you didn't know? My father didn't tell you?"

I'd've slid to the floor had she not pulled me to herself. I put my legs up and lay beside her, and she pressed my head into the crook of her neck, below her Norman jaw. "Oh my poor cousin, my poor, poor cousin."

I was traumatized all right, but for reasons my solicitous cousin couldn't in a million years guess. The divorce itself was immaterial, for in effect it meant nothing different than the separation. I'd still live with my mother, and my father would come take me to an occasional Bison game. My despair hinged not on the proximity of my parents to either each other or me. It hinged on baseball.

I had Larry to thank for my living death. I hadn't believed him the time he told me the Browns were trading Jim Brown to the Packers for Bart Starr. And I had my doubts when he said he'd copped a feel off Susie DiAngelo in her garage. And I certainly didn't believe his stuff about Jimi Hendrix in concert playing guitar with his pecker. But right after I'd applied to St. Leo's he told me, "It's a good thing your parents are only separated and not divorced." "Why?" "Why! Are you kiddin', they get divorced, you might as well brand a 'D' on your forehead. The Catholic Church disowns you. No more religious instruction, no more CYO dances, and you can kiss St. Leo's goodbye. I think the pope gets your name on a list." Larry was an altar boy and spoke with a certain authority. And of course, he'd hit my tender spot. If it hadn't been tender, he'd certainly made it so. And I believed him.

The 'D' now emblazoned on my forehead, as if the iron came out of the sky over Saint Cloud that night, I knew I'd not play for St. Leo's. They were the best, and I had had every intention of becoming the best of the best. Their best player from two years ago now played for a Yankee farm club (and as a matter of fact was called up at age twenty-two). I felt like the rabbit in the claws of the gargoyle.

But in fact I lay in Odile's arms.

"I heard them talking on the phone late last night." I'd seen a phone in the upstairs hall, more proof of my death. "I knew it was your mother. My father asked, 'Do you want me to tell him? Maybe I could explain.' I don't know what your mother said, but I knew it was over. It was official."

She lifted my head and kissed one cheek, then the other, then the first again. I took this as my cue to leave, to go to my room and face the darkness like a man. Then I realized she was still kissing me. "My poor, poor cousin," she whispered between kisses. And the kisses fell everywhere, even on my lips. She didn't pause on any one spot too long, for she meant to quell what burned across my entire face. I fell asleep on her blanket. When I woke at her side in the early morning, I saw someone had covered me with another blanket. The puppets looked on from the limbo of early light. I suddenly remembered the divorce, and my horror and despair, having disappeared in the folds of the night, rushed back to me.

The diary: "June 18. (Last entry) I'm going to the Eiffel Tower to jump off. My life is over. I'm making it official. I only want everyone to know my blood is on his hands. It's his fault. His his his! His fault for fixing up the Packard, his fault for being a hero, his fault for learning about wine, his fault for being Frenchified, his fault for making it impossible for my mother to love a man like my father. Uncle Charlie, take a douche."

I left the diary open on the desk and went down to the kitchen. Feeling drained and hungry, and needing nourishment for my final journey, I ate an apple and a piece of chocolate cake, washed down with milk. France has perfect milk, I remember thinking. I decided it was time to go and tried to open the back door. I couldn't.

"You need the key," my aunt said behind me. I turned and saw her there in a robe, her hair in curlers.

"Oh. You need a key to get out?" Perfect milk, ill-conceived locks.

"*Bien sur*. That way, if a thief comes in the window, he can't go out the door." I supposed that made sense.

"But what if there's a fire and you can't remember where you left the key?"

"The idea is, don't forget. Where are you going so early?"

"The Eiffel Tower."

"It doesn't open for two hours yet." From a bowl of fruit on the counter she picked a kiwi.

"I wanted to beat the crowd."

"Did you sleep well?"

"All right, I guess." She was peeling the fruit, its skin like thin suede. My aunt had beautiful fingers, the nails long and painted red.

"You looked very comfortable when I covered you with the blanket."

When Odile had held and kissed me, I only knew she was keeping the bottom from falling out of the bucket. Standing before my aunt, I felt my despair turn to some kind of shame.

"Odile was teaching me French." She set the skin aside and got a knife from a drawer.

"And you fell asleep with your arms around each other?"

Obviously, the laws concerning intimacy between brother and sister had some corollaries for cousins.

"It was an accident." She took a plate from the dishwasher, set the kiwi on it and began to slice it.

"Well, you two will have to make a point of being more careful, won't you. I'm certain such accidents can be avoided if you make sure you're in your own bed by, say, eleven."

"Yes, Aunt Babette."

"You wouldn't want to accidentally get serious about your own cousin, now would you."

Serious? I wasn't even sure I liked her. "No, Aunt Babette."

"Kiwi?"

She held out the plate, the crossections looking kaleidoscopic. I took a slice and ate it.

"I know Odile's at the experimenting age, but I won't be calling your mother trying to explain what happened between you two."

Already I was beginning to forget I was on my way to jump off the Eiffel Tower. Did Aunt Babs mean it was naturally agreeable for Odile to experiment, only not with her own cousin? Did she mean Odile, in the throes of this "age" (maybe one year did make all the difference), might even call upon her cousin to assist in an experiment? Did she mean she—Aunt Babs—wouldn't mind but my mother might?

"Don't worry, Aunt Babette. You won't have to explain anything."

"We pride ourselves on open minds." Who? She and Uncle Charlie? Odile? The French? Me? "But there are rules."

"Yes, Aunt Babette. I understand perfectly." We finished off the kiwi, as if sealing some pact. Then I went upstairs and put my diary away, but not before writing, "Suicide off. It has come to my attention that O might have the hots."

After my uncle and aunt left that morning, Aunt Babs last giving me a remember-what-we-said look as she worked a dab of hand cream with her beautiful fingers, I immediately went springing past the kings of France and knocked on Odile's door. She said come in.

I kissed her cheeks in greeting, then sat on her bed. I began weighing her every gesture, her every word, but soon discovered the pity of the night before was only that. In fact, even Odile's pity had waned, for she hadn't even asked how I felt today.

"I bet you have a lot of boyfriends," I said.

"I'm quite selective about who I date."

"I mean I bet guys are asking you out all the time."

"No. Most of them know better." My cousin with the hots was sounding like a prude. "Although, there is Audrey's brother, Philip."

"You like Philip?"

"I adore Philip."

"Your mother like Philip?"

"She adores Philip."

"Philip like you?"

"His parents have a summer house in Saint Tropez with a pool and tennis court, and Philip asked me personally to join him."

Perhaps I responded in the only way possible. "Why? Is he coming apart?" And I laughed high in the throat, "Hmmn-hmmn-hmmn," like my father would have.

"That's silly." Then she reeled with laughter. "That almost sounds like my mother when she's having her orgasm."

"You've heard your mother have an orgasm?"

"Well—once. At the Eugenie Hotel in Biarritz. She goes '*oui-oui-oui-oui-oui*,' like a squeaky bird. I bet she could break a glass."

"Yeah? What about your father?"

"Didn't hear much out of him."

"Really? And he usta be a Screaming Eagle."

"Screaming Eagle!"

We both got giddy with laughing. Finally Odile said, "And what are you doing today?" She rubbed my cheek with her fingers. "You feel better?"

"I feel great! I'm going to the top of the Eiffel Tower." Suddenly I wanted height, though not to plunge from.

"Oh. But when will you ever go to the Louvre?"

On the kitchen phone I called Wretch to see if he'd come with me. "Sure, okay," he moaned in his fog. During the bus ride to town I asked him what he knew about Odile, how she got on with guys.

"She's been known to put out," he finally got around to saying.

"Christ, who for?" I felt that last brush of her fingers across my cheek.

"You're the one who asked. So don't act pissed."

"Just tell me who for."

"Well, a guy has a nice car, she goes for a ride with him."

"A guy like Philip Lennon? Does he got a nice car?"

"An MG. That asshole. Why the questions? You horny for Odile?"

"No. "

"Right. Hey look, these French kings were always ballin' their cousins."

"Yeah, well I'm no French king."

When we got to the Eiffel Tower, Wretch bought tickets for the elevator to the top. Actually there were two sets of elevators. One set rolled up the curved legs to the second level. The next set shot straight up through the neck of the tower. Somewhere along that neck, as the girders and rivets steadily diminished till I felt we'd be spit into the open air, my legs turned to rubber and my stomach rose. All I could think was, if we ever go to war with Russia I'll never make a paratrooper. I couldn't even pull my hands off the railing in the elevator when the door opened. Wretch saw what must've been terror in my eyes and didn't bother getting off. We rode back down, and as we walked away from the Eiffel Tower he said, "Don't feel like a wussy. Even my brother can't handle heights."

We crossed the bridge to Trocadero. I still hadn't got my legs back and sat down on a bench.

"What you need is a good run," Wretch said.

A minute later he walked over to a man trying to take a picture of a woman, probably his wife.

"Let me get the two of you," Wretch said politely.

"You sure you can handle this machinery?"

"Lieca. Fifty milimeter lens. No problem." Wretch looked around, evidently judging the light. "At f-22, I can get some flowers in the foreground."

"Very good." The man gave Wretch the camera and went and put an arm around the woman. "Where you from?"

"Baltimore." Odd, I thought, because he wasn't from anywhere in the States. But I knew he loved the Orioles.

"No kidding. We're up the road in York, P-A, ourselves. Make sure you get all of the Eiffel Tower now."

"Yeah, sure," Wretched answered. The camera had an adjustable lens which Wretch turned.

"No, no," the man said. "It's all set. Just push the button." He started smiling again.

I heard the camera go click, and the next thing I knew Wretch was flying through the crowd, a halfback slicing across a broken field, the camera cradled like a football, all at a speed I'd never have guessed him capable of.

It seemed a few seconds before the man started screaming. "Come back! Thief! Thief!" And another few seconds before he turned and saw me frozen on the bench and charged toward me. I bolted in the opposite direction as Wretch and ran for what seemed an hour, only to find myself back at the Seine. Certain I was downstream of the Eiffel Tower, I followed the river, knowing it would pass under the bridge to Saint Cloud.

I reached Uncle Charlie's by three. Downstairs I phoned Wretch. He sounded like nothing was new under the sun.

"Christ, why did you do that!"

"I don't know. It's something I do. It's in my blood or something."

"Well, I never want to see you again, got it?"

"Yeah, okay. So long." And he quietly hung up.

Saturday morning my uncle went out and brought back a bag of croissants. He asked if he could take me to the top of the Eiffel Tower.

"I think I'm afraid of heights."

"I thought you looked a little wobbly at Notre Dame. It's nothing to be ashamed of, son."

"I know."

"Speaking of Notre Dame, I just heard at the bakery that Corny MacDougal got caught stealing a camera out in front of it yesterday." Christ, I thought, two cameras two days in a row. Maybe idiocy was in his blood. "It turns out he's got a whole drawer full of stolen cameras."

"I guess you were right about him."

"And I guess you wouldn't know anything about those cameras."

Had Wretch implicated me? What had I done anyway?

"As a matter of fact, he showed me the cameras."

"He showed you a drawer full of cameras? Did you suppose a boy his age has the money to buy expensive cameras anytime he likes?"

Apparently, mine was a sin of judgment, not action.

"What do I know about cameras?"

"Don't be flip."

I expected him to bring up my father. I'd've had to admit there was something as well about the company he once kept, back when he was working for Bethelem Steel. I could only remember the vague tension in my mother's face whenever he spoke some name or another. About that time, things began to sour between them. Getting laid off from work shortly after didn't help. But Uncle Charlie let it go.

"I hope you've learned something. Now, what do you want to do today? You name it."

"I don't feel so hot. I think I'll go to my room and read."

Except to share dinner in Odile's room the next few days, I kept to myself. I'd seen kids playing soccer in a Saint Cloud field and told my aunt and uncle I'd been invited to join and couldn't get enough. A profound lie, for a sport in which a player intentionally hits a ball with his head seemed preposterous. What I actually did was ride the bus into the city and ride it back again, never getting off. Three round trips could kill the better part of a day, and I didn't care what the bus driver might think. What I was thinking was bad enough. I had begun to sense I had problems considerably deeper than never being Saint Leo's best, or having poor judgment in choice of friends, or being afraid of heights, or sounding like a puppy who had to go out (or a bird having orgasms), or never being adored by Odile—even if we weren't cousins. What I sensed was something wickedly unnerving—that I could not be anyone other than who I was. Facing my inescapable fate, I began singing in my head, over and over, the Simon and Garfunkel song about the rat in the maze.

Then, a week after the first wine-tasting, and a week before I was due to leave, my uncle and his friends were on the patio drinking, when I came in from three hours of aimless wandering around Saint Cloud.

This time, when my uncle saw me, he invited me out. He found an empty glass and handed it to me.

"I don't think your mother would mind if you tried a bit of Mouton-Rothschild, '29."

I was in my cut-offs and tie-dye, as usual, and the circle of men paused to watch. My uncle filled my glass half full, then took the glass from me, swirled it around, and handed it back.

"Take a sniff."

I sniffed.

"What do you smell?"

"Roses."

Everyone laughed, looking at the bushes surrounding us.

"Concentrate on what's in the glass, son."

I did. After a moment I began to smell something like the wild blackberry patch Larry and I knew over near Mount Carmel cemetery.

"Blackberries. Near Carmel."

A round man with a round face, covered in a beard, resniffed.

"Blackberries," he said. "Approaches caramel—*oui, oui! Il a raison!*"

My uncle smiled. "You have a good nose," he said. "Now, taste. Like this." He took a good draw and swished it around his cheeks and lips gyrating slowly like he was coating the whole inside of his mouth. I did the same.

"What do you taste?"

Everyone waited in expectation. I was truly amazed. It was like Odile had said, a production in your mouth.

"Warm berries. But something like cream, too." The men nodded their heads. "And funny, but a small taste of—tar, just in the back of my mouth though."

"Bravo," the round man said. "Bravo!"

"Apparently you have good taste buds as well," my uncle said.

I drank the rest of my glass, hurriedly, and said I had to leave. I ran upstairs to Odile's room and entered without knocking.

She was reading the erotic poetry. I hadn't seen the book since the first night.

"How dare you come barging in!"

"I'm sorry. But I had to tell you—" Then I realized she was slightly flushed and excited. I wondered what she'd been up to, abashed to think what it might have been. "Listen," I continued as if I hadn't noticed her state. "Your father just let me try some wine. Odile, it was fantastic, exactly like you said."

"Come here," she said. She slapped the book shut with one hand, then pulled her other hand from under the covers and patted the bed. I finally looked her in the eyes, and I didn't see any hint of embarrassment. "Sit with me."

Her window was cracked open, and men's voices and laughter drifted in from the patio below. I sat down beside her. The book thumped to the floor opposite me.

"Would you kiss me?" she asked.

So I kissed her cheeks.

"I was hoping to taste the wine."

"Why don't I run downstairs and get you a glass."

"I only want a little taste." A hand came up—the one from under the covers—and a finger made a windshield-wiper motion across my mouth.

"Odile, we're cousins."

"So what? It's not as though we're always meeting at family get-togethers." Somehow that line sounded rehearsed.

I felt warm and heady from my glass of wine—I think it was the wine—and held out my lips tentatively. She touched them with her own and drew back. Her tongue flicked out and swabbed away.

"I can taste it."

She repeated the procedure several times, each time closing her eyes. I knew this because mine were wide open. I heard the Righteous Brothers sing, "You never close your eyes anymore when I kiss your lips." And the astounding thought occurred to me: someone couldn't know that unless his eyes weren't closed either. My eyes closed. My brain drifted. My uncle's laughter shook the flagstones on the patio.

Odile kneaded my lips for maybe ten minutes. I didn't have the courage to resist or to reciprocate, but I was enjoying things exactly as they were. Then I heard my aunt's voice, out of place among the men's, and broke away clean.

"That wasn't very exciting was it," she said.

By dinner time in her room, she'd adopted a teacherly tone. She said I couldn't put off the Louvre any longer. She'd like for me to go to the Dutch wing and tell her afterward what I thought. I said maybe. After I set our trays aside, I sat next to her. I tried to kiss her, and she averted my strike.

"First, promise you'll go to the Louvre tomorrow."

I hesitated and then agreed. She held her face to receive my kiss. But the heat of the afternoon was no longer there.

"I think I'll go to bed."

"The Louvre opens at nine-forty-five."

"June 24. O wants to Frenchify me. Maybe I should let her. I'm aching in parts I never ached before. So what if she's my cousin? The French probably have some way around that, or just don't care—though my mother would. But how could she not want me to be like UC?"

The next five days I went to the Louvre and reported back to Odile. Creating a game, she gave me the name of a painting, and it was my job to find it, without asking anyone where it was. "Then I want you to study it. And when you come home, tell me what you saw." So I wandered the tall corridors of the Louvre, a Lilliputian dwarfed by paintings and statues. At first I raced through, looking only at nameplates. Then, slowly, I found myself pausing to gaze at the paintings themselves. I also found myself saying things to Odile I didn't quite know the meanings of, as I had to the wine-tasters. There is only one painting I can remember now. A Rembrandt—the name will come—where an angel, a woman, leans over the shoulder of a man writing, one of the evangelists. "Mathew Inspired by the Angel."

"I think she's whispering something dirty in his ear," I told Odile.

"She's guiding him."

"Guiding him to the sack!"

"I wonder . . ." She studied the space before her, summoning the painting. "Maybe that is a naughty look coming to his eye. Maybe Rembrandt is being ironic."

"See, I told you."

That night she said, "I've never spent as much time with any boy as I have with you."

Everyday Odile would reward me with kisses, and I felt propelled toward a leap over the walls of my maze. But the kissing was not the same as the day of the wine-tasting. I went through the motions, but forgot where I was. My mouth flat against Odile's, I saw in my head figures from paintings turn into New York Yankees. Concentrate, I'd tell myself, concentrate. Your future depends on it. Whatever ache I had now became a numbness. Always Odile's blue blanket was between us, neither of us willing to pull it away. It didn't seem my leap had fuel enough to happen.

Suddenly it was our last day together, a Tuesday. The Louvre was closed, and I wondered what effect that would have. I didn't go to Odile's room until shortly after noon.

"I don't understand. I thought you'd want to spend every second of today with me."

"Why? I'll leave here tomorrow, and we'll probably never see each other again."

"If that were true, then all the more reason we should take advantage of today—but we will see each other again. I'm going to ask if I can come visit you at Christmas."

I didn't doubt she'd ask, but I doubted she'd come. "I hope you like snow."

"I love snow. We don't see much. I mean, we do when we go skiing at Chamonix, but not here. Do you ski?"

"No."

"You could learn."

A ski-lift stretched like guitar strings to a mountain peak at the top of my brain. "I don't think so."

"Oh, yes! You're very capable. You could be a Rhodes Scholar if you put your mind to it." I didn't know what that was. "Already you have the athletic abilities, though you'd have to learn cricket. I doubt Oxford has baseball. And you'd have to study very hard. But you'd be set for life—"

I flew at her.

"Odile, what's the point!"

I suddenly grabbed her by the shoulders and kissed her

closed-mouth and hard. I yanked the blanket down and pressed my tie-dye T-shirt against her nightgown.

She shook her head. "Your libido's overwrought, isn't it?"

"Yes!"

She pulled me over and crushed herself down on me. I felt her small breasts flutter like birds. Then, whatever rashness had led me to grab her in the first place turned to implacable fear—God, I thought, what have I done? Then I thought of Wretch, or rather of his brother. *Laid when he was fifteen*. And I knew I myself could join that Olympus of rare beings, and even be installed a notch above Wretch's brother, who had met with Odile's slap. But, however bold my thoughts, Odile must've sensed the timidity coursing through my body.

"It might be easier if we had some wine," she murmured. "Why don't you go to the cellar and get us a bottle?"

"Take a bottle of wine?"

"It's my father's wine. Maybe a half bottle."

"Jesus, Odile. Don't ask me to take something from your father."

"Okay. We don't need the wine at all, do we." She pressed a cheek to mine.

"Wait—where's your mother?"

"She's shopping. Then she's going to the beauty parlor. Hair-do, manicure, pedicure—she won't be home for hours. They have to treat her extra special."

"Why?"

"Because she owns the shop! You don't think we live this way just on a high school teacher's salary, do you?"

"Your mother owns a beauty parlor?"

"Two. When her father died, she parlayed his apple orchards into beauty parlors."

We looked at each other as if we'd both forgotten what we had in mind.

"All right then," Odile said, rolling off me. "Go down to the corner, to the Esso station. In the men's room there's a machine you can buy *preservatifs* for five francs."

"Buy what?"

"*Preservatifs*—rubbers."

"I thought you were talking about jam or jelly or something. God, rubbers at the Esso."

"You won't get cold feet between here and the gas station, will you?"

"Cold feet, rubbers. That's pretty funny—" I almost whined.

"Will you?"

"No, no."

I got up and started to go, stopped at the door and turned around.

"We don't have to do this with them watching, do we?"

"Them?"

"Them." I made a sweeping motion with my head.

"My puppets?" She laughed and jumped out of bed. Without crutches she walked to the shelves. "Now, children, you aren't going to watch." Very slowly, like opening a cap on a hot radiator, she turned a puppet's head. "You'll have to get the ones higher up." So I climbed up on her desk chair and began twisting heads.

"Odile, how did they get this way, all facing you?"

"My mother. When I broke my foot, she said they could keep me company—I guess she meant till you showed."

"Didn't she expect anyone else to come over?" A useless question, for no one had.

"I told you, everybody is in the South of France for the summer." Who beside the Lennons I didn't know.

We were at the desk now. There were two puppets left. "There, does that make you feel better?"

"Yes, much."

"Hmmm, that's real nice," she said in a strange voice.

She'd picked up the sticks—with the strings and was lowering the puppet to the floor. "Try yours."

"I don't know, I—"

"Hmmm, come down here with me." Her puppet was a woman

with long eyelashes.

I tried to maneuver my puppet, a man dressed like, I guessed, a troubadour. He flopped down hard on the floor.

"Gently, gently."

I got him on his feet, but he tottered like a drunk.

"That's right, easy. Now come closer. Closer."

God almighty, I thought, rehearsal.

She spouted something in French, maybe by Villon, maybe by the woman with the bursting dam. Her puppet fell on her back and, whether he meant to or not, mine tripped over her and fell on top.

"Oh, like that! Yes! *Oui, oui.* Ah, *oui-oui-oui-oui*—"

We both heard the footsteps in the hall at the same time. I jerked my puppet up, and as he swung at the end of his strings, my aunt entered the room.

"Oh, hello, mother," Odile said calmly.

"What is going on here?"

"Rodolfo was just comforting the dying Mimi while Musetta fetches her muff." Aunt Babs stared silently at the incapacitated Mimi. Rodolfo, whose feet I had managed to get on the floor, reeled with uncontrollable grief. "Why? What did you think we were doing, mother?"

"I came to tell you I won't be going to the shop. I have a migraine. And what are you doing on that foot, young lady?"

"It's much better, mother." But, setting her puppet back on the desk and making her way to bed, Odile hobbled dramatically.

"And you, young man, I think you can spend your last dinner at the table tonight."

"Yes, Aunt Babette."

"I'll be in my room." She turned and walked out, again having thwarted my plans. As with the first time there was some part of me that deeply rejoiced. Actually, the very same part.

"Come here," Odile said, low.

I looked at the door. I heard my aunt go into the bathroom and a faucet turn on.

I set Rodolfo next to Mimi and went to Odile.

"The Esso."

"Are you crazy?"

"Tonight. Come to me tonight."

"Goddam, what if they hear us?"

"We will be very quiet. Wait until three." She kissed my mouth, her heat on full blast. I turned and left the room without looking back, and then left the house.

At dinner, luckily, my uncle brought up baseball. He'd really grown out of touch. Thought Yogi Berra was still playing catcher. Despite my mind being full of Odile, I rattled off stats—RBIs, ERAs, singles, doubles, triples, homers. My uncle was impressed. My aunt couldn't care less but seemed satisfied I could conduct baseball talk with considerable ease. It must have proven something to her. Then my uncle brought up the matter of tuition for St. Leo's.

"I told your mother I'd help because she doesn't have money enough."

"I'm not going to St. Leo's."

"What? They were the best when I was in those parts. They still are, aren't they?

"Yes."

"Then why not play for the best?"

"You know why."

"I have no idea." If he didn't know about the Pope's list, couldn't he at least feel destiny's hand moving through his house?

"I don't think I'll ever play baseball again."

My uncle stood up and shoved his own hands deep in his pockets, and I half expected him to say, "June, I'm a little worried about the Beaver here."

"Don't be frivolous with a God-given talent, son."

"There are more important things in life than baseball." Uncle Charlie was stupefied. Aunt Babs narrowed her eyes, and I envisioned her a sentinel in the hall that night.

Which wouldn't have mattered. I actually had made it to the Esso in the afternoon sun, but walking home I suppose I already knew I'd never go to Odile. Around four in the morning my virginity concluded it was good for one more trip to France.

Up and packed by nine, I went to her door, which was open. She was looking out the window, and I went and stood beside her. I'd heard her running the bath earlier, and now she smelled like a bouquet.

"You must think I'm terrible," she said.

"Terrible? You're the most wonderful girl I ever knew."

She turned to me with glassy eyes, which I mistook for contrition's relief.

"It is better we wait, Odile. At least till next time."

"There won't be a next time."

"Of course there will."

Why else had I waited! Intending to prove the future was ours, I kissed her. Yes, I wanted her to know, our destinies would merge, our juices would commingle. And to back that I had spit to swap right now. I let my tongue wander between her lips. They parted instantly and drew me in. There was no savory production, as there had been with the wine, but the safe taste of toothpaste. Her own tongue battered away. After a few seconds, like the day on the elevator, I felt my legs go rubbery and my stomach rise. I thought I'd be sick. She chewed my tongue and drew on it till I thought it would come out by the roots. I didn't understand the fascination with this method of kissing. But I held on. I felt myself, by a supreme act of will, leap the walls of my maze. At long last she stopped.

"I'll miss you, Odile." It was an effort to speak.

"Me, too." She resumed looking out the window. I walked away a moment later swearing I'd write her everyday. "Yes, do," she said.

I'd once had my hand trampled by baseball cleats, and I don't think that hurt as much as my tongue did now.

When I went downstairs with my suitcase my uncle was sitting in his chair, and my aunt was standing beside him. By the expressions on their faces, I knew something was wrong.

"I just went to get the wine for today's tasting." He nodded toward the fireplace mantle. There stood two bottles side by side. "While pulling out those, I discovered another bottle was missing. Only a half bottle, of nothing special, but missing just the same."

The love of my life had ripped off her father, who also happened to be my uncle. I wondered when. It must have been since the last wine-tasting, a week ago, or wouldn't he have noticed then? That was the day I'd run to her with berries, cream and tad of tar in my mouth, only to catch her with a hand under her blanket. Maybe she'd already been into some wine.

"I don't know anything about your wine, Uncle Charlie."

My aunt rolled her eyes, as if she had expected this of me all along. What was worse, I could only mumble.

"This camera business with the MacDougal boy, now a missing bottle of wine—what am I suppose to think?"

"You can think whatever you want, I didn't steal either."

"I really suppose I should tell your mother about this."

"About what?"

"Don't be like your father!" My aunt burst in. "If you stole something, at least be man enough to own up to it!"

"Babette," my uncle said.

"Listen to him! He's so full of lies he can't even talk straight!"

"I bit my tongue in my sleep," I explained. "And my father never stole anything from anyone."

"He swore up and down he didn't, son, but they fired him anyway."

"You mean Bethlehem? He was laid off."

"He was fired—for thieving."

I went to the fireplace. I took hold of a wine bottle, clubwise in one hand, not knowing who or what I intended to clobber.

"Take it back, Uncle Charlie."

"Your father was a thief." He stood up. Though he seemed to loom, his voice went very soft. "Everyone knew."

"No."

"They knew."

"Then how come he didn't get arrested?"

"They couldn't prove it."

"Bullshit."

"Son, someone had the evidence, all right—"

"I'm not your son! Just tell me—who had the evidence—"

"Your mother, that's who. Imagine her having to live with that."

I had the bottle by both hands now, like a Louisville Slugger, and I was about to unleash a furious smash, right across the other bottle. For I could imagine very well what living with that was like. Suddenly Odile appeared at the bottom of the stairs.

"What's the commotion?"

"Odile, I told you to stay off that foot."

"My foot is fine, mother."

Something dawned simultaneously in Aunt Bab's and Uncle Charlie's eyes. And then in Odile's. I was prepared to save her.

"Son, listen. You no doubt have a good swing—save it for the bats at St. Leo's."

"I told you, I'm not playing for St. Leo's."

"Why in the world not!" He laughed loudly.

"'Cause I stole the bottle, and thieves don't play for St. Leo's."

I looked at Odile. Yes, I'll take the rap for you, Odile. I tasted her spit on my aching tongue. She tilted her head. *Dignity, my love, dignity. A baseball player smashes bottles, the person you are to become doesn't.* "Besides, I've got better things to do with my time," I said, placing the bottle on the mantle, my eyes fastened on the girl I now knew, somehow, was forever mine. A second later, as luck would have it, the bottle crashed on the floor.

A curious smile broke across my aunt's face, not at my clumsiness I believe but at what she must have known was about to issue from her daughter's mouth.

"Petrus! My God a bottle of Petrus!" Odile screamed. "You big colossal jerk!"

"Odile!" My uncle snapped. "Stop! It was only an accident."

Now, strangely, she walked toward me. She stooped down and in what had been a shoulder of the bottle dipped her fingers and licked the wine off. "You will never taste Petrus in your life." Her voice sizzled and her eyes peered at me as if from the bottom of a well.

"Odile!" My aunt screamed. "Get up this instant!"

"June 30. At Orly they said they realized O took it (but didn't seem in a hurry to punish her). Jet take-off not as fast as first thought. The pilot says we're at 38,000 feet. I think I finally get it. She took it last night. Last night. For the two of us. A real special occasion, like Smokey Robinson says. Snuck to the cellar. Took it. Waited." She had reason to expect me.

Some years ago, in honor of Charlie and Babette's fortieth anniversary, a bottle arrived at their door on the outskirts of Paris. It held forty-year-old Petrus, a wine whose reputation—I solemnly learned—is surpassed only by its cost. I didn't think the extravagance wasted, despite my wife's protest. Now she asks me about the reading light and I reply, "In a minute." She rolls over and returns to sleep, her breathing contentful. True to his word, my uncle paid my tuition and I became indeed St. Leo's best. The spring before graduation I brazenly tried out with the Bisons as a walk on, finding my name on a list in the War Memorial Stadium locker room after the first cut, but not the second. On scholarship in college, during sophomore year, while stealing home off a wild pitch, I ripped the ligaments in my left knee and never really recovered. These days I play with my son, age eight, and he laughs at my Spaulding artifacts. In a window at the mall, his eye is on a glove the size of a bushel basket. "No fair," I say. Among my fears is loss of memory, which I find ironic, being a computer programmer.

Two years now I've taken my son to join my father for the Bison opener. My father is working on his twenty-first year with his wife Claire. It was to clear the way for her that he divorced my mother. I don't know that they are destiny's darlings, but she brought a change in him. Not once in twenty-one years has my father cracked his joke about losing the opener, and whenever he laughs, which is often, it is downright infectious.

I never saw my cousin again, but I hear she runs her own travel agency with offices throughout Europe. No surprise, given her multilingual talent. I never saw my aunt and uncle again either. But tonight, in the evening paper, on the same page as my daily crossword, I happened on an article about a man, his wife and their daughter—Hope—who work in the Southwest restoring adobe buildings that suffered last spring from unusual rains. They mix mud and straw, then apply it by hand. The man's skin has benefited from the sunshine. At least in the picture I have of him. His name is Cornelius B. MacDougal, and I wonder how many can there be in this world. Who but a "Corny," dubbed "Wretch," would name a daughter Hope? I turn out the light and wonder some more.

RESOURCEFULNESS

Peter Owen, rousted from sleep by persistent knocking, answered his door to find two men in black rubber coats and chrome helmets.

"Evacuate the building, please."

"What is it, a fire?"

"No. A crack's been discovered in the main support wall—"

"Long as a lightening bolt."

Peter Owen stayed calm, if not insouciant. Recently his business had collapsed, and Katie—her warmth still in the sheets—had deserted Paris. If the floor now dropped from under him, so what?

"You may remove personal things only."

From his window he saw people defying orders, and like ants defying weight, hauling out large pieces of furniture. Peter Owen's flat came with a few spartan scraps, and his evacuation required but three suitcases, and several crates scavenged from the nearby wine store. A neighbor across the street, Jean-Luc, had storage space in his cellar, dry and warm—habitable, if times turned desperate. One year earlier, Peter had stored things with a neighbor in Poughkeepsie, and now all he owned was neatly stacked on basement floors on separate continents, waiting for him to make a move.

Surprising himself with a burst of resourcefulness, Peter found a furnished groundfloor studio that very afternoon in the 15th Arrondissement. He and Jean-Luc loaded the trunk onto the rear seat of a cab, and Peter took a last look at his old building. A rumored meeting spot for insurgent Communards in the late 1860s, it seemed stout as ever, even as gendarmes girdled it in an orange ribbon. The new apartment, modern, had a single window, facing the constant noise and fumes of a busy street and an elevated Metro line. But Peter reasoned this was a temporary arrangement. As he moved boxes in through his window, a boy came out of the lobby, paused briefly to examine Peter and his possessions and walked away. A handsome boy in sparkling white clothes, he reminded Peter of an ice-cream vendor.

He put his things in order and lay down on the bed, its mattress misshapen by who knew how much humanity or what antics. Yet the coils at his back were not so relentless and discomforting as thoughts of Katie. "What Paris needs is a good chocolate chip cookie," he heard her say. A summer ago. She was knap sacking from Amsterdam to Rome, like a kid, though she was past thirty. He had matching suitcases at his hotel, bought for his first vacation in four years. In line at a patisserie, she rescued him from a cashier about to shortchange him on his purchase of a *mille-feuille*. They made introductions—Katie was South Carolinian—and walked in sunshine. Then his *mille-feuille* got out of control. Not doing much better with her *tarte aux pommes*, Katie licked and shook her fingers. "Yes, a good, solid chocolate chip cookie!" How much would one need to start a cookie business? Peter wondered aloud. They toyed at first with estimates, but by day's end spoke with precision, as if of a grid network, of dollops on the cookie sheet and sums of chocolate chips. Her business sense impressed him. He himself managed a chain of Hudson Stationery and Office Supplies stores, from Red Hook to Peekskill. His joke: "Stationary man." The next morning they contacted French authorities, who were delighted to welcome foreign investment—even in cookies. Peter flew home and—sweetly deaf to the consternation of boss, family, friends—sold off his car and furniture. Katie cashed in some stocks. They bought the lease on a closet of a shop, exorbitant, its rent no steal either, though it did open onto the popular rue St. Honore. Beside a used oven they pinned up Katie's recipe and began to bake. Round, hefty and neat, their cookies made sense, like the invention of the wheel itself, and it wasn't hard to imagine tourists on the go, fueled by a Michelin guide in one hand and one of "Katie's Cookies" in the other. Come winter, tourists were a trickle. Parisians themselves showed little fascination, even with the introduction of oatmeal and oatmeal-raisin. By spring, the fresh supply of tourists who would be their lifesavers streamed past the shop. In June the oven caught fire. Peter tore an extinguisher from the wall and foamed the flames. After airing the place out, they locked up shop. Gazing on their cookies, molehills after a blizzard, they grew hysterical laughing, dropped to the floor and, hands gummy with dough, made love for the first time. The more business matters worsened, the more solace they sought; then, finally, on Bastille Day, Katie flew to New York, connecting to Charleston. "No hard feelings," she said, leaving her recipes pinned to the wall.

"Stupid! Stupid! Adults behaving like children!" Peter cried out loud. A great black wave rolled across him, and he thought he would drown. His eyes were wet. He got up and pulled the sheets away, found two blankets, laid them on the coily mattress, put one sheet back, then covered himself with the other. That was better, and he went to sleep. He woke hours later, disoriented. There were no curtains, and a blade of light sliced his room. When he opened his window and reached for the shutters, he saw the street deserted in the night. Then he saw the boy in white returning.

He was more handsome than Peter had first realized. He had the promise, should he fill out, of an athletic physique. He wore his silky black hair like an old Beatles haircut. The boy stopped and faced him squarely. Now his hair showed the faintest hint of copper. His skin, nutty brown, seemed so smooth, like porcelain. If pricked with a pin, he might not bleed. An angel's face. A dramatic arch to his eyebrows. Long, delicate nose, with nostrils that turned slightly up. Angular jaw, carved cheekbones, and straight, full lips. His eyes were mysterious: nearly black, but with thin spokes of gold.

Peter wondered at how beautiful a thing the human form could be. People considered Peter himself handsome, that he knew, but in this boy he saw perfection.

"You're American, right?" The boy said brusquely in French.

"How would you know?"

"I saw your stuff in the boxes."

"I see."

"Teach me English. I know alotta words already."

"I don't know."

"Why not?" He sounded affronted. "One lousy hour a day. I live upstairs on the top floor. Convenient. I'll give you seventy francs, say, per lesson."

"I'm just getting settled and have to find work."

"I'm offering you work."

"Let me find something a bit more substantial, and I'll let you know."

"When?"

"Soon."

And he started to walk away.

"Wait. What's your name?"

"Abbas. A-B-B-A-S."

"I'm Peter Owen. What's that name?"

"I just spelled it for you."

"I mean, what nationality?"

"Americans." He shook his head and snorted. "I'm Persian, okay?" And he walked into the lobby.

After Peter closed his shutters, it registered. The boy's agitation, indeed rudeness, was a defense. For Persia had been a land of magic lamps and peris. Now occupying the same space was a land of horrors. Except from papers and TV what did Peter know of it? Heat and dust, names like mouthfuls of barbed wire, painful even to speak. Robed masses, wrapped heads, veiled faces. Human cobblestones at prayer. Pitiless baggy-eyed men. Fanatics, terrorists, perpetual hostages. Impenetrable, all, reducing Westerners to fistshakers or handwringers.

"But here am I," Abbas seemed to say, "the Persian!" Dressed in white no less.

The next morning Peter made phone calls from a *cabine* in the hallway, only to find that, though French law permitted him to run his own business, he could not in his present status work for someone else. This required different papers, complicated to obtain. They scheduled an appointment to review his case, but that was five weeks off. Meanwhile he'd have to do something. He recalled another American, Jim Smiley, who had attended the same three-day course with him a year ago, How To Start A Business In Paris. Now Peter entered a bar off Saint Germain—called "Smiley's Oasis"—and asked to speak to the owner. Clearly the place was a huge success, crowded already in the afternoon, and Peter reckoned on employment here for a fellow American. As a barmaid with a British accent and a tag that said "Beverly" went to fetch Mr. Smiley, Peter looked around: brass rails going in every direction; highly glossed oak; fake tiffany lamps; three TVs; the Detroit Pistons beating the Boston Celtics. A tape, Peter realized.

Jim Smiley—all smiles—couldn't remember him. No matter. Peter explained the situation, wanting to stress his urgency, but without sounding like a failure or a dolt. When he finished, Jim Smiley—who hadn't stopped smiling—said, "That's the way the cookie crumbles." Peter detested him but said, "I need work." Okay, Smiley said. "Ever bartend?" In college, years ago. "Under the table, you understand?" Of course, Peter said, knowing this meant piddling wages and no benefits. "You start tonight. Six to two AM."

From a row of upside-down bottles, so many fangs dispensing poison, Peter concocted seven-and-sevens, screwdrivers and rum-and-cokes for droves of Americans, hankering after a week or two of Paris for the tastes and voices of home. No price too dear, they gobbled cheeseburgers, gnawed Buffalo-style chicken wings, and swapped tales of perilous Gallic expeditions. They booed or cheered the tape of the Pistons beating the Celtics (Jim Smiley was a Motor City man himself), and danced to Bruce Springsteen pouring from the juke box. Amidst this stampede of refugees there was, for Peter, one bright spot—Beverly. Round face glowing—Rubenesque Peter thought—her British voice spouting orders, tireless and jovial, she might be a woman he'd be interested in, except she seemed a bit too happy working for the likes of Jim Smiley.

Asleep by four AM, Peter was awakened at ten by fierce knocking. Orders again to evacuate? In pajamas he opened his door to find Abbas.

"Yes or no," he barked in French, "will you teach me English?"

Peter scratched his head.

"Ninety francs a lesson—that's the limit."

"Okay." Money was money, but Peter may have been more curious to learn how venom spewed from such beauty. Abbas would come at one o'clock, Monday through Friday, beginning that day.

Peter insisted Abbas speak only English at his lessons, which reduced the boy's bluster to intermittent gusts. After a few lessons, Peter asked Abbas if he remembered anything of—Persia. Abbas narrowed his eyes. "No," he nearly shouted. "A child me then. Must carry out. I know later we lose much." Then, fuming, added, "Ten years my mother upstairs and hardly leave. She read books, old, oh yes! and talk to old birds."

"She has some birds?" Peter asked calmly, trying to bring calm.

"Two. Touracos. Orange here." Index fingers drew simultaneous circles around each eye.

"And what about your father?"

"My mother only. I say we lose much."

Embarrassed, Peter said, "I usually make tea and muffins for a snack. Would you like some?"

"Yes, please."

"Do you like jasmine?"

"Yes, please."

Peter made tea and toasted muffins, which he served with butter and honey. While he clanked his spoon in his cup, Abbas stirred quietly, his storm subsided.

"You know, Mister Owen," Abbas asked, now almost dreamily, "jasmine it is Persian word?"

"No."

"So also candy, lilac, azure, sugar, lemon, orange, magic, paradise, caravan, musk, tiger. I say julep?"

"No, you didn't," Peter said, sipping his tea and drinking up the Persian words and the Persian face.

At the beginning of August Abbas asked, "What means the word 'buttercup'?"

"The name of a flower. Also, what someone who likes you might say." Abbas' eyes gave away nothing. "You have a girl who calls you buttercup?" "Teach the English," the boy snapped. He's at that age, Peter thought. Starting to unlock small windows in young girls' hearts—and how this boy will unlock them! Fling them open and climb in! Maybe an English-speaking girl? Of course! Peter tingled, a tutorial Cupid assisting the quest. Two weeks later, Abbas showing commendable progress, Peter mused out loud, "Maybe a certain somebody appreciates your new and improved English? Hey, buttercup?"

"Screw off, Mister Owen."

"Now that's new and improved. Abbas, has your mother ever taught you manners?"

"Lots."

"That's good. I'd hate to think she wasted all her time on birds."

"No more birds."

"No?"

"Birds dead. One one day, the other two days after."

Though Abbas didn't seem the least bit saddened, Peter was. "It happens that way," he reflected.

"Mother cry like end of world." Peter had yet to see the woman—or at least didn't know it if he had. He imagined her ensconced above, drawing on finances and memories rescued from another era.

"Sometimes it's difficult to let go of things dear to us, Abbas."

"Even ship that sinks."

"That may be true, but—"

"Sink, sinked, sinken? Yes?"

"That's a tricky one. Let me show you."

Didn't Peter know about clinging to sinking ships.

Every time he opened his shutters he had a notion of what a perfect store his apartment would make on this bustling street. Then he'd remember the diet of unsold cookies, sickly-sweet. Even worse, Jim Smiley, like some specter of business savvy, would rise up in his mind. "And what will you sell from your window, Owen? Maybe Cracker Jacks? Maybe to the pigeons from the girders under the tracks?" Then, in the mid-August heat, an idea blossomed with such clarity Peter marveled it hadn't come sooner. Having learned from Smiley's Oasis something about Americans' indomitable taste for things American, he wrote Katie. "Cookies alone," he said, "lacked variety. But imagine shelves of Cheerios, Campbell's soup, baked beans, corn chips, diet soda, etc. Imagine 'The General Store,' here to serve the thousands of Americans living in Paris! I am not seeking your investment," he continued, though he knew well enough of the fortunes from her father's factory, which churned out paper plates, cups and napkins. Toothpicks, too. "Simply,I miss you." Missed especially—he didn't write—her dulcet serenades in French—spicy, tangy, obscene French—when they made love. Did she sing like that in Carolina? "So, Katie, if you ever miss Paris, or maybe need an ear that understands French, I'm here." He signed it "*Amoureusement*" and mailed it before he could debate its lack of subtlety.

Later that day, Jim Smiley said he needed a hand with something from the car. "This'll knock their socks off!" Following the boss outside, Peter saw a life-size wooden Indian tied to the roof of Smiley's BMW. They carried it in—Peter gripping the ridges of a headdress—and posted it next to the bar. Six times that night someone posed alongside, asking Peter to snap a flash camera, which he did, stonefaced as the Indian in the viewer. Suddenly, between making drinks, Peter realized how perfect a wooden Indian would be outside The General Store.

When he next saw his concierge, a sallow woman forever smoking a cigarette, he broached the possibility of converting his apartment to a store. She nixed the idea with a phlegmy laugh. "We're not zoned." "But there," Peter pointed across the street beyond the shadow of the Metro rail, "an optometrist, a Thai restaurant, a *presse*—" "That side is zoned. We are on this side, unless maybe you want to fight city hall." Easier to cross the Alps on elephants, Peter figured, considering he'd yet to get over the hurdles barring his working papers. But he'd keep an eye open for something properly zoned.

The very first thing the very last Monday in August, Peter found himself at the Prefecture de Police, *tête-à-tête* with, and aching at the desk of, one Mademoiselle Prieure, a redhead. She shook her hair, puckered and unpuckered her lips, squirmed rubbery and lithe in her seat, conducted short symphonies with long fingers —ringless—and exuded the faint smell of raspberries. Round and round they went. He might only obtain his working papers, she *tsk-tsked*, should some firm first guarantee him work. Of course no one would offer him work, Peter *hmmm-hmmmed*, unless he first presented working papers. He had applications in for an accountant position, a stationery store manager and, inspired by progress with Abbas, an English-as-second-language teacher. She picked up a pen—a Waterman, Peter noticed, classy—held it to her lips flutewise and blew. With the same instrument she caught a stream of hair from a cheek and hooked it behind an ear. "Perhaps," Peter ventured, "we might better discuss my case over lunch, say at noon." He'd gladly foresake his lesson with Abbas—that foul-mouthed Persian. Mlle. P. stiffened, setting the Waterman between them on the desk. "Do not confuse matters, Monsieur Owen. You are in no position. If anyone wanted you badly enough, they'd do the paperwork themselves and send it to us. They are being nice saying you have to get the papers or their hands are tied. But don't let them kid you."

Ten minutes later, burning with a sense of rejection, by potential employers in general and Mlle. P. in particular, Peter tramped across the Pont au Change and searched for the bus to take him home. Then, along the Quai de la Megisserie, when opposite the outdoor bird market, Peter thought he saw Abbas. By the time he fought through cars, buses, trucks and buzzing motos and reached the spot where Abbas—or some twin—had stood, he was gone. There were only hundreds of cooing, chirping, squawking birds in stacked cages. Peter turned to see, in a cage in a store window, two birds—green crested, perse bodied, red feather-tipped—peering at him through orange-ringed eyes. Touracos Persa Afrique, the sign said. 4500 francs for the couple. Not cheap, these cheepers. Had Abbas' mother decided on replacements? Peter looked up and down the street.

"Didn't I see you this morning at the bird market," Peter said that afternoon over tea and a grammar book.

"No," Abbas said.

"Sure. I assumed you were looking to replace the ones that died."

"I do not know this bird market."

"On the Quai de la Megisserie, everybody knows—"

"I say I do not know," Abbas flared. "Should I care for birds! Be like my mother!"

Peter sat silent. Easier this day to ascertain the truth reading dregs in the bottom of a tea cup, or for that matter, a bird cage.

By now Peter was working from four in the afternoon to two in the morning and saving nine hundred francs a week, a broadening ray of light. He'd even managed to buy a new mattress. Still, he hadn't heard from Katie, not that he expected her to zoom to his arms via the Concorde. Maybe missing her magnified something that wasn't there at all, but it seemed Beverly had grown fond of him. Lonely or not, he still balked at showing interest in a woman who had made a career of Smiley's Oasis.

"How long have you worked here?"

"From the beginning, so that would be one year, two months, wouldn-tit," she said. He was never sure if she was making a statement or asking a question.

"At least not under the table," he said.

"Indeed under the table!" She said. "You want to feel the lumps on my head!"

"But Brits can work in France without papers."

"Yes, straight away, but I'm American."

"You?"

"Quite. I spent my first twenty-two years in Sandusky, Ohio, twanging up my voice, and the last nine here, untwanging it. I prefer French, but if I must speak English, I speak English."

Peter shook his head.

"Astonishing, isn-tit."

"Rather!"

She loved art, she explained. Spent all her spare time in museums, studying and learning, hoping next year to land a job—anything. Ten years a resident, she'd be legal, allowed to work wherever qualified. In the meantime her sister back home sent in a yearly *attestation* saying she supported Beverly, an artiste. The French authorities—ever solicitous to the arts—gladly issued a residence card. "Despite everything I know about art," Beverly joked, "I couldn't sketch a smile button."

"Ten years!" Peter gasped. Well, would someone attest to supporting him? Beverly asked. No, he didn't think so. That's okay, she reassured him.

"There are ways, I suppose, to lead a totally untraceable life in Paris." That seemed impossible, he remarked, if not premature. Then, the very next day, he received a notice from Mlle. P.—as in prick teaser—saying the government was to revoke his residence card if he did not by September twelfth—ten days!—present proof of an income-producing business. End of notice. The rest was obvious. His welcome terminated, he'd be declared illegal. Would they wrest him from his apartment? He could always move for the price of a taxi fare. Leave no forwarding address. An untraceable existence might not be as impossible as a traceable one.

That afternoon Abbas pleasantly suprised Peter and took his mind off his worries by asking if he knew anything about "football

American."

"Adjective first. Yes, a bit." He was being modest. Quarterbacking a dormitory to an intramural championship, he had a good arm once, maybe still. Was that fifteen years ago? "Wait a minute."

He went to his closet and pulled out a football. He handed it to Abbas, sitting at the table. Peter adjusted the boy's fingers as if giving lessons at a piano. "Like this, by the laces."

"It has a need for air."

"It needs air," Peter said.

"It needs air. If I had to be American, I would be a quarterback."

"It's not as simple as that," Peter laughed.

Then Abbas stood abruptly, fading to pass, bumping the table and knocking over a cup of tea that spilled across the table and onto Peter's legs. "I am sorry," Abbas said, at once timid, dropping the ball and running to get a dish towel. "I am sorry." And he bent over and dabbed at Peter's knees.

"It's okay. It's okay." Peter pulled Abbas upright by the arm. "It's okay." He looked at Abbas' eyes and saw the small spokes tremble.

"I am stupid."

"Abbas, it's only tea, and these are old jeans."

"I go and come back tomorrow."

"Don't make a big deal—besides, tomorrow's Saturday."

"I come back Monday."

"Okay, suit yourself. But listen, I'll buy a needle and get the ball inflated. Then we can toss it around."

"I would like this."

Strangely quiet his next two lessons, by Wednesday Abbas was back to his old self. "Will we throw the football?" He barked. "Yes or no?"

Peter had forgotten. Five days he'd been scouting for space to set up The General Store. To buy out a lease on even a small place cost fifty thousand francs! And that in neighborhoods Americans never went into. To say nothing of stock or initial reparations.

Refrigeration was out of the question. He felt the black wave lapping at his toes. Soon, too, he'd hear the knock at his door.

"I'm sorry, Abbas. Let's make a definite date. Saturday? Sunday?"

"No. Possible Monday."

"Possibly."

"Possibly."

"Okay, then. Monday."

"Tuesday we begin school."

"Oh. Will you still want tutoring?"

"No. I will be busy with school, I take serious."

Peter said, "That's good," but sensed something escaping from his life, an exotic aroma about to blow out the window of an otherwise bland room.

"Next year I begin business school. That's why the English. A must. By thirty I am a millionaire, dollars not francs."

"Oh." The exotic aroma suddenly had the dubious scent of a Jim Smiley.

"American football begins on Sunday. Here on TV the game will be Chicago Bears up against New York, Giants not Jets."

"I'm an old Giants fan myself."

"A joke. I bet you two hundred francs, I take the Bears."

"But—" Peter almost explained those games were tape-delayed a week, condensed into one hour with no commercial time-outs. In the international paper Peter had read, "Giants Tame Bears, 35-7." Why not teach a lesson other than English? "I take the Giants. For four hundred francs."

"No problem. You want six hundred?"

"Eight."

"Okay, even thousand."

Had the boy no concept of money!

Abbas pulled out his wallet. "Here is TV schedule for September. I got from magazine." As he read it off, his wallet lay open on the table. Peter saw a color photo of a woman. She looked as beautiful as Abbas—his face, eyes, nose, cheeks.

"Is that a sister?"

"... Washington against Miami, and Detroit against Minnesota. No. I have no sister. This is my mother."

Peter looked with wonder. She seemed too young to be Abbas' mother. Maybe—how? by arrangement?—she'd married early and had a baby.

"It is several years old. Mother is much tireder now."

"More tired."

"More tired. Soon is another birthday and she will stay home like always."

He had not yet met the woman living right above his head, Peter realized, feeling he had squandered a chance, though at what wasn't clear. Thursday he reminded Abbas of their date to toss the football, not to forget. He couldn't stop thinking of Abbas' mother. In the picture, mostly facial, he had made out a cowl or a lowered hood around her neck, black with yellow speckles, and he wondered what it meant.

On Friday, asking Abbas if there was absolutely anything else he wanted to know about English, the boy said no. Peter could barely stand the thought of him going off to school, his mother's picture in his hip pocket. "Okay. Monday then, eleven o'clock, we meet here and take the Metro to the Bois de Boulogne."

"Okay."

Then out of nowhere, Peter said, "Maybe your mother would join us."

"She does not know about American football."

"I'm sure. But maybe she'd like to watch. Get out in the park—I could make a picnic."

"She is no *feu d'artifice*."

"Fireworks. That's okay, me neither."

"I will ask, but you do not know."

"Can I call you tomorrow and see?"

"We have not any phones. I will come down and tell you."

No phone? —Privacy? —Fear? —Threats? He couldn't imagine.

The next morning Abbas came, beaming, to say his mother would "company" them.

"At first she is scared, like her usual, like a mouse. And I scream at her. You must get out! Ten times I scream. For your birthday give this to yourself—get out! And then she says okay."

Peter's heart swelled. He went immediately and bought a needle and inflated the football at a gas station. Flipping it in the air on the way home, he decided on a French picnic of cheese, bread, fruits and nuts, wine (did Persians drink alcohol?) and water. The phone in the hall rang. It was Beverly.

"I decided to have a party tomorrow night."

"What's the occasion?"

"Smiley called. He's giving us off Monday, to have some new toys installed. Something about holograms."

"Figures. He's probably one himself. Okay, I'll be at your place with bells on."

"Well, I haven't invited you yet, now have I?"

"There was a young girl from Sandusky, who had something that smelled rather musky—"

"Well, Peter, you're getting on brilliantly today, aren't you."

"When I asked her to see what that might be, she replied..."

"What did she reply?"

Peter pinched his nose making it sound inoperable.

"Why, goodness gracious, ask me?"

"That's 16 rue Sablon. Till tomorrow, Peter. Till tomorrow." It was the first time since Katie he had made someone laugh. He was in top form.

Tomorrow, Sunday, seemed beyond reach. Monday seemed beyond time. How could he wait? He went out to look at a store front advertised in the paper. Got halfway there and decided no. Who needed The General Store? Who needed anything but those two faces—Abbas' and Abbas' mother's? To think they might have been there all along, his for the asking. Now he would have them side by side. What would he say to her? Had they anything in common? He had never been mangled in the treads of a revolution, no, but he knew what it was to be down on the ground and have to raise oneself up. In sleep that night, he vividly dreamed of Abbas, happily polishing the wooden Indian as lightbulbs flashed.

Sunday night, trying to make the time go, he took the Metro and mingled at Beverly's, a glass of Rhone wine in his hand. He wouldn't drink much. He'd leave early. Get a good night's sleep. Yet every time he finished a glass, prepared to depart, Beverly refilled it.

Only English-speaking people were at the party, including Jim Smiley. What a pathetic lot, Peter thought, listening to Smiley berate the French. "They treat their dogs better than people." What was he in Paris for? Peter wondered. The smile, the wink, the punch line—that's what. He was an American among Americans here. Emperor of the islet. He didn't allow dogs in Smiley's, he was saying—"Know why?" "No. Why?" "No dogs, no frogs." Everyone cackled.

"Bloody idiot," Beverly said, coming up behind Peter.

"His own caricature." He paused to look at her. "You've done a nice job on your place here, Beverly." Every inch of wall space was covered with pictures, smartly framed.

"They're all prints. Someday I'll have a few of the real things."

"In the meantime."

"What's that look? 'How does a poor girl working under the table do so well,' is it?"

"I'm sure you're a very resourceful woman, is all."

She yanked Peter into a doorway, as if in reproach for some insinuation. "Very resourceful—especially when I do the books."

"Bev? You?"

"Bozo out there makes it so easy, doesn-tee."

"Well, well. You are full of surprises. But don't you think Bozo out there is gonna look around and realize nobody lives quite this well on the chickenfeed he pays?"

"He thinks I'm subsidized by a rich sister in Sandusky. Him and the French."

They laughed softly. She laid a hand on his arm.

"I've got to get going, Bev."

"You don't have to leave, do you?"

"Yes, really, I do."

"I mean, Peter, you don't have to leave."

"I'm sorry."

"If trouble hits, Peter, if you need a place to stay in a hurry—"

"Thanks, but—" He appreciated the offer of refuge for the night, and the future. Still, he felt drawn toward tomorrow as if toward a lighted space he had never seen or known, where everything would work out, better than ever. "—I gotta go." Beverly was great—fleecing the fleecer. Brilliant, truly, wasn-tit. Yet that was it, she was the girl from Sandusky who aped Brits and stole from the boss. What wonder in that?

Peter walked briskly, foregoing the Metro. Drinking too much, he wanted to clear his head, maybe break a sweat. He trotted down the steps at Trocadero, the Eiffel Tower glowing on the other side of the river. He jogged past fountains shut off for the night, into a park along the quay street, and now he darted and feinted, a quarterback with intelligence and agility, attributes to impress even a woman who knew nothing of football. Suddenly he stopped. His mind lurched as the real, physical presence before him jostled with the images so long on his mind. There stood Abbas himself, at the edge of the park, near the curb. No mistake—as there might have been at the bird market. It was Abbas.

He was talking to a boy smoking a cigarette. Peter didn't think Abbas was a smoker. He hoped not. Abbas spotted him and sharply nodded the other boy off. The boy looked at Peter and moved down the curb.

"Abbas! What are you doing here?" Peter caught his breath.

"Remember? I live across the river like you."

There were others, Peter saw, strung out loosely along the curb, on the gravel strip between the sidewalk and the street. All of them boys, he slowly realized. And how quiet they were. The streetlamps here made Abbas' clothes salmon-colored. A car stopped, and the boy smoking the cigarette bent and put his head in the passenger window.

"The Bears were beat bad by the Giants," Abbas said blankly. "I owe you one thousand francs."

"The Giants beat the Bears badly. Don't worry about it. I only hope you won't be so careless with your money from now on."

"Yes, but I pay you, fair is fair."

The other boy flicked his cigarette away and got in the car and drove off. Peter felt a hairline crack in his heart, though why, he didn't know.

"Shouldn't you be home, resting up for tomorrow?"

"It is early."

"Quarterbacks need their rest. You can't just hang out, Abbas, for no good reason."

"I have reason." He ran his foot in a small arc in the gravel. "Why are you here, Mister Owen?" Then his foot kicked at the ridge of gravel, spattering Peter's shoes. "You are stupid to walk down this street this night," Abbas said. "After tonight, okay. This I swear. But not tonight." His eyes were glassy, his mouth gnarled. "Why tonight, Mister Owen?"

And now he wished he had not stepped foot from Beverly's apartment. "Abbas, listen. Whatever's going on, we can leave here."

Another car raced up and stopped. It was a big car for Paris, white with tinted glass. It turned the same color as Abbas' clothes, and Peter's chest hardened like a breakwater.

"See? I must go now," Abbas said.

"Abbas, you and me, we'll walk home together."

"Do not act stupid. It is too late."

The driver's door opened and a man stood up, looking across the rooftop at Abbas. He had a pointy face, blond hair combed straight back, a red shirt unbuttoned halfway, revealing curls, glasses the same tint as the car windows, and tanned skin, not the nutty brown of Abbas, but oily tan.

"I believe this is Sunday night," the man said, his voice American, beseeching, his arms reaching straight and parallel across the rooftop, his hands palms-up like a beggar's. "Please, buttercup . . . ."

"Abbas? You and me, com'on, we leave here, right now."

"Don't break my heart," the blond man said, and got back into the car.

"Come home with me. Abbas."

"It is too late, Mister Owen." Abbas opened the passenger door and got in. "I leave an envelope under your door."

An eruption of darkness flooded Peter's heart.

"Abbas—wait! God damn you, wait!" He caught the door. "What about your mother, Abbas? What about her?"

"Go, go! She is there, she is always there!" Peter's hand slackened, Abbas slammed the door and the car pulled away.

Peter watched, the car slowed for a moment, as if looking to pull to the side, but the brake lights went off, and the car went on its way indifferently. Peter started to chase it. There was no traffic, and in a matter of a moment the car disappeared in the night.

Breathing heavily, he entered his apartment and banged his shutters closed. He lay on his bed. "Stupid! Stupid! Stupid!" He cried out loud. What kind of place was this? Why was he here? How had he given up a stable, productive life for one of shock after shock? Back in the States he had a job and friends. Here he was a drone, the bee who gathers no honey and has no sting, ineffectual and useless, swatted at from all sides. He drifted in and out of uneasy sleep, until light came. Then he heard voices in the lobby.

"... for her birthday."

"Aren't you the thoughtful son!"

"She has not been the same since the others died."

Through the peep hole in his door, everything as if in the wrong end of a telescope, Peter saw his concierge and Abbas. By a ring at the top, he held a cage, tightly fitted with a white cover.

"My son should be so thoughtful!"

On Monday he stayed in, eating what food remained in his cupboards and refrigerator, and making phone calls, local and long-distance. The movers would come after he was gone, to put everything in a crate, not very large. Payment and key would be with the concierge. A thousand francs appeared in a blank envelope under his door. Peter addressed it to Abbas, put on a stamp and, venturing out Tuesday morning, mailed it. But one thing left to do, he went to Smiley's Oasis. There he saw, built into the walls, strange new boxes glowing with faces—no, entire heads. Cooper, Bogart, Wayne, Monroe, others, looking trapped in cubes of marmalade. Beverly was behind the bar, loading the register with coins. As he approached she picked up an envelope and held it out.

"Smiley says he doesn't need you anymore."

"The man's a hologram himself." He felt like trying to explain something to her. Though what did it matter what she thought? In less than three hours his plane would take off. Hudson Stationery and Office Supplies awaited him. He was needed. And his departure from this place would be timely, for today was the day his residence card would be declared invalid, the revocation and expulsion process set in motion.

"What will you do now, Peter?"

"There's nothing left here for me."

"Around here, you gotta learn to be resourceful." She leaned toward him, over the bar. He caught a whiff of something, not the fruity scent of a Mlle. P., but a fleshier sweetness. She smiled, as she often did at him, vaguely, her mouth curled with a wry promise. Unlike other times, when her smile didn't catch, it caught now, and pulled gently. Was she to be believed? Slowly, his mind began to whir with the possibilities. From here on, in Paris, he would be illegal, an outlaw. He thought about his desk, his office, the safe smells of ink and paper. He moved down the bar, sidling up alongside the Indian.

"Beverly, let me have a whiskey. Me and Injun Joe here must cogitate on the future."

She brought over a bottle and two glasses.

"Smiley's best stuff," she said.

"Bev, suppose I needed a place to stay in a hurry?"

"Peter, I like you."

"We don't know anything about each other."

She poured him the expensive whiskey, and some for herself. "A woman should never let a man drink alone."

"Can I tell you an idea?"

"Sure, why not."

"Well, picture this. A store, a general store."

MY RED DESDEMONA

She was standing at the top of the stairway in La Gare, the restaurant where my troupe of players and I were about to celebrate the finale of *Hamlet*, our offering that August for Shakespeare in the Bois. La Gare was an old train station, and we were seated right where the tracks would have been, now covered over in fine oak planks. There were maybe a dozen of us, and I, as their director, was determined to lead us into a riotous night of food and drink. As hot a night as it was, the terrace to the rear of the station, down the tracks, was shut, because of an impending storm. They had left the doors open for the air, and you could smell the rain coming.

I don't know how many times I looked up at the red-haired woman, but I realized she was searching the platforms below, as a woman years earlier might, waiting for someone to arrive. I had not seen Sheila in at least twenty years, and at first I thought her appearance here in Paris, at the top of those stairs, an improbable coincidence. But the more I looked the more I realized it was her. La Gare was immense, cavernous, and to muffle the crowd noise thick sheets of white cloth hung from the girders. I made her out—some fifty feet away—between two of these sheets. She herself wore white, a summery, sleeveless dress, and all that whiteness made her orange long hair all the more shocking. She seemed anxious, like a woman waiting for her lover.

"Hey, Joe," someone asked me, "Cote du Rhone okay with dinner?"

"Sure." I rose and stared at her. She saw me. Then turned and walked away. "Excuse me," I said and rushed after her.

The last time I had seen Sheila was during a cold Upstate winter. We were in amateur theater, she acting, I directing, and we lived together in an attic atop an old Victorian house. The attic formed an A-frame, but the wood was unfinished and uninsolated, and between the joists the points of the nails holding down the shingling outside poked through old brown slats. There was one cast iron radiator that clanged and hissed. From the high roof beam I had hung a swing, and we were always warning visitors who wanted to try it out —often drunk or high—not to get a face or butt full of nails.

We were rehearsing *Othello* at the small Salt City Theater, a few blocks from our attic. Sheila played Desdemona. Her red hair and fair freckled skin made her unusual for the part, since in those looks one might expect a fiery Maureen O'Hara, which in turn made Sheila's subtle innocence seem all the more confounding. Our Othello was played by Ahmad, from the Bronx, a big black guy with a thunderous voice, ideal for the Moor in Shakespeare's eyes. The Bard was a bit blind when it came to geography, but he just had to have the ram tupping the ewe be black. That night we finished rehearsal about five-thirty. I had a dinner date with my father at six at his favorite steak house, to talk business, that being his business, heating and air-conditioning. I told Sheila I would meet her back at the attic, and walked off into a blustery February evening, thinking of how we would keep each other warm that night under our big down quilt. About halfway to the restaurant, maybe five blocks, I realized I had left my calculator in the director's office at the theater. I hurried back. The side door we used was locked, but I had my own key. Inside, I flipped on a light to a corridor leading to the back stage area. Before I reached the office, I heard voices. They came from the room where we stored props and what modest scenery the theater could afford. The voices were low, throaty, incoherent. I turned a corner into darkness and saw a flickering light escaping from a partly opened door. By now I knew what the human sounds meant. I slid quietly along the wall, until I reached the door. I looked in. There on a bed—the Desdemona death bed—lay Ahmad, supine and naked, his feet on the floor, his dark body barely visible. A candle had been lit, the most bitterly ironic candle in all of theater. "Put out the light, and then put out the light." Kneeling on the floor between Ahmad's legs was Sheila, her red hair and white skin impossibly radiant.

For years afterward I reflected on that moment, wishing I had been capable of a mighty Shakespearean rage. Instead, I slipped away silently, holding the fury and pain inside. Indeed, there was a greater influence at work that night, more massive than jealousy. My father. Who was not the kind of man you cancelled a business dinner with. I ran to the attic, pulled out a suitcase, and stuffed in everything of mine that I could. I thought about slashing the ropes of the swing, but the ladder I had used to hang it was hidden away in the cellar. Outside, the snow fell harder and pelted my face, flakes melting and mixing with tears. I caught my breath outside the restaurant. By the time I actually entered, I was forty minutes late and surprised to see my father calmly going over computer printouts and biding my tardiness. A Tuesday night, slow, my father had taken over a table meant for six. I approached. Looking up, he said, "I thought we agreed on six." He studied my face, read the obvious, then allowed himself to see my suitcase.

"She fucked you over, didn't she. I'm not surprised." I sat down, and he called Heather over, our usual waitress, and ordered big, like we had something to celebrate. Two sixteen-ounce Porterhouses, rare, a bottle of Dewar's and a small bucket of ice. "You'll get over it. A man can get over anything. "

He showed me plans, projections for his move south into the mid-Atlantic sea board. Spread sheets, numbers, graphs, my father's incessant tapping of his pen on the rim of his glass, bites of near raw meat—it helped my head. But the image, her red hair, was burnt into my chest.

"Where's your calculator?"

"I left it at the theater."

"Christ, almighty. Texas Instruments. Best they got. Make sure you collect it with the rest of your stuff. Tomorrow." He saw a split with

Sheila as a split with theater. Something he had no use for, unless it meant a building he could equip with a compressor, fans and air ducts. It was my mother's love of theater that had led to amusement for my sister but infection for me. She took us to local plays, and later, on train trips to New York City, Broadway, which lit up at night like a carnival, a million miles from our hometown. My father had no use for Sheila either, though he had met her only a few times, briefly. She was from Long Island, "Something hanging from an ass that thinks it wags the dog."

"We'll set you up outside DC, along the I-270. It'll be the biggest industrial corridor on the east coast in three years." He mopped away some bloody juice with a piece of bread. "You know, maybe the old suspicion is true. Redheads have no souls. So they try to suck the soul out of you. You finally see that, Joe?" He knocked back the last shot of scotch. "A man can get over anything."

A few years after that dinner, my mother died of a stroke. The day after the funeral a Salvation Army truck arrived and took away her clothes. I had to get back to DC to oversee the heat and air in a renovated theater on Fifteenth Street.

I thought less and less often of Sheila. But it amazed me how often the attic rose up in my dreams, as if it had pyramidal powers. Even two decades later I still dreamed of the attic, several times a year. The space was always shifting, different levels, different planes, like a stage set, all made in wood, and clearly within the A-frame. So often I would see the swing and at first Sheila would be seated in it, going back and forth. I think she was happy. But slowly she disappeared from the dreams. And I never dreamed of her at Desdemona's bed, with Ahmad, though often, early on, waking from my attic dream, my mind would collide with that memory, her white skin, the movement of her head, her red hair. But even that memory had seemed to have faded out by the time I saw Sheila standing at the top of the staircase, peering onto the platforms, in a station with a pitched ceiling, all of which seemed itself a variation on our attic.

I ran up the steps and into the bar. It had the same brick walls from years ago when it was the entrance to the station, no doubt with ticket counters, maps, a newsstand. Now it was chic, softly lit, with a zinc bar and tables where people met before going downstairs to eat. I saw Sheila standing by the door, looking out. The forecasted rain had arrived, in blinding sheets. She couldn't get out, and when she turned I was standing before her.

"Hello, Sheila."

She acted confused. "*Pardon*?" She said, the French way.

"Sheila, it's me. Joe."

"*Qui? Est-ce-que je vous connais*?

I could connect the dots and remember. The freckles on her forehead and cheeks, constellations I had once memorized, like a budding astronomer.

"Sheila, I know it's you."

Finally, she cleared her throat. "I didn't know if I would be able to talk to you." She looked young. So much so it scared me. "I followed you after the show. You still head for the nearest bar. I'd seen your name on a poster in a bookshop. *Hamlet*. Directed by Joe Dunn. " It had been at least half an hour before we left the theater, which meant she had to wait somewhere, and remember.

"Not exactly a billboard in Times Square or Piccadilly Circus."

"It was a good show, Joe."

"It was what it was."

La Gare was normally packed, but the weather was keeping customers away. I found a table, she followed, and we settled into low seats, padded, swiveling. A waitress swept in, clearing away debris, giving the surface a wipe and asking what we wanted. Sheila ordered chardonnay and I ordered Dewar's on the rocks. Lovers-meeting -after-twenty-years. What a strange scene to play, because it couldn't possibly matter, couldn't possibly change anything.

"So," I said, "where were we?"

She swiveled, and her legs cleared the table, one crossed over the other, her dress pulling back above the knee. "As I recall, you made a sudden exit. I don't think it was in the script."

"I'm sorry. Was that an exit left? Right? Or did I simply drop through the floor? I forget."

"I figured your father's strangle hold had finally gotten to you. He probably had you evacuated by private helicopter."

Had she no idea what I'd seen? I laughed. Should I be bent on making her acknowledge the truth? The waitress brought the drinks.

"Sheila, I saw you. Do you understand? I went back to the theater. I had forgotten something."

She looked at me strangely and sipped her wine. "Honestly, Joe. I don't know what you're thinking." Her voice rose a bit. "I only know I went back to our place and you were gone. Your things. Jesus, Joe, you even cut down the swing."

"I never cut down the swing."

"Yes, you did, Joe. You did."

I leaned into her face, spoke low, almost growling. "I never cut down the swing."

"Upon my knees, what does your speech import? I understand a fury in your words, but not the words."

"Sheila, don't play. Who cares now? Who cares? Why lie?"

"To whom, my Lord? With whom? How am I false?"

"Stop, Sheila."

"Alas, the heavy day! Why do you weep? Am I the motive of these tears, my lord?" She brushed a finger across each of my cheekbones.

"Bravo. Okay, okay. 'What? Not a whore?'"

"You left, Joe, and I never knew why. You hurt me."

"Is't possible?"

"I loved you, Joe. How many times did we tell each other?"

"I cry you mercy, then: I took you for that cunning whore of Venice."

She carefully set her glass down. "At least my father wasn't my pimp." In one breath, she admitted whorishness and accused me of the same.

"What does it matter, Sheila? We were together six months.

That's twenty-year-old blood under the bridge."

"I know. The stream moves on. Now you're married. French wife. Two kids. Boy and a girl. When you're the son—slash—partner at Dunn Air and Heat, you become Google worthy, not to mention head of European operations. You air-condition the Eiffel Tower yet?" She spoke a little too jovially, an old buddy proud of what I'd done in life.

"Did you also read my old man died? A year ago, almost to the day."

"They only said, suddenly." Yeah, I thought, no details. Not allowed. Which was good.

There was someone standing beside our table. A young couple, dripping wet, both in blue jeans, him with a Yankee baseball cap, her with hair done up in braids and beads.

"You're Joe Dunn, the director, aren't you?"

"I suppose I am."

The girl spoke up, gushing. "We just wanted to say how great the production was." They were Brits.

"Yes," the boy jumped in. "Excellent. We're in theater, too." Then they fluttered off and squeezed in at the bar.

I laughed. "See, the critics are raving."

"Like I always told you, the next Lee Strasbourg."

I looked at the kid with the Yankee cap. Ahmad had worn one of those, too, always bragging about his Bronx Bombers.

"So, aren't you going to ask why *I'm* in Paris?" Her green eyes bubbled up.

"A zillion visitors each year. Why not you?"

"My oldest daughter starts Beaux Arts in a few weeks. I'm moving her in, helping her set up house."

As good as I was in math, I couldn't imagine the addition. "That means at least two daughters. Well. Life does go on."

"I'd like to tell you all about it." She had worked her chair around and her knee touched mine. "I'm at the Hotel Saint Martin. Nice view on the canal. My daughter's staying with her future roommates. Come spend some time with me." She leaned across and kissed me on the lips. "You remember how good we were?"

"Apparently not good enough."

"Honestly, Joe, I don't know what you're thinking."

"I can't compartmentalize like you."

"Everybody compartmentalizes. I hear the French are good at it. A spouse here, a lover there." She rubbed her hand along my arm. "Aren't you the least bit curious? Can't you just imagine?" Imagination. Memory. They seemed to curl up into one. Her apricot smell—now as it had been then. The thick long hair. The opalescent skin held together by freckles. She rose, drew a breath, sighed. "Just imagine, Joe." She bent and kissed me again. "Hotel Saint Martin, three nights." She walked toward the door. Suddenly, she stopped and turned.

"You know something, Joe. I still have dreams of the attic, even now, after all these years. You ever dream of the attic?"

"Don't be daft."

"And Joe, you did cut down the swing." She sashayed out, into the night. The rain had stopped, and the streetlights made a glow she disappeared into.

I'd lied. More than once. When you are the director of Dunn Air and Heat, Europe, it's easy to compartmentalize. And when I'd been on the road for a week or two and returned home to my wife, kissing her hello, sweeping up the kids in hugs, I'm sure she compartmentalized as well. The swing? I honestly couldn't remember cutting it down. I had thought about it, that I remembered. Memory and imagination. For sure there are certain images I would always remember. My red haired Desdemona with her Othello, for one.

I looked at my watch. After midnight. One year to the day. There are also images you remember but have only imagined. I imagined my father in a strange arid land, driving a truck on his way to double check the finishing touches on the biggest job Dunn Air had ever known, when suddenly the truck blows up, and he doesn't get out. The day before, I had heard from him. He said the airport job at Basra was nearly done and we were up a quarter mill.

But he was sitting on four thousand window units. "It's 121 degrees today. They drive around in their cars to keep cool. Can't afford a lousy window unit for the house. Plus the electric shortage. The heat never stops. No wonder so many blow themselves up. Must be cooler in paradise. Hey, how bout it! –Dunn Air, Paradise Division. Virgins not included. I luv ya, Joe."

"Hey, Joe, Joe, where you been?" I turned to see our Horatio. "You up for this? You OK?" He put his hand on my shoulder, squeezed. "Maybe this wasn't a good idea."

"Ah, Horatio, there is a divinity that shapes our ends." I took a sip of Dewar's. "I'll be down in a minute."

"Sure, Joe. You take your time."

I thought about ordering another drink. They would understand my need to be alone. They might not understand my need to lose myself in her red hair, scan every inch of her skin. I left a twenty on the table and went to find a cab, fleeing one ghost in search of another.

AUBADE

Manda had the phone in her left hand as she stirred honey into her tea with her right.

"Yes, an American couple from Worcester, Mass. Republicans. I didn't think Massachusetts even had Republicans."

"You forget Romney?"

"He's practically a Democrat."

"Wait till he runs against Barack. Look, don't get into politics with the customers, Manda."

"I know, Mom. The wife's okay. Quiet. But if the husband makes one more crack about Obama. Thank God they're heading for the D-Day beaches today."

"Manda, I'm proud. The way you've run L'Aubade this past year. I know how prickly clients get. Say, how's Claudette?"

"Fine. Sends her love. Her brother Pierre was working in the garden yesterday. You wouldn't believe the spring we're having!" She sipped her tea, looked out the kitchen window. "The wisteria along the back wall is going crazy."

"That was Dad's favorite."

"Maybe it's putting on a show just for him."

"Oh, Manda, I wish you were here."

"Mom, Sonoma is literally the other side of the world from Normandy."

"I know, dear. Well . . ." Manda could hear her mother inhale. "So, Tuesday. Be thinking of us."

"At least Robbie's there."

"Yes, if your lazy brother will get out of bed. I'm tired of being his alarm clock."

"Dad's death took a lot out of him."

"It's been a year! His moping. How can he be so . . . listless!"

"I thought you said Uncle Max was putting him to work on the vines. Isn't now when they have to do that tricky pruning?"

"Actually, once Robbie *does* get up and going, he's all right. Max says he could be a natural."

"Well, there you go. Don't worry, Mom. Robbie'll be fine." She sipped her tea. "Oh, I didn't tell you about the Frenchman. Pascal something."

"What Frenchman?"

"He came in last evening. Said he didn't even realize L'Aubade was back in business."

"How old is he?"

"Thirtyish."

"Good looking?"

"Good enough. Very nice. From Provence. He must have spent time here. Asked if I'd get him the local paper."

"*Normatin*? You two might have a lot to talk about."

The daughter laughed.

"Manda, you've been going there for what, ten years now, and living there almost two?"

"I'll never be a local."

"You know you can always come home to Sonoma."

"Why do you always say that? I spent a grand total of, what, four weeks there?"

"Oh, my poor Manda, a woman without a country."

"Stop, mother."

"What do you think your father and I were for thirty years?"

"Yada, yada, yada." Manda watched as two birds raced and somersaulted over the garden. "Mom, one other thing. I've got a road test tomorrow. Number *four.*"

"That's great, honey. Just don't get all nerved up again. Hey, maybe you should get Monsieur Provence to give you a massage or something."

"Or something. If I thought it would help. If I have to take one more driving lesson with that moron from *auto-ecole*."

"You'll pass! I'm sure. Listen, hon, I gotta run. *Homeland's* coming on. Boy, that gets you going. You don't know *which* side that Brody character is on. It's one of Obama's favorite shows."

"You and Barack enjoy yourselves. I'll be thinking of you and Dad on Tuesday." She looked at the clock. "Yep . . . love you, too. Talk to you next weekend." In ten minutes, the bakery would open, the bread and croissants still hot. Then she'd stop at the café that sold papers and pick up the local for Monsieur Provence.

"More coffee? Juice?" Manda found herself squinting, the sunshine through the dining room window so bright.

"No, thank you, Miss," said the wife.

"I'll have some more of that bread, if you've got more of that jam," said the husband."What's that again?"

"Black currant. My neighbor, Claudette, makes it. From the bushes out back. That's the end of that jar. I could run next door."

"No, no. It's eight in the morning. Besides we have to head to the beaches."

"Here," said Manda, "I got the paper for you. Yesterday's. Not bad for the middle of Normandy."

The husband took the paper. "*International Herald Tribune*. That. Condensed version of the *New York Times*. Obama lovers."

"You know you love the weekend crossword, dear," the wife said.

"'Bout all it's good for." He glanced at the lower corner. Then opened the paper to the crossword. "*All's Well that Ends Well*. Wonder what that's about?"

"You'll figure it out, dear. My husband's a whiz on crosswords. You do the crossword, Miss?"

"I try."

Just then the Frenchman walked in. Manda seated him at a table apart from the Americans. They spoke French. Then she laid out bread, a croissant, butter and marmalade, an apple, a plain yogurt, and black coffee. He had grey eyes, friendly, close cut black hair and a closely shaved beard that looked like it would grow in before evening. A dark blue sweater draped his shoulders, the way a Frenchman wore it, like it was giving him a hug from behind.

"Seven letters," the husband was saying, "Division of biology."

"Come on, Joe, you get started, we'll never get out of here. We owe you anything, Miss?"

"No. All paid up."

"Let me have another hit of that java," said the husband. Manda carried the pot over and poured. "One for the road. By the way, Miss," he sipped loudly. "What part of the States are you from? Can't place that accent."

Manda got the look she always got when asked that question. She never followed her mother's advice – just tell them Sonoma.

"Actually, I've never lived in the United States."

"You're American?"

"Yes, I am."

"And you've never lived in the U.S.? Where were you born?"

"Tokyo."

"And you're American?"

"Do I look Japanese?"

The man turned to his wife. "Sounds like one of those Obama things."

Manda raised the pot of coffee a bit. "My parents were foreign service."

"An American who never lived in America. Damnedest thing I ever heard. So why live *here*, I mean it's a nice place to visit . . ."

The Frenchman started coughing. "*Mademoiselle*," he coughed. "*S'il vous plait, un verre d'eau. Vite!*"

There was no water in sight. She ran to the kitchen and came back with a bottle and a glass she set quickly before the Frenchman and poured.

He sipped. His coughing had stopped.

"Close call," he said in French. "I thought you were about to break the pot on his head."

She looked. The Americans were gone.

"Not all of us are that bad, believe me."

"Surely not." He smiled, patted his lips with the cloth napkin. She never used paper. "Mitosis."

"Pardon?"

"Division of biology." He spoke English now. "Mitosis." He rose from the table and stood at the windowed double door. "Would it be all right to go out and look around?"

"Of course."

He pulled open the door. "After you." She was quite tall, so no surprise he was slightly shorter.

The garden was surrounded by old Norman buildings from the 17th century, half-timbered. The entire building to the right leaned slightly to the left. Perfectly squared-off hedges, about waist high, divided the garden into sections. There were gravel pathways dividing rose bushes from hydrangeas, day lilies from irises, raspberries from black currants. In the center was a well with a roof. All the roofs were covered in undulating clay tiles splotched here and there with silvery-green lichen.

The Frenchman turned this way and that taking it all in. He looped around toward the well and paused at a statue of a woman kneeling, facing the well. She was naked and bent low, her back arching; her hair, as if it were wet, covered her face. Her buttocks rested on her heels. The Frenchman ran a hand along her spine, just visible in the limestone.

"My grandparents used to own L'Aubade—gave it its name. When I was a child I used to ride this like a pony. My grandparents scolded me until I learned not to do that anymore."

Manda drew closer. The Frenchman looked into the well, pulled a coin from his pocket and, without looking to see how much it was, dropped it in. Manda heard it splash. Once she had set a glass of wine on the edge, and a few moments later heard a splash, not realizing she had bumped her glass. The well was crisscrossed with four black bars, like a tic-tac-toe board. The three houses that formed a horseshoe around the garden once had shared the well. There were some smaller buildings further back where horses and wagons had been kept, though now they served as garages. In one was Manda's parents' Volvo, which she started occasionally, though never had driven.

The Frenchman quickly went over to a small shed.

"May I?" She gestured. He opened the old wooden door and disappeared inside. Years ago this had been an outhouse, a three-seater with walls for separation. A luxury in its day. Now it stored garden tools and the like. After a few minutes the Frenchman emerged.

"I don't believe it!" He held up his hand. In it was a pack of cigarettes. *Gaullois*. "I hid these there, oh, twelve, thirteen years ago. My parents hated my smoking."

She went to the shed and pulled our four cushions.

"Let me help you," said the Frenchman. He slipped the pack of cigarettes into his pants pocket. "These'll make a nice conversation piece later on."

"*Merci, Monsieur*."

"Please, call me Pascal. And I like speaking English when I have the chance."

"I'm Manda."

They walked toward the white-painted metal table and four chairs on the terrace behind the dining room and set the cushions in place.

"And you were born in Tokyo! How exotic. You know, I've never been outside of France."

"That's not so bad. Keep talking. I'm listening." She went and opened the double doors wide, stepped in and returned with a bowl of fruit and some napkins.

"My father was a mason – he worked a lot on that back wall – and we lived on the other side of town. But we'd often come here on Sundays. The men would play *boules*. At Easter we would roast a lamb on a spit over a cherry wood fire. I can still smell it."

Manda ate an apricot. "Help yourself."

"Thank you, but no."

"Are you a mason?" She looked at his hands. Well manicured.

"God no! I hate the smell of cement. My father used to come home reeking of it. On his hands, his clothes, in his hair. I adored my old man, but never wanted to smell like him. Listen, I've got a couple of hours before I must head off for a Sunday meal. Could we walk around town together? I'll be your tour guide. Fill you in on all the secrets of Livet-sur-Risle."

She pulled an apricot pit from her mouth and set it on a napkin. "I'm afraid I'm very busy today, Monsieur . . ."

"Pascal, please."

"Pascal. I have an exam tomorrow. I must study."

"Oh? In what?"

"It's a road test."

"How do you study for a road test?"

"I have some computer programs—"

"On a computer screen! Huh! You have to get out in a car, see the streets, the signs. Please, come, come. I have an idea."

She thought a moment. "You're probably right. Okay."

They walked out the driveway to the street. At one time, it was lined on both sides with buildings very like the inn. But most had been destroyed by British artillery during the war. Now there were many modern apartment buildings five or six stories high. She followed Pascal until he pushed a button on a key and a car *bipped* and flashed its lights. It was a medium-sized Peugeot, not much different from the one she drove at *auto-ecole*. At the car, he handed her the key.

"You drive."

"I can't do that."

"I'm sure you're a fine driver."

"I mean, that's illegal."

"It's Sunday. Not much traffic yet. It'll be fine."

"What if we get pulled over?"

"Do not worry. I have a cousin. He's an obnoxious twit. The French equivalent of your American friend. But he owes me. And he happens to be the *Préfet* for the Department."

"I really don't think so."

"Everything will be fine. Drive, baby, drive." He held the door open.

Finally, she got into the seat and belted up, adjusted the mirror, and pushed the seat back a notch. The side mirrors seemed fine. And off they drove.

Pascal had a soft, patient voice. He was like a conductor. "Slow. Downshift, second. Yield, right, clear. Speed up, shift, third, speed limit fifty. Traffic circle, downshift, now, second, slow, yield left, looking, looking, clear. Stop ahead, downshift, second and stop. Full stop . . ."

So it went for an hour. All around town. Over streets and past signs and signals she had observed dozens of time, but never really felt. Now she and Pascal were at the edge of town where the forest started.

"Go straight. You need some speed. Haven't hit fifth yet. Accelerate. Forty, third, faster, shift, sixty, fourth, good, and yes, shift, seventy, fifth. Hold at eighty. About a kilometer ahead there's a right turn, take it in second."

The sunshine filtered through the trees. She had never felt so good behind the wheel.

"OK, slow down, shift, fourth, good, signal, right, downshift, third, good, downshift second, make turn . . . perfect. Speed up, shift, third, hold at sixty--"

Suddenly a wild boar crashed through the brush at the road's edge. She slammed on the brakes, missing it by two meters. It was followed by three long-legged hounds. Then a few seconds later, two men on horses.

"Bastards!" Pascal shouted, "They are way out of season!" His eyes were wide, his face flush. He pressed a button and his window hummed down. "You see. They have no guns. They just like to terrify the boar, give the dogs a thrill."

They sat there stalled on the road. It was a narrow road. She lowered her own window. The air felt good, smelled fresh. But she felt unnerved.

"Do you want to drive?"

“Me!” He laughed. “You are a much better driver than I am!”

Feeling extremely confident, she kept herself busy the entire afternoon and avoided thinking too much. Above the old wooden door that led into a staircase, a box was attached to the wall, from around 1900. It had a glass door and a peaked roof covered by two pieces of slate. Inside was a ceramic statue of a Madonna and Child, which Manda was able to retrieve using a ladder. She washed mother and son in the kitchen sink and, after cleaning the glass with window spray and paper towels and wiping away cobwebs, she returned them to their lookout. In a pantry off the kitchen she found some dahlia tubers stored in plastic bags full of dry straw, left there by Pierre last November. From the shed, over several trips, she carried large clay pots and bags of soil. Each trip, she looked around the shed trying to figure out where a young Pascal had hidden his smokes. There was no place obvious, but of course that's what a hiding place was.

Before starting the potting, while her hands were still clean, she remembered to get the sheer curtains from the washer and hung them on the clothesline in the sun. She laid a sheet of plastic over the white table and started potting, enjoying the smell of soil. She planted one dahlia per pot. She had just finished burying the last knobby root when Claudette came out. Claudette was 73 but strong and wiry. People called her Madame, though in fact she had never married. She attended church and when she saw the freshly bathed Mother and Child, she smiled. She helped Manda position the pots around the edges of the terrace, advising not to water until shoots started showing.

“A man checked in last night,” said Manda. “His name is Pascal. Says his grandparents used to own L'Aubade.”

“Oh, Pascal! Always so sweet. Like his grandparents. But he hasn't come to see me!”

Manda didn't mention the driving lesson but simply said Pascal had to go off to some family meal.

"His family! Most of them are complainers and hypocrites. And that cousin – totally corrupt. Everyone knows it. *La loi, c'est moi*!"

Claudette excused herself, saying she had to go bake, something for a charity sale. "But have Pascal come see me. Tell him I'm waiting."

Manda went to the kitchen to prepare a salad for dinner which she could set aside until she got hungry. She pitted black olives, cubed feta and made honey-mustard dressing. She had a bag of spinach leaves, pre-washed, *prêt-a-consumer*. Normally she would use half a bag, but while she had been pitting and cubing she kept thinking she would make enough for two and now emptied the whole bag into a bowl. She had a nice *pain-cereale* she could slice up.

Admittedly, Pascal had been in the back of her mind all afternoon. His voice mostly. So different from instructor Mme. Guichet's. She had never really instructed, only growled when Manda made mistakes. Claudette's "sweet" comment about Pascal got her thinking more.

She had had three lovers in her life, never a French lover. Here in Livet-sur-Risle, all the local men were shorter than her, nice enough to talk with as they peered up at her but not inclined to attempt anything more. There was a Dutchman who owned a cottage overlooking a weir just up river from the town. Manda had Dutch roots on her father's side, which probably gave her her height and the blond highlights in her brown hair in summertime, the latter less and less so the older she got. The Dutchman came here on long weekends and holidays and Manda had met him at a café on market day. Pleasant, funny, he could speak French or English. More than a few times, they made love at the cottage, the window open to the sound of the rushing water. Back in Paris, there had been the Canadian from Montreal. He was big, strong. Probably ate hockey pucks for breakfast, she'd told her mother. He spoke that funny French that always brought a smile to her face, which he mistook for an invitation. She didn't mind. Her fondest memory was Juan Miguel from the International School in Madrid when, at the relatively late age—these days—of eighteen, she had decided she could no longer stand her virginity. Despite the accounts she'd heard of how awkward and clumsy the first time could be, her first time with Juan Miguel was anything but. In fact, nothing had ever topped the three times they made love. Her family were tennis fanatics and whenever she watched Rafael Nadal, she thought of him. Of her three lovers, only Juan Miguel was shorter than her. Age twenty-seven, three lovers. She felt under accomplished. Her mother's comment "a massage or something" made her wonder. Sure, something to relax her, settle her nerves, but in fact she had no nerves, hadn't even thought about tomorrow's test.

She went upstairs to an office that overlooked the garden. She had to do a mass e-mailing of invitations. She had offered L'Aubade for the July 4th picnic that the Normandy Democrats Abroad held each year. There were many members, though she knew only about 30, plus spouses, ever showed. It was always on the Saturday closest to the 4th. Nearly all the Democrats were married to a French spouse. The Americans came from places as varied as Idaho, Louisiana, Maine, Oregon, Texas, North Dakota. Manda could tell you the capitals of every one. Getting around the "where-are-you-from?" question was simple. "I'm registered in Sonoma, California." No lie, as her parents' house there was her legal US address. The house her parents had bought 30 years ago, then rented for nearly nothing to her mother's sister and her husband who tended the small but profit-turning vineyard.

Manda had been to several Normandy Democrats meetings, where people seemed to get worked up over nothing. As if they were compensating for being ex-pats. Manda had realized long ago, when you were an American abroad, there were only two things you could do for your country, pay your taxes and send in your absentee ballot.

She had just finished her mass mailing and was about to go have her salad when she saw Pascal and Claudette walking in the garden. He had his arm around her shoulder. They walked slowly, all the way to the back wall, and smelled the wisteria. Claudette broke off a cluster and they walked to the well where Claudette dropped the flowers in. They paused again at the statue. Manda would have to ask Pascal what that was all about, then thought that might be too impolite.

After she finished her salad, she sat at the dining room table doing a crossword puzzle, the French one. Sometime after seven, Pascal walked in.

"Hi. Would you like some salad? A glass of wine? Something?"

"No, no, thank you," he said, patting his stomach. He looked tired. "I've been eating all day. Claudette just plied me with her *quiche au saumon*."

"She's a fantastic cook."

He had something in his hand which he now laid on the table. "Congratulations, you passed."

She knew what it was. The form for the driving test. It listed categories and then had two words that could be circled, either "*Favorable*" or "*Insufficent*." The first was circled.

"My cousin was at our little family reunion. He carries a briefcase wherever he goes. Need a building permit? A hunting license? A driver's license?"

"And what will you expect from me in return?"

"Ha! My cousin asked me the same question." He drew close to her. "You know what I want?" It was a question, not a statement.

"What?"

"To have a *digestif*, a calvados, in the salon."

"Yes, sure. But I think we're out of *calva*, only have cognac."

"I think I know where there might be a bottle."

The salon was one floor up. The best views from the inn, of course, were over the garden, on that trip back in time. The windows of the salon faced the street, the modern buildings and a parking lot. But when in the salon, you didn't bother with the windows. The room was the view. It stretched the length of the house, incredible oak beams above, polished clay tiles on the floor. The walls were covered in linen with floral patterns. At one end was an upright piano. At the other, a grand fireplace. Scattered in between were leather chairs and carpets, and a coffee table with a marble top before a sofa that faced the fireplace. There was a bar off to one side.

Manda rummaged around, found two brandy glasses. "Sorry, only Remy Martin."

Pascal walked to the end of the room where the piano was. At the wall, he fiddled with something, then easily slid a panel aside and took out a bottle of calvados.

"My, oh my," Manda said, more amused than surprised. In a four-hundred-year-old house, who knew how many caches there were?

He brought the bottle over and set it on the coffee table next to the glasses. It was a third full.

"Before WWII, when the Germans were closing in on Livet-sur-Risle, my grandfather buried all his calvados in the space between the garages. About 30 bottles. After the war, he dug them up and slowly, sip by sip, went through every bottle. This is the last one. He had to start hiding it from Grandmamma who scolded him more and more the older they got." He looked at the fireplace, so tall he could probably stand in it. "You know what? We need a fire." There was wood set up. That's the way Manda's father had always done it, and her mother afterward. Once a fire had died out, and the ashes were shoveled away, crumpled paper, kindling and wood were set in place. Guests became impatient and didn't like to wait for you to build a fire. Manda reached in a basket near the fireplace and pulled out a plastic bottle of *allume-feu*. She squirted a shot across the paper.

Pascal poured the *calva*, then sat at one end of the sofa.

"Do the honors?" Manda asked him, holding out the match box.

"No. No. You're the driver."

She struck a match and bent to light the fire. It caught slowly, spread smoothly. She walked to the windows and drew the drapes, closing out the last of the day's light.

She sat on the sofa, reached over and took a glass, handing it to him. Then took a glass for herself.

"*Santé*," she said.

"*Santé*." They clicked glasses. A few minutes of silence passed. Then Manda began to tell Pascal how the wild boar that morning reminded her of the poachers in South Africa.

"South Africa!" Pascal gave his head a quick shake. She told how the family lived in a guarded compound with high walls, barbed wire and cameras. Quite luxurious and lush. "A paradise prison," she said. She was chauffeured to a school no South Africans attended. On weekends, they would venture out, her father at the wheel of a Land Rover. One Sunday they were headed for Sun City, "a Disneyland for adults." Her father, who loved adventure, set off on a side road. The land was practically desert. They bounced along, then spotted a mound. When they got close, they realized it was a rhino carcass. The father parked, telling them to stay in the Rover. When he came back, he said they had sawed his tusk off. They didn't bother with Sun City.

She told Pascal about surfing on Bondi Beach. Doing museums and shopping in Madrid when she was eighteen. Skiing at Chamonix not far from their house outside Geneva. She talked of London, Paris, where she'd gotten a Masters from Sciences-Po.

"Stop, Manda! I'm out of breath! Phineas Fogg around the world in twenty minutes!"

"At least he had a place to return to. Like you. Family. Roots."

"Roots! Ha! Consider yourself liberated. My father got so sick of the nonsense, he moved us all south. Blamed the Normandy weather."

"This place is about as close to a home as we've had. About ten years ago, my parents discovered L'Aubade and fell in love with it. It was run by a Monsieur Arnault and his wife. We came here at least twice a year. Then, almost two years ago, when the Arnaults could no longer make a go of it and were deep in debt, my parents bought it. I helped them run a B&B for about a year. Then my father died suddenly. Heart attack."

"I'm sorry."

"We buried him in Sonoma, not two kilometers from the high school where he and my mother had gone to their senior prom."

"So, they went full circle. That is magic."

"For them maybe. Standing over his grave, I just kept thinking how badly I wanted to be back here in Livet. Like I say, the closest thing to a home we ever had."

"You know, I remember the Arnaults. Monsieur was too ambitious. Too fancy, shooting for the stars. Michelin stars."

"I remember the changes in the menu. And the prices."

"He almost got his star, too, and when he didn't, he fell into a pit. Depression. Chefs have committed suicide over those bloody stars."

Pascal suddenly popped up and walked quickly across the room. "You play piano?"

She rose and walked toward him. "I had a very isolated childhood. My best friends were piano teachers. They became a kind of constant." She sat on the bench. "So, I can finesse Beethoven." She played *Fur Elise*. "Or Chopin." She coaxed a few bars from *Polonaise Fantasie*. "I can tinkle out Cole Porter." Now she played *Begin the Beguine*. "And sometimes I just like to bang out some Jerry Lee Lewis."

"Now you're talkin'! Slide over!"

The two of them started banging away on the keys till finally they cried in unison—"Goodness! Gracious! Great balls of fire!"

They looked at each other again and this time they kissed. Very gently. After a moment, Pascal pulled his head away. "This really is not a good idea at the moment. I want you to go to bed. And *sleep*. You need your energy for tomorrow."

"I thought you said I passed." She stroked his face, the beard had indeed returned.

"Yes, you did. You have the paper, and it's official. But certainly you realize official isn't always true."

When she went downstairs at 8am Pascal was in the dining

room. He had laid out a spread. Fruit, yogurt, juice, butter, jam, croissants and bread, still warm.

"This is a first," Manda said.

"Tea, right?"

"Please." He poured.

"Honey?"

"Please." She stirred in a spoonful, amazed he had even noticed the day before.

"Just think of what kind of shape you'd be in this morning, after all that incredible bouncing-off-the-walls sex we nearly had last night."

"Hmmm." She buttered a piece of croissant and applied a bit of jam.

"You're not a mason, so tell me. What do you do?"

"I'm a farmer."

"Sorry, but you don't look like a farmer."

"I own a solar farm. I harvest sunlight. Make electricity."

"Really?"

"Only a few hectares so far. Supply about a hundred-and-fifty homes."

"That's fantastic. Not only a great lover, but a man of sustainable energy."

Just after 8:30 they left the house. Pascal said he wanted to be with her, wait at the curbside till she got back. On the way out the door, she happened to glance at the guest book. There was an entry from yesterday. "*To our wonderful, sweet and worldly hostess, best of luck. I envy you. By the way, I voted for Obama. Don't tell my husband.*"

She pulled up in front of the test center. Pascal was waiting. The *examiner* looked at her. This was the same one she had had the first time around. *Examiner*—sounded like something from the Inquisition. He smiled. Laughed. Scribbled a few last things on the form attached to his clipboard.

"Normally, we must mail the results. Safer that way, we

painfully discovered. Time was, some people, upon learning they had failed, committed serious harm upon the examiner." Now he made one last notation, circling *Favorable*. "Congratulations. You can use that as a license till the permanent one arrives by post. Safe driving."

She opened the door and ran to Pascal waving the paper. They kissed and walked back to the house. "I have to get going," he said. "Long drive ahead."

"Oh? Could we do one more number on the piano? For old times' sake?"

When they got to the top of the stairs, they didn't go into the salon but turned and went into the bedroom.

They stood naked at the window looking through the clean sheer curtains out onto the garden. They didn't speak for a long time but caressed each others' shoulders as they looked.

"What happened at the well?" Manda finally asked.

"I hesitate to tell you."

"Go ahead. I'm a big girl."

"At the end of the war, after Livet had been liberated, a lunatic circus broke out. I'm sure you are aware of the things that went on. Several days into this frenzy, Claudette, who was eight, and her brother Pierre who was five, were in an upstairs room, when they heard a commotion. They went to a window. That one there, over their kitchen door. All at once, they saw a woman run naked into the courtyard, for that's all it was then, not a garden. The woman was Minette, their aunt. Their mother's younger sister. Minette screamed and pounded on the door. But their mother had bolted it. Now a gang of men came racing in. One man had a mechanical shaver he could operate in one hand by squeezing, back and forth, back and forth, rapidly. My grandfather ran out. He knew about Minette. She had showed up here several times with German soldiers—*les boches*—and stayed in a room there." Now he pointed to the right. To the building where the guests of L'Aubade slept. "When a soldier showed up, you didn't turn him away. Now, my grandfather had his arm around Minette, but before he could get her to the door to the stairwell below, the men rushed them and overpowered my grandfather – though he was twenty-six and strong. Minette slipped away and the pack followed, moved in, closer and closer. She backed up. Further and further. When she got to the well, she stopped. As they drew closer, she sat on the well, leaned back her head, pushed with her feet and vanished."

Manda gasped.

"Claudette and Pierre saw everything."

Manda rubbed Pascal's back, but it was more to comfort herself.

"The man leading the charge was my grandfather's own brother. So, sister against sister. Brother against brother. Some liberation."

The two stood in silence a long time. Manda felt the afterglow from love-making turning into a sickly emptiness.

"I really am sorry I told you this," Pascal finally said. "I have ruined your day, if not more."

"No, no, no. Like I said, I'm a big girl. Horrid things happen." Even in your own back yard, she thought. "Oh, I have something for you!" She rushed, naked, from the room and returned in a moment with a bottle of wine. "Take this. It is from the family vineyard in Sonoma."

Pascal took the bottle. "*Rougemont*. I will save it until you come visit. Very soon I hope."

Wanting to get there before it closed for lunch, she hurried over to the small office that handled their car insurance. Her mother had never let it lapse and to add Manda cost eighty-four Euros, which she paid on the spot.

She walked down the gravel driveway toward the garages. She glanced at the ground where the calvados had been hidden. Above that, in the eaves, was a nest and she could hear the sound of baby birds. Then on the ground she saw one who had fallen out. She went and got a ladder and passing the well, going, coming, and going, she felt a chill air rise out of it. She wondered how Claudette and Pierre did it. In fact, she now realized, he had built a memorial to Minette. She had asked Claudette once about the origins of the statue and she had responded it was just something her brother had found at a *foire-à-tout*.

She drove and drove aimlessly around the countryside. To add to her confusion of feelings, there was the Volvo's automatic transmission. She had only ever driven a stick as the French had insisted, and now her left foot kept seeking a clutch that didn't exist and she had to force her right hand to resist the urge to shift. Very comic by comparison. At one point she stopped for gas, filling a tank for the first time in her life. She bought some tuna sandwiches and a bottle of orange juice which she downed slowly at a roadside picnic area. Into the GPS she typed *Vinsobres*, the town in Provence where Pascal lived. The calculations came up. In eight hours and forty-two minutes she could be with him. But she had obligations here, tomorrow.

She parked the car in the garage just after dusk and walked to the back door avoiding any looks toward the well or the statue. Approaching the door, she glanced up at the Madonna and Child, their small beatific smiles forever indifferent.

Finding it nearly impossible to fall asleep that night she stood for a while at the window looking out on the garden. The well was illuminated by a spotlight on the ground that Pierre had rigged up. It was on a timer and she watched it suddenly turn off at 10:30. She cracked the window and went back to bed, leaving on a low-wattage lamp. She could make out artifacts she had collected around the world – African masks, a kimono, Spanish ceramics – objects that had absolutely no meaning, no connection to anything that mattered. She heard an owl.

She thought of her brother Robbie. How for a year, while she was setting up house with her parents at L'Aubade, Robbie was at university in Rotterdam getting most of his higher education out of a bong. How the day after Dad died and Mom was out making arrangements for the family to escort him back to Sonoma, she and Robbie were alone in the garden and he broke down, blubbering and clutching his gut. He and Dad had gone to play tennis, he said. And Robbie kept hitting the ball deep to corners, back and forth, pushing his father, because his father was pushing him, screaming how he had no direction, no ambition, screaming how he had already dropped out of three universities, as many as he himself had degrees from. "Then I come in and do a little volley. The ball catches the net cord, Mand, rolls along it, seems to hang forever. Dad and I both run to the net, then the ball finally drops, in my favor. Dad has his racket raised. God, the disgust in his eyes. 'You are squandering your mind!' he screams. Then he tucks the racket under his arm and jogs away." Robbie went off to stew in a bar. When he got back to L'Aubade, the ambulance was taking Dad away, but by then it was too late. "I literally – literally – broke Dad's heart."

Manda knew how her father pushed, had always pushed. "I don't think that's so, Robbie. But you listen to me. Do not tell any of this to Mom. Right now she thinks Dad was a fifty-eight-year-old who pushed himself like he was still eighteen. Don't forget, they met when they were eighteen. Let her remember him that way. Do you understand me?"

She looked again at things hanging on the walls. Felt them swirling around, swirling into a vortex, going out the window and being sucked into the well. She hugged the pillow next to her and could smell Pascal. She closed her eyes and thought of Provence, one of the few parts of France she'd not seen, though from descriptions and what people said maybe the most beautiful. In her mind, she saw fields of lavender and vines and olive trees strangely being supplanted by rows and rows of glinting solar panels.

On the terrace she had set up her father's favorite lounge chair. She had a basket full of wisteria clipped from the back wall. When passing by the well, she felt something like she felt all those times walking in the American Cemetery near Omaha Beach. A solemn sense of sadness. But the cemetery was different because there she also felt something singularly uplifting she didn't feel here.

She put two opened bottles of ice cold beer on the table between the lounge chair and a wicker chair. She laid the flowers in her father's chair, sat in the wicker, picked up a beer and *clinked* the other.

"*Santé*, Dad." She felt her eyes going moist like the sides of her bottle.

Suddenly Claudette was there. "I'm sorry. I'm not interfering?"

"No, no."

"I did remember." She walked over and stood looking up at the Madonna and Child. Then her head bowed and her lips moved silently. When she finished she turned and smiled at Manda.

"Claudette, if I wanted to go away for a while, maybe a week, could you and Pierre look after things?"

"Of course, dear."

"I mean, guests are booked. Two tonight till Thursday and three on Friday for the weekend."

"Don't you worry! Put a note on your door telling them to knock on ours. I know this is a hard time for you."

"You have no idea." She looked over at the Volvo which she had pulled out of the garage into the sunshine, opening the four doors to air it out. In the trunk was a suitcase to unpack at Pascal's. She took a sip of beer, then noticed that her father's was untouched. Never would be.

"Listen, Claudette. Never mind I asked."

"Whatever you wish, dear. I must go prepare lunch. Will you join us?"

"No, thanks. I have a lot to do."

There were the ads that had been sitting in a desk drawer for months: Piano lessons available. She would hang them in the library, the small music academy, and the music shop. Then she would come back and prepare some dishes to welcome the guests, salmon on blinis with dabs of dill sauce, tapenade on small squares of toasts. She would fill the guests in on places to visit: churches, abbeys, the best route to see thatched-roofed houses, or the cliffs along the Channel. Where to eat the tastiest oysters or *Veau Normand.* And the guests would stroll in the garden. Hers. They would sniff at flowers, marvel at the buildings, follow the lines of old beams, hear the birdsong—all it of joining in a collaboration of unassailable beauty. And if they asked about the statue, she would explain it was just some curiosity her neighbor had picked up at a rummage sale.

HOW IT WORKS

Going to check for mail on a bright October morning, I pause a moment outside our house in Normandy. Across the road, down behind a thatch-roofed house belonging to our dear friend Jacques, flows the Seine, right to left, toward the English Channel. The Seine is an estuary here, and at this moment the tide is rushing in, making the river run backward. Riding the tide inland toward Rouen is a container ship, stacked with metal boxes full of who knows what commitments. It's so massive I can see its top layer glide over Jacques' rooftop. A typical Norman thatch, his roof is capped with a row of plants, mostly irises, rooted in tightly packed clay that seems never to erode. Though we didn't think to imagine it when my wife and I bought this place, also in October years ago, we watched next spring as the irises blazed purple, making the passing of a container ship seem all the more surreal.

From the mailbox near the side of the road, I retrieve a letter I've been expecting and go seat myself in a chair on our front terrace. I open the envelope and remove the results of a blood test I recently had in Paris. My eyes flit quickly down a column listing a small sample of my blood's make up.

Bingo. Amylase. 329. I'm not alarmed, but disappointed. Next to my 329 are numbers indicating healthy levels of amylase. 30-110. At very best, I'm still three times over that.

On a Thursday six weeks ago in Paris, the pain began. Abdominal at first, it spread after two days to my back and chest. My nights were feverish and sweaty, and I vomited anything I ate or drank. My wife was on a work trip in Stockholm and our fourteen-year-old son told me I didn't look well. Sunday morning I arranged for him to stay with friends, left a note for my wife due home that evening, and checked into the American Hospital of Paris. I knew what the pain meant, for I had suffered two bouts of acute pancreatitis before, both times admitting myself to a hospital in Normandy.

By comparison, the American Hospital was a luxury hotel. Single room (I don't think they have doubles), tasteful décor, and doctors who understand English. In Normandy, I had found translating my pain and symptoms into French somehow once removed from the truth, but here at the American Hospital I was practically loquacious and cheery. In no time, they had me in a frock, riding on a gurney, an IV inserted, feeding me crystal clear nourishment I couldn't vomit and —more importantly—painkillers. They took X-rays, did a CAT scan, inserting me prone and feet first through a whirring metal donut as a hot, strangely enticing, liquid coursed through my body. Back in my room, I was excited to catch Andre Agassi on TV, playing in the last tennis match he would ever win, since he would lose two days later in his career's finale.

Our good friend Barb stopped by. She's a doctor at the hospital, working the emergency room. Her youngest son is a schoolmate of our son, her husband one of my best buddies. Though she was aware of my pancreatic history, we chatted like two Americans bumping into each other at a Paris café. Before leaving she gave me a handful of pages, instructing more as a doctor than a chum,"Read this carefully."

Indeed I did. An article from MayoClinic.com on pancreatitis. How it works. The pancreas secretes digestive enzymes and also insulin. Pancreatitis occurs when an overabundance of these enzymes —amylase for one—backs up into the organ itself and begins to digest it. Repeated attacks—I was in the throes of my third in four years—can cause irreparable damage. MayoClinic.com speaks of serious, life-threatening complications: infection, pseudocysts, abscesses, shock, kidney, lung or heart failure, and—if one survives those—diabetes and pancreatic cancer. The causes of pancreatitis can stem from environment, genes or just plain gluttony, but the cause that leaped out at me was "excessive alcohol intake." Of course I had been warned of this before, from doctors at the hospital in Normandy and from my GP in Paris.

In English from the Mayo Clinic "pancreatitis" sounded closer to home. Still, two readings of the article had the ring of a news bulletin issued by the likes of Monty Python. Picture a young John Cleese. "In the Pancreatic War today, angered Amylase, driven into battle once too often by their power-intoxicated leader, rebelled and devoured him." Slapstick news right there in my gut.

Now, sitting on our front terrace with blood results in hand, I am faced with the prospect of a battle longer than I want to admit. I've not sipped a drink in six weeks, but the amylase still rebels. In the hospital my enzyme level had registered over 900. If 100 is normal, 329 has to seem encouraging, and patience a virtue. An English friend up the road who has great tufts of gray hair sprouting from his nostrils is a doctor specializing in acupuncture. He told me I should quit drinking for a year and let my pancreas heal. If the inflammation scars the pancreas, it'll no longer produce digestive enzymes. You'll have to take about eight enzyme tablets with every meal. And the pain—you ain't felt nothing yet. Probably get hooked on high octane pain pills. Any alcohol whatsoever will be out of the question. We two have knocked down plenty of wine together, so his advice was tough, he knew. A few years back, he had easily cured my stubborn sciatica with one serving of his magic needles. The jury, he said, was still out on treating pancreatitis with acupuncture and couldn't recommend it.

I rise and face our house.

It is 225 years old. My wife and I bought it in 1990. Having lived five years in a Paris apartment, we sought a weekend refuge, a *residence secondaire*. More the size and feel of a large cottage, the house is typically mid-to-lower class Norman, one story plus attic—*grenier*, half-timbered. In between the columns a mesh of branches pried into place holds a blend of mud and straw, finished off by a smooth mortar-like mix. The roof is slate, though originally it would have been thatch. There is a foundation of limestone and flint stone, two feet high. The house is narrow and long, probably the lasting influence of early Viking – Norsemen – settlers, who were also boat builders.

Our house. This boat. This vessel. I have poured my soul into it. I was born in Buffalo, NY, and my upbringing had informed me early of do-it-yourself necessity. For various reasons I had always worked on various houses, though never one of my own, and everything I'd ever learned about how an abode worked seemed prelude to a passion I instantly felt when I first saw this Norman fixer-upper. I am now 55 years old, and the notion of having a vessel that contains my soul is intriguing. For fifteen years I have sawed, sanded, drilled, plumbed, wired, tiled, roofed, floored, cemented, mortared, spackled, painted and varnished. Our house is built into a gradual slope that pays homage to the Seine. I have pushed the earth behind us back. One weekend two buddies—an Austrian and an Australian my wife worked with—and I shoveled out a ton of dirt. I have spent hours and hours rummaging through used-lumber yards, measuring tape in hand, seeking just the right oak beam. My two favorite beams, running five meters lengthwise in the dining room I've added, originate from an old hospital in Rouen. It took me three days to strip them of a dozen coats of oil paint. It's surprising deposits of leaden dust never showed up in my CAT scan.

My work at first was eyed suspiciously by the neighbors, who probably feared I'd slap on aluminum siding. "These Americans, they think they can go anywhere and do anything." But I have stayed true to the Norman half-timbered style, for it was love at first sight. I hanker for the sight, smell and feel of wood. Ironically, there was very little visible wood when we bought the house. Everything inside had been plastered over during a strange trend in the 20's and 30's that valued concealing a Norman house's skeletal wood. Probing with a mere pen knife, I discovered that a good deal of the lower beams along the front of the house, the north side that gets sun only in summer, had succumbed to rising damp, and rotted away. As needed, someone had gouged out the rot and whacked in cement, then plastered over everything and painted on chocolate stripes where the beams would be. I stripped it all back, my nostrils full of the odor of damp and rot. I found more rot. Cozy dens full of sleepy woodlice. I spliced in necessary sections of oak and replaced a foundation of rubble and clay with waterproofing, clean cut stone and mortar.

When I wasn't in Paris—teaching or editing or raising our son—I was in Normandy. Sometimes, when I couldn't write in Paris, I comforted myself here, where it was easier to knock out a wall than a short story.

Knocking out much of the wall space on the house's south side, I always cleaned up and left intact any original beams that didn't absolutely need replacing. I have added a dining room and, carving into the slope, a two-story addition with a recreation room and bathroom downstairs, and an office and full bath upstairs. Between the dining room and the rec room is a small bar—a slab of recycled oak and barstools from IKEA. Since these additions face south, I have installed as much glass as possible to let in the sunlight that rolls down our slope. It took eight of us (mostly locals who by then had learned to trust me) one sunny Saturday to raise the beams for the two-story bit. Sometimes, when I gaze on, even run my fingers over, our house's original beams and joint work, I can imagine, actually watch in my mind, a group of Normans years ago raising beams. My village friends and I had done a modern impression, using Skil, Bosch, and Black-and-Decker power tools. *Sans electricité*, our predecessors, Amish-like, had sawed and drilled by hand, pegging together tenon-and-mortise joints. We had used steel angles and bolts, later made invisible once I had filled in the walls. I sometimes think the long deceased Normans watch me the way I have watched them. "Hey, Pierre," one shouts. "Come look what the American is concocting now!" I sincerely hope they appreciate my construction as I theirs.

My wife and I have convinced our son never to sell the house. He promises he won't, whatever a fourteen-year-old's promise is worth. (I promise more homework, less computer, a clean room, shampooed hair). In any case, I can say this: our son has an aptitude for this house. His understanding of how it works is turning into affection. We save money for his college education, but if he becomes a plumber, mason, carpenter, we will be proud. His attentive eye and do-it-yourself dexterity reassure me. Maybe he senses, when I explain electricity or plumbing to him, I am purposely imparting the know-how he'll need to maintain this place when I am no longer around.

When I am no longer around. How my soul used to rage against the thought. Rage against the dying light—though I was only twenty. In those days of "Nietzsche is peachy," I was the existential hippie, full of Sartre's *Nausée* and Kierkegaard's *Fear and Trembling* . As much as the angst hurt, it was cool. Many years later, the novelist Jane Smiley would put a new name to it, "The Age of Grief," though her version of it attacks people in their 30's. She wonderfully evokes the image of Christ in Gethsemane, sweating blood and begging heaven, "Lord, if it be thy will, let this cup be lifted." But it cannot be lifted, and the cup comes round for each of us to drink from. My own age of grief smoldered a long time, but in the last few years it has subsided. My only *nausée* these days comes from pancreatitis. Maybe I simply seek a resignation with dignity. Maybe I am consoled by this house, my soul's vessel, which will be tended to by our son.

Fifty-five years old, I can still throw a football that many yards, though I can't imagine that clean age-to-distance ratio holding up even another year. When not threatened by rebellious amylase, I feel I could really enjoy another twenty-year stretch of highway. But I know how it works at this age. My wife and I have watched close friends, more or less our age, die, four to cancer (two other friends have beaten it), and one to heart attack. The last was overweight and diabetic, and in that strange, I dare say, smug way people can have even toward dear friends, we saw it coming. Also, about the time I was fretting turning fifty, I received word that a woman I had lived with after we'd graduated college and traveled with cross country in an old Dodge van, had died of a heart attack, leaving behind a husband and two children. I hadn't seen her in twenty-five years, and quite frankly our own relationship had been a mismatch, but remembering her washing dishes in a Wyoming stream, I felt the clear jolt of the unexpected. So, as long and pleasant as that last stretch of highway might look, there is occasionally a sudden great patch of black ice. Trouble is, there's no road under the ice.

I guess I was attracted to women who love to travel.

My wife and I have traveled the world for twenty-three years, beginning with Greece soon after we met. We have made love on every continent but Antarctica. Back when, while I lusted after literature, she was becoming a PhD economist. These past two decades her work for an organization in Paris has allowed her wide travel, and much of the time our son and I are with her in the seats we have together after she has given up her business class. These days we are often stopped at airport security checks, and she once again must produce the doctor's letter explaining the syringe in her purse. For a dozen years she's injected herself twice daily, pricked her finger three or four times daily, and slipped a paper strip into her portable glucose reader. One time we were on a cruise ship, sitting around a dining table with friends, having to wait much too long for food after my wife's injection. She began shaking and sweating, her eyelids fluttering. While I coaxed bread and beer into her mouth, a friend swept our crying son away. That's the only time such a thing has happened. As far as I know. For my wife is not the kind of person to talk about her troubles.

Besides a love of travel, my wife and I share a love of wine. Wine nurtured our love for each other. One of our shared heartbreaks is the theft of wine from our Paris cellar, and we know that makes us fortunate by comparison. We have sat a thousand times on our terrace out front drinking wine, watching the Seine flow, ships pass. In summer, when the garden's in bloom, we look at our roses, toast each other and joke, "To the days of wine and roses." Because of our property's slope, the front terrace actually sits atop a garage at the roadside. On nice days we often call down to passersby—the village is small, about sixty people—to come join us for a glass of wine. We have the only roadside terrace in town and so it has become something of a drinking dais.

Our village is named Vieux Port, so called because the Romans had a port here, "Portus Tutus." Bacchus would have loved this town, where the wine flows as sure as the Seine. Most of the houses now are *secondaire*, whose owners—Parisian, English, Dutch—come to kick back on weekends, during holidays, much as we have done, though we spend the most time here besides the *permanents*, and will soon retire and live full time in Vieux Port. The locals enjoy us *étrangers*, not just because we pump money into the economy, but maybe because we connect them to the eccentric world. A few here have never even seen Paris. In this town everything flows—the talk, laughter, music. In summer barbecues smoke and in winter fireplaces blaze. We never tire of watching the Seine, our river that starts as a trickle in Burgundy. Till recently, everyday at precisely 11:31, the Concorde—on its way to New York where it would land three hours before it took off—streaked over our heads, several miles up, and by the time you heard it you had to look quickly along its vapor trail to actually see it. About every four years, a majestic armada of tall ships gathers at Rouen. Then, always on a Sunday, they sail one after another down the Seine, bearing flags from around the world, past Vieux Port whose population that day swells to a thousand. Some ten miles upstream, in the town of Villequier, where Victor Hugo visited and wrote, his daughter, son-in-law and another couple, their boat capsized by a sudden storm, drowned. A statue of the great man stands on the bank, his head downcast, and beneath are written his words, "the grass lives and the children die."

In 1944 the Germans were pinned down in Vieux Port, back in the days when the town had a number of *auberges* serving food and drink, and the Germans, too, used Vieux Port for rest and relaxation. (The *auberges*, tainted perhaps, disappeared after the war, never to return. I keep meaning to write a story based on the German presence here. The villagers old enough to have lived through it have never brought it up, and I have never inquired. But

I do wonder what went on behind doors we so easily pass through these days.) From the flat farmland above the woods, the English fired a few shells, just to remind the Germans the war had turned and they really should be on their way. One shell hit the house next to ours, killing the resident, whose name is on a plaque at the church, where a number of us gather on VE day. Next to the cemetery that surrounds the church someone decided to place the green bin where we recycle our bottles, *clink-clank*, and after some weekends or holidays the bin overflows. My wife and I plan on being buried in Vieux Port, within earshot of the bottle bin.

Up behind our property, behind a field—which some absentee landlord lets to grazing horses who get occasional carrots or apples from our son and his friends at our split-rail fence—is forest, mostly beech trees. Hidden there you find the ruins of the 12th century *Chapelle de Saint Thomas*, where lepers would pray. It is built on the site of a Roman temple, though no one knows to whom it was dedicated. I vote for Bacchus. It is a charmed life we lead in charming Normandy. Ah, Vieux Port! Ah, Veritas Partytown!

I am sitting at our dining room table, drinking tea, *orange cannelle* with the slightest suggestion of spice, indeed a superior vintage. In the past six weeks I have found different flavors of tea and infusions interesting. Alas, the tastes of currants or vanilla gotten from a brewed bag will never replace those of fine wines. I sip, read from one of the many articles on pancreatitis I've downloaded since first discovering MayoClinic.com. I've come to think the alcohol aspect a bit overplayed, at times preachy. While my own choices are beer or wine, some people around here knock down vodka, whiskey, gin and have no apparent problems, though some pancreases evidently are more delicate than others. Now I'm reading the news I somehow have been waiting for. The University of Maryland Medical Center gives the usual spiel how alcohol not only hastens enzyme output, but then, with a follow-up punch, allows those juices to pass more easily through duct walls and damage the pancreas. But umm.com turns upbeat, speaking of things that are actually good for your pancreas. Anti-oxidants, like soybean extracts, may be beneficial, and certain traditional Chinese medicines "are effective for the prevention and treatment of pancreatitis": licorice root, ginger root, Asian ginseng, peony root, cinnamon Chinese bark. I knew it! Ah, pancreas, heal thyself that I may drink my wines again!

Just because I can repair sinks and toilets, am I daft enough to think I can repair a leaky pancreas? ("Pass the duct tape, son.") The last doctor who treated me at the American Hospital, a Frenchman who amazingly had done his residency in Cleveland, Ohio—and so could relate to Buffalo winters—told me my pancreas was a keg of dynamite ready to go off. I didn't admonish him for clichés. My French GP in Paris, perhaps whose *joie de vivre* hasn't been chilled by a stay in Cleveland, says, sure, once the enzyme level returns to normal, I can have a few glasses of wine now and then. That's not bottles per day, as so easily happens around here. I can control, moderate. Drink only nice wines, not the stuff on sale we all buy just because it's cheap fuel for conversation and laughter.

Still, there is that other voice of late. Quit. Just give it up. You know and admire a number of ex-alcoholics—no one from this town, of course—and they converse and laugh with gusto and wit.

This table came with the house. It's made of simple planks, I think beech, and seats six easily, more with some squeezing. Hundreds of meals we've eaten here, with so many guests and friends, as the wine and chatter flowed. What's most interesting about this table are the small markings in it, as though someone spilled a box full of apostrophes across it. According to the previous owner, the table came from a WWII German mess tent, and the markings were made by knife tips. The owner said he and his wife bought the table in Germany and transported it here. I've always found that odd, and I wonder if that's because the owner found it less—what? Scary? Discomforting?—than telling us new homeowners the table was here all along, that Nazi soldiers sat in our house, at this table, stabbing at their food.

Tonight we have Francoise and Raynald coming for dinner. My wife is making duck breasts. She is easily the best cook in town, and I'll bet one of the best in Normandy. We will break out bottles of burgundy, maybe a Morey-St. Denis, and I will make my little joke of late. "None for me. Why, I'm so far ahead of you all, I gotta give you a chance to catch up."

I hear my wife and son returning from Pont Audemer, the nearest town with a supermarket, and must help unload the car.

My wife and I don't talk to each other as much as we used to, and it would be easy lately to blame my lack of drink, but it is bigger, something that has been happening for I'm not really sure how long. I must remember to explain to our son how love works. You fall into it full of passion, my boy, discovering so much to share. You get married, have a kid or two, hopefully as fine as you. Then twenty-three years down the road you find yourselves tiptoeing around each other some days, sharing only the most necessary information: what goes on the shopping list, the fact the vacuum bag needs changing, and the guests arrive at seven. By day, you accuse each other of snoring the night before. Sometimes you think her stoicism expresses itself as impatience with other people's problems. She goes around turning lights on, you turning them off. She thinks you enjoy agonizing over choices rather than simply making decisions (maybe an old existential hippie does). You think she buys distractions too readily for your son. She thinks you have a pretentious chip (you think, aren't they all?) on your shoulder. You think maybe you do, a great big Buffalo chip. Your master bedroom, in the only house the two of you will ever own, feels more and more like Antarctica. Still, you know you are lucky because in the guest bedroom, on the top shelf of the armoire, there are seventeen albums of photos, most of which you have shot but your wife has put in order and labeled.

The groceries are stowed away, sunlight fills the kitchen, and my wife begins snipping the ends off green beans. It's a beautiful kitchen I've built for her. Oak cabinets, black granite countertops with small gold speckles, a range, two big ovens, and a microwave.

A spotlighted island chopping table in the middle and lights in the ceiling made from some leaded windows with touches of red and gold I found cheap in an Amsterdam flea market.

There is a sudden crack! and I know instantly what it is. Once in awhile a bird, its eye unable to distinguish between reality and reflection, slams into one of the many windows I've installed and breaks its neck. "We need to stick on some do-not-enter decals," my wife says and I enjoy her words. This time it's a blackbird, its body warm through the paper towel as I carry it up to a barrel we keep for the likes of pulled weeds and deadheaded roses. When the barrel's full I drive it up to a big recycling yard where there's a giant bin for *dechets verts*. They turn it all into mulch, and in the spring I can get a few free barrels to sprinkle around the rosebushes. I look at our house.

One hundred years from now, perhaps a great-grandchild, curious to know what life was like back then, will read my stories searching for clues. Two hundred years from now I don't know that my words will be read. But I do know this. Someone will walk around this house and wonder how these beams have stood so long. Even during the shortest days of the year, the sun will roll its light down the slope, across the field, through a few bare apple trees, in through the glass wall, across a bar and into the kitchen, where it finds a woman happily preparing food, though in the back of her mind is the slight worry that her husband really needs to change the bag before he starts vacuuming.

David R. Poe, born in Buffalo, has lived and written in France for thirty years. He continues to live in Paris and Normandy with his wife and son.

32763242R00146

Made in the USA
Charleston, SC
22 August 2014